D0042242

blue
rider
press

Shirley

Also by Susan Scarf Merrell

FICTION

A Member of the Family

NONFICTION

The Accidental Bond:
How Sibling Connections Influence Adult Relationships

Shirley

A NOVEL

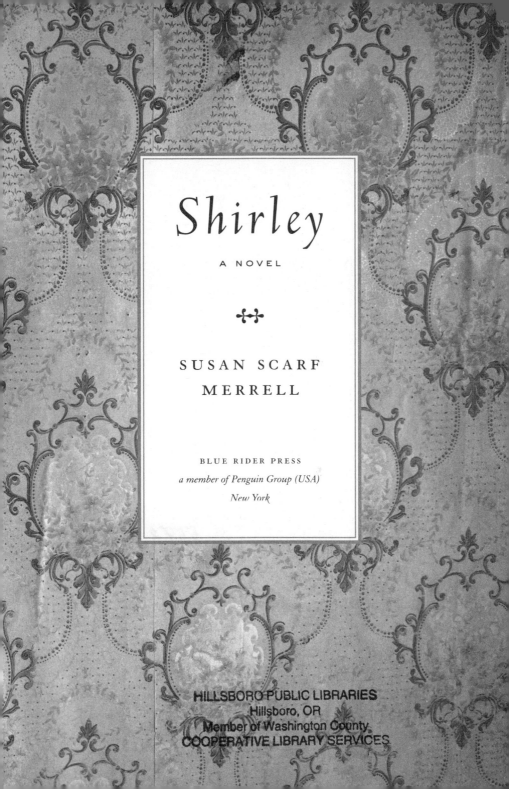

SUSAN SCARF
MERRELL

BLUE RIDER PRESS
a member of Penguin Group (USA)
New York

blue
rider
press

Published by the Penguin Group
Penguin Group (USA) LLC
375 Hudson Street
New York, New York 10014

USA • Canada • UK • Ireland • Australia
New Zealand • India • South Africa • China

penguin.com
A Penguin Random House Company

The author gratefully acknowledges permission to quote from "Not Waving but Drowning"
by Stevie Smith, from *Collected Poems of Stevie Smith*, copyright © 1957 by Stevie Smith.
Reprinted by permission of New Directions Publishing Corp.

Library of Congress Cataloging-in-Publication Data

Merrell, Susan Scarf.
Shirley : a novel / Susan Scarf Merrell.
p.   cm.
ISBN 978-0-399-16645-7
1. Jackson, Shirley, 1916–1965—Fiction.   2. Entertaining—Vermont—Bennington—Fiction.
3. Psychological fiction.   I. Title.
PS3563.E7426S55   2014   2013046531
813'.54—dc21

Printed in the United States of America
1   3   5   7   9   10   8   6   4   2

Book design by Gretchen Achilles

For Jim

No live organism can continue for long to exist sanely under conditions of absolute reality; even larks and katydids are supposed, by some, to dream. Hill House, not sane, stood by itself against its hills, holding darkness within; it had stood so for eighty years and might stand for eighty more. Within, walls continued upright, bricks met neatly, floors were firm, and doors were sensibly shut; silence lay steadily against the wood and stone of Hill House, and whatever walked there, walked alone.

—*The Haunting of Hill House*

Shirley

One

"You have green eyes," she said. I handed her my end of the fitted sheet and she tucked the corners deftly together, folded again to make a smooth square, her knob-knuckled fingers making quick work of a task I'd never had to do. Bed-making I knew all too well, but, oh, the luxury of a second set of sheets!

"No," I said. "My eyes are blue."

The closet door opened easily for Shirley, mistress of all the warped wood in this eccentric house. She stacked the folded sheets, nodded for me to follow her down the cramped back staircase to the kitchen. There were breakfast dishes to do. She washed, her hands reddened by the soapy water. I dried. Finally she responded.

"Envy. It's wanting what other people have."

Well, that was pointless to deny. I added two chipped saucers to the stack on the cupboard shelves. One of the black cats, the one with the white splash of fur on her paw, undulated irritably from behind the teacups, tail high. Shirley emptied the water from the basin, splashing the faucet stream to rinse the scummed soap left behind. "I only want what I have," she said. "I want exactly what I have." She wiped her hands on the dish towel, pushed her wedding band back on with a grimace.

"You know who you love," I said.

She laughed, as if I'd said something terribly clever. And then she added, "I'll do what's needed to keep what's mine."

"I see." I could picture my mother waiting outside the playground fence when I was very young, feeling herself unwelcome— or unworthy—while I played with schoolmates. Was it love that made her hover there? I didn't know. She did what was needed, just as Shirley claimed to do. "You protect what's yours."

"Yes," she answered calmly. "I do." She pointed to the packing box on the wobbly kitchen table. "I brought that down for you. Things for the baby, attic treasures. You're welcome to use any of it."

Confused, but eager to please her, I undid the flaps and opened the carton. Withdrawing a crinkled ball of newsprint, I carefully unfurled the paper until a child's cup emerged. "Pretty!" Easy to be enthusiastic about such a solid piece of china, the limpid-eyed bunny painted on the side. The child I was making could one day hold this cup in his or her hands, would never know what it was like to come into a world without Beatrix Potter china, and look, stuffed among the wrapped baby dishes—a green sweater with a cheerful button-eyed polar bear sewn onto its belly. Already I knew my baby would be far luckier than I had ever been.

"The cups were from my mother."

"One for each child?"

"We could have used help with the rent, but she sent us china and silver spoons. That's Geraldine."

"I love them." I was breathless at the thought of having a mother who provided such bounty.

"We had to buy each child on layaway," Shirley said. "Couldn't pay the doctor or the hospital. But she sent bunting. For the crib we couldn't afford. And christening gowns. You can imagine how well those went over with Stanley." Her laugh was not a happy one.

Whatever Shirley disliked about her mother had to be small change compared to what I'd grown up with, I thought. I wanted Shirley's baby cups, and the silver spoons, and the bunting if she offered it, and the clothes her four babies had worn. I wanted things, for I had never had them. I pulled a piece of newsprint off a cereal bowl, straightened it out, laid it on the table. "Who's this? Missing student?"

She peered at the photo. "Oh my, that's from a dozen years ago at least."

PAULA WELDEN MISSING SINCE SUNDAY FROM COLLEGE CAMPUS: SEARCH IS MADE OVER WIDE AREA: GIRL'S FATHER ARRIVES HERE FROM HIS STAMFORD HOME; WHEN LAST SEEN MISSING STUDENT WAS WEARING RED PARKA, BLUE JEANS AND THICK-SOLED SNEAKERS

Eighteen years, in fact. "She looks like you, Rose, doesn't she?"

A hole in the fabric of one day and entry to another. I glanced around the kitchen, anywhere but at Shirley—if I were Paula Welden, I would have been thirty-six that September morning.

"Did they ever find her?" It seemed terribly important, immediately so. It wasn't that we looked alike; it was something more. It mattered, oh, it mattered more than anything, to believe that if there had to be women in danger, there would be those who found them.

I shivered, felt the walls of the kitchen shiver with me like so many sheets flailing on a clothesline on a windy day. I pulled out a rickety chair and sat. I had to.

"They found her, didn't they?"

Shirley began to unwrap the other cups, smoothing page after crumpled page. "No, never. I remember some people thought she'd run away. With a boyfriend. And our local police came under the gimlet scrutiny of the FBI."

The girl was lovely, her blond hair smooth and cut to the shoulders, her smile relaxed. She was from elegant Stamford, Connecticut—a far cry from South Philly—and her father came up to aid in the search. He must have loved her. If I had seen Paula Welden's picture, knowing nothing else, I would have wanted to be like her.

"Me, too," said Shirley softly. I'm not sure I had spoken.

"Did you know her?" I asked.

A pause.

The black cat on the windowsill stopped licking his paw, tongue protruding through tiny, sharp teeth. The house itself held its breath; not even a floorboard creaked. "I never met the girl," Shirley said finally, her voice light. "Not once."

She was an honest woman, or so I believed. But can anyone who makes up fictions hour after hour and year after year be wedded to the truth? Even now my memory recircles the events of my year in Shirley Jackson's house, what I understood at the time and what I now trust to be fact. Conditions of absolute reality have a glare all their own, like sunspots on water or the glinting of ice against a mountain boulder on a cold Vermont afternoon. You think you know where you are, you are sure of what you've lived through, and yet, at the same time, the whole thing seems a dream.

Perhaps this makes it easier to believe.

Two

But that wasn't the beginning. My story starts with a single word.

Money.

I'd never had any, you see, and though Fred was wealthy by my standards—his father owned a small candy store and they could afford three meals a day—we knew nothing about the rich but what we gathered when we could swing an afternoon at the movies. My own family wasn't dirt poor. Nothing so romantic. We were city poor, meaning that I was invisible every single day of my young life. Invisible on the street, in school, at home. Invisible, except when creditors came looking for my parents: Mr. Hoffman the butcher, Sam Rabinowitz the grocer, Mrs. Schumann from the store where my mother regularly stole underclothing for me and my sister.

Yes, she was light-fingered. But not greedy, and for the most part I think the neighbors respected her. Under similar circumstances, wouldn't any mother hope to be as determined? People were pragmatic about my father as well. Of course they didn't like him—perhaps feared him—but when his services were needed, there was little hesitation.

I loved both my parents, despite the way they clawed at life, but with none of the compassion of my elder sister Helen's parental adoration. I felt sorry for her. All I ever wanted, once I was old enough to see my family clearly, was to be free of them. Not a day went by that I didn't feel two things: fear and yearning. And I guess I was greedy because of it. I ate too fast, when there was food. I went to my friends' apartments and lusted after their dresses, their books, their mothers' hugs. I didn't know I was lonely. I didn't know there was another way to be.

That was my childhood.

After high school, I worked as a cleaning girl at the Bellevue-Stratford, a hotel in center city, close enough to the Broad Street line that I could get there right after my classes at Temple University. I ran the carpet sweeper, checking under the bed for buttons, forgotten stockings and loose change that I conscientiously delivered to the head of housekeeping. My mother received ten dollars a week so I could remain in the cramped bedroom I shared with my older sister. When I bought my first pair of high-heeled pumps I kept them in my schoolbag to make sure no one borrowed them. One day, I would be in charge of something, a store or a family. Literally anything. I dreamed of firm decisions, impeccable in their correctness.

In the meantime, I cleaned toilets and made beds. I kept my eyes low. Oh, and I read every book my English professors assigned, swallowing Wharton and Dickens and Eliot whole. How their women lived! Such writing! It untangled tragedy from the banality of day-to-day, rendered it beautiful, artistic, worthy. Like Catherine Morland in Austen's *Northanger Abbey*, I knew myself a heroine.

No better way to clean a stranger's hairs from a sink basin than to imagine oneself a poetic figure burdened by an unraveling story—

I'd wanted to take a business course, but most of the girls I knew from South Philly were studying to be teachers. And when I went to register, the woman at the main desk glared over her reading glasses and told me taking business was a dishonest way to find a husband. I couldn't bear for that stout crone in the pilled cardigan to know I was less womanly than she. Half sick with resentment, I registered for English.

But Fred was the graduate teaching assistant for English 2022, the nineteenth-century British novel, so Mrs. Feldman in the registrar's office turned out to be the canny one.

I already knew of him, of course. We'd gone to neighboring schools. Everyone knew who the Nemser twins were: Fred's brother, Lou, won a writing competition and was hired for the cops beat at the *Philadelphia Examiner* straight out of twelfth grade, and Fred edited an underground literary magazine. They were tall and thin and very serious. Not rebellious, exactly, but able in argument. Lou was popular with girls; when I was a lowly seventh-grader, and they were lording it on the street corner outside their father's store, Lou dominated my fantasies. I doubt he ever noticed me. Then we were evicted from our apartment—another fed-up landlord tired of waiting for rent—and we went to live with my father's cousin in Germantown, and I switched high schools for the second time. We moved twice more before my junior year ended. It wasn't until my father left us for good that my mother and sister and I got to stay in one place.

Fred walked me to the Stratford, making me a good half-hour late for my shift, the very first time I went to his office.

Now that I was a college student, and Fred was my teacher, I could see he was the handsomer of the two brothers—shyer, his nose slimmer, his teeth a bit crooked, and his heavy-lidded eyes invasive in their interest. Blunt fingers riffled my first paper, a discussion of authorial point of view in *Pride and Prejudice*, and it seemed to me that even my childishly scrawled sheets looked beautiful as he flicked his thumbnail at the edge of the pages, making a *click, click, click* as he complimented me, said I had a gift for literary criticism. He wanted my conclusion rewritten, drawing a clearer parallel between Elizabeth Bennet's instinct toward self-awareness and Austen's intrusive narrative position. I nodded enthusiastically, feeling my hair bounce on my shoulders (I was proud of my hair, straight and blond, an anomaly not merely in the Jewish ghettos of South Philly but even in my own family), delighted by his approval.

He was walking my way, he said. And when I said I wasn't heading home, but to work, to the Stratford, he reddened. "That's okay," he said. If I didn't mind.

I didn't.

We cut across the campus, stepping around dingy snow that insisted on drifting over the shoveled paths, ice crackling under our boots. My navy coat, the one that had come from my sister Helen's employer, was barely needed. The heat between us embarrassing, a public nakedness. To his credit, Fred remained able to talk, telling me about his interest in folklore and ballad, about his dissertation, about the feelers he'd received from English departments as far away as Syracuse, as prominent as Harvard. As we passed the faculty club, Fred stopped to greet Professor Bricklen, the creative-writing instructor I'd had the previous semester. "This is Rose," he said. "Rose Klein."

I almost wished I were invisible then. "Rose Klein, yes." Professor Bricklen's gaze scraped down me, from head to toe. He was one of those very large men with piggish eyes buried under the folds of his brows and cheeks, and yet his glare was ferocious. "She took my intro course, Professor Nemser." I stood my ground, silently meeting Bricklen's gaze with what I hoped was pride, if not defiance. Of course he remembered me. He was the kind of man who would remember girls like me more than the others. "I can only hope that her work ethic has improved."

Fred took me by the elbow. "This is my friend Rose."

I suspect, looking back, that this was precisely when we teetered over into love. We walked steadily down Broad Street for nearly half a block before I thought to thank him. But I didn't. I pretended it hadn't happened, as did he. I never told him that Professor Bricklen liked his female students to sit on his ample lap while he critiqued their work. I let Fred think Bricklen found me mediocre rather than stubborn.

Five months later we were married. I was pregnant, with Natalie, although I didn't know it. Two months after that, we were in North Bennington, Vermont, spending our first night with Stanley Edgar Hyman and his wife, the novelist Shirley Jackson, in their sprawling, messy, book- and kid-filled home, on the hillside just off the Bennington College campus.

It was about money, because we needed it, now that I was nineteen years old and pregnant. It was about money, because Stanley's department wanted to hire Fred, even though he hadn't finished his dissertation. It was about money, because money was the nutrition I'd been starved of, and what I would always crave.

Oh, why pretend? Money was what I called it, not knowing any better. But of course it was always about love.

I KNEW WHO SHE WAS, Shirley, and I'd read some of her essays and stories, in *Ladies' Home Journal* or other magazines. I knew she was supposed to be a witch, that she had lots of children, and I thought she would be slim and tall, with a wicked sense of humor and a stylish haircut. I was nervous on the train, trying to focus on the novel of hers I'd taken from the Temple University library, a book about a haunted house and a crazy girl named Eleanor who goes to stay there. Eleanor hated her sister, I'd gotten that far, but I couldn't identify with the character at all. She had no instinct for saving herself. How could I respect a fragile girl like that? The other character, Theodora, was crazy in a different way, loud and outspoken, the kind of woman who embarrassed everyone around her.

The story made my head ache. Every time I closed the cover and tried to nap, the first line popped into my thoughts, inscrutable and irritating: *No live organism can continue for long to exist sanely under conditions of absolute reality; even larks and katydids are supposed, by some, to dream.*

"What does that even mean?" I asked Fred, pushing the open novel onto the papers on his knee. He glanced at the lines, shook his head, and slid his typescript back out from under, lifting the pages up in the air as if he'd suddenly become farsighted.

"It doesn't make sense," I said stubbornly.

"Well, don't waste time wondering. You can ask her for yourself when we get there."

Funny, thinking back on it. I didn't tell him how thrilled I was about the adventure, so excited to meet a famous writer, to stay in her house. In my mind, I was not only traveling with Fred, I was journeying toward Shirley. And there you go—traveling with Fred; journeying toward Shirley. As if I already knew how much she would matter.

The train coach was loud and full of smoke, and Fred scrawled pencil notes in the margins of the typescript he was bringing to show Professor Hyman, sighing as he did so in a way that added to my distractibility.

I patted his arm. "It's going to be fine," I said.

He turned to the next page of his manuscript.

"Fred. Fred, honey. You'll be fine."

"Not now," he said. He jotted something in the margin, pressing the papers against his raised knee to make a surface.

"Fred?" I said. "What if she doesn't like me? If she thinks I'm . . ." He took my hand, not even raising his eyes off his work.

"Everyone likes you," he said absently. He'd obviously forgotten the things his mother had grumbled when we announced we were getting married. *Go find a nice girl, Freddy. Someone you can be proud of.* If she liked me, she certainly hadn't shown it yet.

I looked out the window. Fields jounced before me, lazy cows and rusted tractors the only relief from endless expanses of late-summer cornstalks massed askew. It was as hot as Philadelphia, but thicker, more claustrophobic, as if vegetable spores clogged the air, snagging on the open train windows as we blew past. I didn't feel that second being alive inside me. I barely felt my own self, my breath's rhythm the unsteady reverberation of the train. Still, that second life was going to make me matter—it would have needs I could fulfill, would give volume and weight to the hardly noticeable manifestation that was me. I leaned my head against the seat, tried again to close my eyes but couldn't. Farm fields claimed my attention, blurring one into the other as time itself blended into mush until, finally, we arrived at the North Bennington train station with a great ceremonial screeching of brakes. My husband shuffled his papers together, grabbed our new suitcase, and assisted his bride down the train steps with solicitude.

"Fred Nemser! Fred Nemser!" Stanley waited for us under the covered porch of the station, shielding himself from sunlight. What an extraordinary sight he was—short, wide, balding, toothy, bespectacled, rumpled, a veritable compendium of academic clichés and yet oddly compelling. I can't, even now, explain why, except to say that when he looked at me, I felt he saw me. And when he saw me, I felt worthy.

"This must be the estimable Rose. Welcome to Bennington! Come meet Shirley and the family." He hoisted our suitcase atop his very plump shoulder and escorted us for quite a distance down the street to a small square. We turned left, up the hill, all of us glistening with perspiration. Along the way, Stanley described the class he wanted Fred to take on for him. It seemed Shirley had been unwell, and he hoped to lighten his teaching responsibilities by sharing duties on his folklore course. "It's the biggest course at the college," he said flatly, in the way of men pretending not to care about those matters of which they are most proud.

"I can do the ballads," Fred offered.

"I've read your dissertation draft. Impressive. You have some perceptive notions about Frazer and *The Golden Bough*, but you miss important links between folk music and folk myth. We'll discuss what you must do."

"Thank you."

"No need to thank me! A pleasure to find a young man with such noble inclinations. A member of the brotherhood already. Not for the faint of heart, our work. Ignore Negro spirituals at your peril, my friend! I'll have you read my jazz/blues writings. You should be able to handle all the musicology."

Stanley was out of breath. Fred tapped our suitcase as if to remove it from Stanley's sweaty shoulder, but it was too late. "We're here," said our host, turning left, onto a path between two gawky bursts of privet.

What a house it was. A huge façade, hulking high on the property, four white columns across a sagging front porch. Shutters painted, but not recently. Bicycles toppled against the bushes. Jars of all sizes (dusty, some with dried flowers, others with pebbles or marbles or brackish water), a bucket, a ragged broom, and a tray of half-full drinking glasses—contents brownish-gold and dry— books on the railings, and a long-forgotten doll abandoned in the weedy flowerbed. But to me the worst were the trees: gargantuan evergreens, trees out of nightmares, monstrous and dark enough to seethe across the yard by themselves, stripping all light and lawn in their paths. "Hill House," I murmured, thinking of the novel in my purse. It occurred to me then that I'd never seen evidence before this of how a novelist constructs a world from fog and fact.

Stanley smiled approvingly but shook his head. "Shirley will show you the one everyone thinks is that house. Perhaps it is; perhaps it isn't. She claims a house in California as the source. The wise man would wager that Hill House came straight from her imagination. Nonetheless, there are a few frightening edifices in North Bennington, good enough for haunting. Ask her to show you the best one. It's down the hill and up, across the main street. A pleasant stroll. This one of ours is demon-free. No need to worry if you'll turn out to be an Eleanor or a Theodora."

My romantic fantasies to the contrary, I'd never considered myself worthy of being a heroine, not really, and I smiled at him, feeling suddenly safe, as if he were a kind of father. The sort one would want to have. As we grinned at each other, I heard a movement on the porch and looked up the ramshackle steps. And there she was.

I'll not forget my first view of Shirley Jackson. Shirley, like her house, was not the surprise you expected her to be. A mountain of a woman, standing over us so that she appeared even more imposing. I would soon understand that—despite her girth—she was quite short. Still, she gave an impression of substantiality. That afternoon, Shirley wore a beige sack of a housedress imprinted with an endless green geometric pattern. Chinese cloth slippers—I would later learn this was her favored footwear. Lank reddish hair held back by a headband. Her spectacle rims a pale brown. The cigarette between her right forefinger and middle finger was burnt halfway, smoke dancing the length of her fleshy forearm. Her smile. Shy, but not so. As if there was a part of her that knew herself to be better than me, and another part, equally powerful, that believed herself to be worse.

If there was any quality to her I recognized, it was of course that. Shirley's was the smile of a woman like me, the abandoned and the never-loved; it was the smile of the arrogantly insecure. It was the smile of the mother-to-be who had never been mothered, the smile of the brilliant person in a woman's body, the beautiful woman in an ugly shell. I loved her immediately, I wanted to be her and take care of her.

Just last year, at a dinner party, a famously cantankerous American history professor proclaimed that the only people who like Shirley Jackson's work are unhappily married women, and I snapped at him that the people who love Jackson understand imperfection and know how to live with it and appreciate it. "Isn't that the better way to be?" His mouth hung open; he'd never before deemed me worthy of notice. But I know I'm right: that was Jackson's gift, to understand the absurd unloveliness of love.

Ascending the porch steps in September 1964, toward Shirley in the flesh, I felt an inexplicable need to exchange a hug.

She spoke over my head, to Stanley.

"That woman called. You promised."

Stanley handed the suitcase to Fred. "I'll talk to her again."

"You promised, Stanley. And we're out of Scotch."

"Send Barry."

"I did. They want the bill paid."

"I'll walk down."

"And you. Nobody said you were pregnant."

I blushed. We hadn't told anyone.

"I'm a witch," she said calmly. "Now come inside and let's get you settled. Rose, is it?"

"Yes," I stammered, feeling very, very out of my depth.

"I'm Shirley. I've put you two at the back, in my son Laurie's room. He's married, lives in New York City with his family, and as green about the ears as you two. They'll come up tomorrow afternoon; you'll have a great deal in common."

I disliked, immediately, the notion of her children being real and present, and old enough to showcase how young I was myself.

"On Monday we can meet with the estate agent, find out about homes for rent near the campus. But there's no hurry. The room's free and only our youngest, Barry, is at home during the week. The two girls are home on weekends."

"You have four?" I wanted to say something sophisticated, something clever so that Shirley would know I was not a child. Despite Shirley's casting him as green, I pictured the married son— elegant wife and pretty baby—as someone who had all the nuances of adulthood figured out.

"Or maybe you'll stay here," she continued thoughtfully, as if she'd seen something in me, something rare and worthy of study. As if I were the heroine I'd always dreamed I might become. Even though I'd imagined Fred and me ensconced in splendid solitude, our first home together, my first home anywhere, I nodded. I felt the exterior of the house thrum slightly, as if I had been recognized.

Inside, I let my hand glide up the warm mahogany banister, an orphan arriving home. "You'll help with dinner, won't you? Our evenings will amuse you." I instantly believed her.

We climbed the broad front staircase. I wanted to touch every painting, look at every family photograph. I heard her breathing deepen. She used the railing and she moved slowly, and while I thought about the size of her, and hoped she would not topple back on me, I also wished she would turn and smile again. Already, I found her moods both dazzling and confusing.

Three

BLOATED WITH INDIGESTION, I must still have slept on the sagging horsehair mattress, because the moon was splashed across my face when I awakened in the otherwise pitch-black room, startled to realize that Fred was not beside me. I peered through the dark, wanting to see the rickety Victorian dresser and the comfortable green reading chair by the closet. All I could make out was the drifting of the window draperies against the muddled glass that had seemed so elegant in daylight. I lay under the quilt, my exhaustion and the persistent discomfort that was almost fear rendering me immobile for some moments.

I could hear the house creak moodily. I'd liked it more in daylight: room after tall-ceilinged room sprawled out on both floors, each fitted out with bookcases, and endless places to lounge, and well-used blankets to throw over chilly legs. During the day, the light had been low and pleasant, flickering leafy patterns passing genially over the book piles on the floors and tables, the discarded shoes and cardigans, the stacks of student papers awaiting attention. The house seemed to have a will of its own. I had the idea the

house had created itself rather than been masterminded by its owners, as if it would produce a bassinet for me when one was needed,
or shorten its staircases if someone was tired.

I wanted the house to like me, I thought, and I placed my hand
on the wall next to the headboard. The plaster was thick and still
beneath my spread fingers, as walls are supposed to be, but I had
the sense not of an inanimate surface but of a sentient being holding its breath. Not wanting to be caught.

Far in the distance—down the long book-lined hallway, down
the staircase, perhaps out on the sagging porch—I detected conversational grumbles, male voices chuckling, the squeak/groan of a
suffering rocking chair. I tipped myself off the high bed, slipping
Fred's jacket over my nightgown. Bare toes on the worn Oriental
runner, I crept down the hall. It was chilly. On the stairs I began to
smell the sweet odor of pipe tobacco. Fred's laugh, sonorous, more
musical than his speaking voice, wafted toward me; I was happy,
knowing how happy he must be, as I made my way quietly toward
the open front door, peeked around the corner.

They sat together under the yellow porch light, Stanley's rocker
next to Fred's rickety stool, one balding head and one curly cap of
hair leaning over the same open book. "This ballad," Stanley said.
"This one has always been my favorite."

"'The Demon Lover,'" Fred agreed, humming the first few
lines in the tuneless tone that passed for his singing voice. Someone had once told Fred that if he couldn't sing well, he should sing
loud, and he'd taken the idea to heart. I was glad that tonight, for
once, he was ignoring that advice. "'Well met, well met, well met,

my own true love, well met, my love, cried he. I've just come back from the salt, salt sea, and all for the love of thee.'"

"Yes, that's it. You'll begin with Lomax. I like to start with Lomax and work the earlier versions in as we go. Connect the Child ballads all the way from the Orient to the Negro in America, through to the blues," Stanley said.

"I could spend two weeks just on the 'House Carpenter' variations. James Harris himself."

"I hoist my tumbler to the demon lover."

Fred sipped his drink, checking to make sure Stanley wasn't laughing at him. But they were cut from the same cloth, those two.

"James Harris is folklore's proof that man has never been trustworthy. We're not alone in our preference for that ballad; it's Shirley's favorite as well. D'you know, her book *The Lottery and Other Stories* was supposed to be subtitled *The Adventures of James Harris?* She's smart about folklore, has read almost everything. I often discuss my lecture plans with her."

"Ah . . ." Fred's envy so new he wasn't yet aware of it. "It must be great to talk like that, with your wife. To share, to work through the details, to be able to think out loud . . ."

Stanley took a long swallow of his drink. In the silence between the men I think some information was passed, but I had no idea what it was.

"She longs for a tall, thin man in a well-made blue suit," Stanley said lightly.

Fred rattled the watery ice in his glass. I wondered what he was thinking.

. . .

I'D NEVER BEEN AROUND PEOPLE as smart as the Hymans, never felt myself surrounded by such brilliance, but at the same time, not knowing why, I felt sorry for Stanley. Just as I'd felt sorry for Shirley earlier at dinner, when the phone rang as she was slicing a pie and he was topping off our wineglasses for the umpteenth time. The look that passed between them, and their three kids—a boy and two girls, ranging in age from about twelve to maybe nineteen; the elder son would come up on the following day with his wife and child—each busily refolding napkins or studying the carpet underneath the long table, well, I didn't have to be older or smarter than I was to know that the phone rang often at this hour. No throat-clearing, no jokes in that moment, just the strange, quick glance, the hard and unforgiving silence, and then the burst of commentary about how glad the children were that Shirley had made the first apple pie of the season. In a moment, Stanley was reciting *Julius Caesar*, and Shirley was interrupting him and they both slipped into Brooklyn accents—*Dis was da noblest Roman of dem all*—and we were giggling again, and the youngest kid, the boy, ran upstairs for his guitar, and all was well. But I observed how hard they had to work, for just that moment, to be happy.

As I stood shyly in the hall, a ragged moth hovering at the outskirts of dim light, while Stanley told Fred how "my Shoiley" often had dreams about her demon lover's appearance, how she used James Harris as a repeating character trope, I wondered if the Hymans would change us very much. Before I could fully ponder the thought, Stanley switched gears, his frame shifting in the chair, his voice speeding off in another direction, talking about how necessary folklore was to fiction writers: "Think of Ulysses the castaway. All the ritual patterns of drama: *agon, pathos, sparagmos*—"

"The messenger!" Fred exclaimed.

"Yes, and then *threnos,* the mourning rituals, *anagnosis, theophany,* and then—"

"*Peripeteia,*" Fred interrupted.

"A fiction writer needs to know all there is, everything possible," Stanley said. "Language and history and music and culture. What we come from, our intellectual past, the beliefs that shape our thoughts. Therein lies the trouble with our contemporary novelists, not Shirley, of course, but the others. Fools and charlatans, and why? One simple reason. They don't know enough." He tilted his head. "As Matthew Arnold noted long before me."

Fred nodded appreciatively. "A virtuosic dilemma. What separates true artistry, true brilliance, from mere hackery."

"I know what we'll do this semester! We'll run a small second seminar, very exclusive—demonstrate theory in action, take our eager-minded students through a handful of contemporary writers, examine what specific knowledge might have profited them! Contrast them with better writers, you know, Hersey versus Hemingway. Penn Warren's *World Enough* against Hawthorne's *Scarlet Letter.*"

"Yes," Fred agreed excitedly. "The cultural patterns. Experience instead of aimless reporting. Faulkner, not Steinbeck."

Hyman slapped my husband on the leg. "Excellent choice. We'll raise the stakes on our young ladies!"

"Stan," Fred said, trying out the name. "This will be great!"

"They're not bad to look at, either, most of them. The students. An enthusiastic coterie of willing acolytes."

Fred nodded. To his credit, he was unsure of how to answer.

I had been about to go out onto the porch, to sit with them and listen. The door was open; I would not have to make a sound. But instead I returned to our room, huddled under the thick quilt, and tried to keep a brave face in case the walls reported directly to my hostess. I wanted beyond anything to spend the winter living in this house. I was amazed by the Hymans. I wanted their approval. Nonetheless, I wondered how safe we were with them.

I SLEPT BADLY under the cold, opaque eyes of the windows, troubled by dreams of a sort I'd never had. Each time I awoke, my body wanted to spring from the bed, panicked and afraid of something real: My sister Helen, resisting the insistent pawing of her employer, Mr. Cartwright. My father in a well-used car: avuncularly proud of a particularly fine storefront blaze as firefighters scrambled to unleash their hoses; unaware of the cops creeping closer in the gloomy alleyway. My mother, outside somewhere dark, alone, missed by no one. And Fred. I dreamed something of Fred I cannot bring myself to recall. Not even now.

Four

In the morning, Fred and Stanley left for the college on foot. Apparently, the campus was just up the road and through a gate. "You're welcome to join us for lunch, Stanley says." Fred had returned upstairs to remove his tie. "There's a new library building, you can take a look. And then walk across the driveway to the main building. Looks like a mansion with columns. It's called the Commons. Or you can walk into North Bennington, but Stanley says you saw most of it yesterday."

"Can we stay here? Will they want us? In this house?"

At home, we slept in the living room of Fred's parents' apartment. There'd been some discussion about moving us into Fred and Lou's room, and Lou moving onto the sofa, but since we intended to be temporary, that hadn't happened. I didn't mind it much; I'd never had a lot of privacy. Still, I could tell that Fred's mother would prefer to be the only woman. When I rinsed my stockings, I hid them under the side table, draped over my shoes. I kept our area neat, and I helped with the cooking, and I did everything I could to behave like a guest, but I knew it didn't help. Downstairs in the candy store, she whispered to the customers as she weighed out licorice drops or Bit-O-Honeys. Whatever I was doing wrong, the old ladies agreed on it, shaking their heads in sympathy as if Selma Nemser's life were one long mourning ritual. When my mother dropped in to say hello, Fred's mother stiffened and came around the counter to exchange hugs. She stayed at my mother's side, escorting her past the table of cut-glass candy dishes. They chatted by the door, friendly as could be, but when my mother left—I would get a cursory hug and inquiry into my health; I never did know what she wanted when she came—Mrs. Nemser always breathed a sigh of relief and went back to the penny candy counter. On the way, she checked to make sure nothing was missing. I suppose she tried to hide this from me, but how could she? I was so ashamed of my mother that I, too, held my breath. Which is all by way of saying that I understood why Fred's mother didn't want me around. I wouldn't have wanted me, either.

He could have married anybody. In our neighborhood, there were very few girls who wouldn't have been grateful to have him. Smarter girls. Richer girls. Prettier girls. But he had wanted me.

Now he gave me a tight, uncomfortable look. "It's good, isn't it, Rosie? They want us to stay here. And the money, I mean, the baby, it would be better to save some money."

I smoothed the well-laundered cotton of the quilt over the nearly imperceptible rise of my stomach. How had she known?

"We'll see," he said. "We'll try it and see."

I nodded.

"What are the child ballads?"

"The most authoritative collection of ballads and their variations. From the 1800s, but still considered to be the masterwork of the field."

"A collection of children's ballads?" I asked.

When he laughed, I always felt a little relieved, even if his amusement came at my expense. "No, Francis Child was a Harvard professor, the first professor of English. Before that, they were called rhetoric professors. It was his life's work to gather all these ballads and their variations from around the world."

"Oh," I said, mollified.

"Why?" he asked.

"No reason. I just wondered."

"Were you listening last night?" He didn't sound angry, so I nodded.

"'The Demon Lover,'" I said. "That's what you called it."

He rolled the length of his discarded blue tie through his fingers. "It's my favorite, and Stanley's. And hers, too." I patted the bed, but instead he went to the closet and draped the tie through a hanger. He described the ballad then, telling me about the cloven-footed sailor who returns to reclaim his lover years after he's been reported dead. The woman abandons her trustworthy carpenter husband and their children, flees to what turns out to be her doom. The devil's request, impossible to ignore. I shivered, patted the bed again, but Fred remained standing, something puzzled and reluctant in the set of his shoulders, the stiffness of his jaw.

"It's British," he told me. "And Scottish, and eventually there were American variations as well. Always the same message, even though the words change."

"Some people are dangerous to love," I said.

We were silent for some moments.

"Shirley works in the morning," he said then. "So you'll have to be quiet. I think the kitchen's fine, and the parlor, but not the library, where the desks are. That back one is her desk."

I nodded again.

"Try to like it, Rosie. Try to like her."

"I do," I told him. "But why would she like me? They're all so smart, so well educated. I don't fit in."

He sat on the bed, took me in his arms. "Rose Nemser," he said. "You don't know yourself at all."

I started to cry. "Her kids. I don't like them."

"The kids?" He was genuinely surprised. I was surprised myself. It was as if I were trying to establish an alibi for a crime I'd not yet decided to commit. Hadn't Sally and I dried the dishes together companionably last night, chatting about her disdain for her new boarding school's rules? I'd admired her sly smile and the daringly straightforward way she dealt with Shirley—thinking nothing of seizing her mother round the middle with both arms and squeezing tightly, her eyes shut in order to better savor the pleasure of it.

"Don't make me go back," she'd said then. Shirley kept rinsing the soapy dishes under hot water, placing the clean plates on the dish towel she'd laid out along the counter.

"Momma, please. I'll be good and study, I'll keep my room straight, and stay away from boys. I'll be delightful." Shirley glanced at me with a wry smile. Sally's grin included me as well, as if I might play some part in deciding her fate. "Delightful, Momma. I promise."

I dried two more of the rosebud latticed plates—faded gold rims did not detract from their elegance—and stacked them on the sideboard before Sally said again, "Please, Momma. And I'll befriend Rose, I'll show her everything, I'll be a hostess par excellence."

I stiffened without realizing it, so that the plate I was drying knocked dangerously on the sharp counter edge. To my relief, Shirley said, "You need to finish high school, my friend, not dangle after our fairy-tale lovers, pretty as they are. We'll finish here. You might as well go upstairs and start your Ellison essay. I'll take charge of putting on the dog for Rose and Fred." The look Sally shot me was cautious, as if she'd noted a hitherto unseen risk in my presence. I met her gaze flatly, then offered to finish rinsing the dishes. In truth, Sally was okay. She was hardly as interesting as Shirley, but how could anyone possibly be?

"Rosie Klein from Pine Street," Fred said now, his breath warming my hair. "My Rosie. Nothing matters but you. Not before, not now, not ever. You are the reason I want to teach here. The reason for everything. To take care of you, to make a life with you, that's all that matters."

What words could answer? I had, I think, tethered myself to the notion that someday a man would love me, and keep me safe, and I would become whole and able to greet the world without fear. I had married Fred believing that he was my chance for happiness. Now I was certain my luck had truly turned for the better. "Go on, then," I told him. "Go see the campus. I'll be fine." Eyes still damp from weeping, I grinned and pushed him off the bed. "Get going. I'll see you tonight. I'll be fine here, Freddy. Go."

His relief was palpable.

I waited in the room until I heard the front door slam behind the men, listened to the sounds of china and glassware clinking as breakfast dishes were cleared from the table. I let my heart quiet and my tears dry, and then I slipped down the hall to the bathroom, to get ready to spend my first full day with Shirley Jackson.

I WAS NERVOUS. The evening before, she had been hard work to keep up with. Half the time I didn't even know who we were talking about: Howard's name came up twenty times before I realized she meant the poet Howard Nemerov. Paul? That was the painter Paul Feeley. They were friends with Ralph Ellison; the up-and-coming writer Joyce Carol Oates had recently spent a weekend. They knew everybody at *The New Yorker*; Stanley wrote for the magazine. At one point, Stanley said something offhand about Shirley's story "The Lottery." I'd read it, a long time before, about a ritual stoning in a New England village, and I opened my mouth, eager to contribute and delighted that I could, but before I could gather words together, Shirley made a joke about a professor of theirs from Syracuse, someone named Brown, and Fred seemed to know who he was and they were all laughing—even their oh-so-knowledgeable kids—and I was left behind again.

So that morning, I admit I went down the stairs slowly, already worried I would be unable to entertain my formidable hostess.

She was in the kitchen, leaning against the sink with the water running. Yesterday's dress again. A cigarette trailing smoke. Her hair caught up in a limp ponytail. She was watching something out the window, staring intently, and I didn't want to startle her, so I cleared my throat before taking a step across the threshold.

"Good morning," she said, not turning. "There's coffee on the stove." Her voice was different from the night before, lower, the sound of countless cigarettes effable.

"What a wonderful sleep I had," I offered, knowing even as I spoke how dishonest the words sounded.

"I have to sleep," she said. "If I don't, I can't work." She glanced over her shoulder, meeting my gaze frankly. Like me, she'd been crying. "And if I don't work, it's bad. We need the money. Four kids, this house, you can imagine." She tightened both faucets, and took her apron off, leaving the dishes in the sink.

We'd not talked about whether I would work, Fred and I. His mother never had; she was pretty and helpless and hardly knew how to open and shut the windows in their apartment. Her job at the store was little more than a social position, a way of visiting with her friends, keeping an eye on their children. Fred's father— most of the fathers I knew, my own the sole exception—would have been embarrassed if his wife had to contribute to ongoing expenses. A wife could work for something specific; if she wanted to buy new furniture she could take a job in a department store and reap the discount, without shame. Though most of the women I knew had been forced to work on and off over the years, no one ever talked about it. A woman freely admitting, without shame, that she was working for money! Particularly an artist, the kind of woman with the right to behave with any eccentricity. That was the brilliant Shirley I'd seen the night before; now her admission of financial obligation—with its implicit confession about financial need—made her only more fascinating.

"You don't love it?" I blurted. "The writing?"

She pulled out a kitchen chair, dropped her heavy frame into it, stubbed her cigarette atop the mound of butts in the ashtray. "You come right to it, don't you?" She was amused, not angry, or so I hoped. On the shelves behind her, dishes were piled willy-nilly, bowls stacked with plates of all sizes, teacups and coffee mugs teetering against one another. A cuckoo clock ticked hollowly, water gurgled in cranky pipes, birds called to one another in the yard. A fly buzzed against the window screen but didn't find a way in, despite the many gaps in the webbing. I waited without speaking for Shirley to continue.

"Sit," she said, and I did, taking the chair opposite hers, my back to the kitchen door.

I have never known any other person, not in all my life, as unpredictable about silence and sound as Shirley Jackson. That winter of our friendship, there were more times like this one, when we sat in placental silence, than there were hours when she skittered out stories the way one might have expected. This very first morning, it was as if we were trying to get to know each other without speech or movement, merely measuring each other against the cadences of our breathing as the morning sun drifted, slowly, down the kitchen hallway and streamed along the dark, scuffed wooden floors.

After the longest time, when I could trace some vital pulsing in her that matched both my own and that of the life evolving inside me, I abruptly began to feel her as invasive, to feel her mind seeping into mine and wandering through the network of my thoughts. As if she, and the baby already growing, were forces larger and more powerful than what I was myself. And then I could no longer process clearly, could not articulate a whole and complete idea any longer. I wanted to say something, to break the silence, but my throat went tight; my hands, against the cool of the kitchen table, were sweaty. I forced my eyes to blink, raised them to gaze at her; her own eyes were closed and she was humming softly, her fingers moving against the edge of the table as if sorting out the sounds on alien piano keys.

I opened my mouth and closed it. I had never felt so hollow or so grounded; I had never felt so *seen*. Not by anyone, not even Fred.

In one of Shirley's stories, one I've read only recently, a young girl travels with her brother and his wife to a solitary hotel on an island made of rock. She steps out onto the rock of the island ahead of the others, and soon discovers that, in her eagerness to be first, she has marked herself the island's next spirit prisoner. She will not be able to leave, ever, and all because of that first excited dance off the boat and onto land. I wonder, sometimes, about such accidents, the turns of fate that determine so much of our lives. I am not a particularly smart woman, nor even a canny one, and yet I have been able to learn from experience. I admit, honestly, that when I thought I loved Fred, back in the beginning, I only loved the dream of love. I wanted a home, to be cared for, to be able to believe in another who would not betray me, who would never leave me. Fred, dear as he has been, has betrayed me terribly, even though he has never left me behind. Stepping onto the island of marriage was a way forward; I didn't know it was an option that would limit what came later. And Fred, bless and curse him, must have been similarly cavalier: Or else why me? And yet our rhythms seemed to match.

Even at our worst, and we have had our share of worsts—even then, we have trusted one another to hang in and fight for what we are. I think Shirley and Stanley had that, too. Despite the terrible things they did, the ways they hurt each other, they needed one another at the core. Without her, he was nothing. Without him, she could not go on.

"What are you thinking about?" she said to me suddenly.

I had not drifted off into the future, as it must seem, but was afloat somewhere equally hazy, pillowed in my own embryonic seas. I lowered my head, embarrassed.

"Do you ever wonder, what if I had turned left instead of right? Just then, when I was heading to the door? If I had chosen right, not left, and walked up the street, or up the stairs, what different fates awaited?"

I nodded. Now I think we had been pondering a nearly identical idea.

She leaned in, her pale fleshy cheeks aglow. There were coffee grounds on the table, but she put her hands right there, in the pocked puddles. She said, "I dream about it all the time. I get in the car, I have to drive Stanley here or there, and he says to go right and I am certain it should be left. I am certain left is the direction. Left, left, left, but I go right. I listen and go right."

I nodded. She told me to wait, to stay where I was, and she moved quickly down the hall, graceful despite her size. She returned with a small moss-colored book: "You must read this."

"I will," I said, nearly breathless with the importance of it. It was an old book, worn along the binding, its pages foxed by damp. I could smell the sweet mold, anticipate the crackling of the pages, and I held it up so I could read the title. *An Adventure* tooled in gold leaf, its authors *Two Ladies*. An adventure. "I'll start it now."

"Girls without mothers, you and me. We have to help one another." How did she know? I put a hand on my belly. "You'll be good to her," Shirley said then, and, as she turned to leave the room, added, "My mother thinks I failed her. I'm not thin or dressed properly, not ladylike enough, don't meet her standards. But she has no idea, not really. At least yours has an accurate grasp on the realities."

"My mother? How could you know about my mother?"

"Time," she answered matter-of-factly. "It slips."

I stared at her, speechless.

"Or we do, rather. We slip in time, some of us. We do. Or I wonder if that's what it is." Her laugh, moderate as it sounded, rippled visibly beneath the surface of her skin. Whatever she was, she was more than just eccentric; this was, to me, an exceedingly exciting notion. I asked her what she meant.

"Read the book and then we'll talk. Now I'm off to write a little thing for the devil." She laughed again. I wondered if Stanley was equally strange, if all academics, all brilliant people, were like this. She stopped in the doorway, tilted her head slightly. "And then this afternoon, if I finish my work, perhaps we'll go grocery shopping, and I'll walk you up to campus. Show you around. You can see where Fred will have his office, get a look at the harem."

"Harem?"

"The students," she said, and I could not tell if her tone was mocking me or mocking herself. "Such pretty, bright young things. Just like you, Rose Nemser. Young and pretty, and ever-so-enlightened. So admiring of the great minds that deign to educate them. Those girls love their professors."

AFTER SHE LEFT, I opened the book and turned the first dried pages but could not settle in, the print scrambling under my overwhelmed gaze.

I want to try to reconstruct the way I felt the first time I read *An Adventure*, but it's difficult, like trying to separate out the first time Fred and I made love from all the rest, or to recall the specific weight of holding baby Natalie in my arms—I recall her damp warmth more easily than the work required by my muscles. It was a moment in a continuum—not so odd, considering the material—and never felt like something new. The book is the report of two young British schoolteachers who visited Versailles in the year 1901 and got lost in the gardens near the Petit Trianon—Marie Antoinette's private "farmhouse," the place where she held her amusements. As they tried to choose between the various paths, everything became excessively quiet, *flat and lifeless, like a wood worked in tapestry. There were no effects of light and shade, and no wind stirred the trees. It was all intensely still.* (I quote from memory, sure that I will always know these words.) From behind them, a costumed man came running, insisting that they head right and not left. Right and not left. They went over a bridge, heard running footsteps, passed a servant and her daughter, and then came upon a woman sitting and sketching in the center of her garden: Marie Antoinette. The sound of horse hooves in the distance. When, months later, they returned to Versailles and attempted to retrace their steps, the path they took was not to be found. It didn't exist.

No one believed the women.

They were unable to reproduce the experience.

Eventually, the friendship dissipated.

There was never any proof.

Shirley loved this story, the bitter sweetness of both miracle and aftermath. She loved this story and she shared it with me and became my friend. Part of being loved by Shirley, I suppose, was always that I appreciated those women, too. And I still see why they matter, what they teach us: that an adventure can begin without warning, that the most minor decisions—right, left—can change lives in a moment. That friendships, even the best of them, don't always survive. Oh, and this: that so much of what happens can't ever be proved—the best we can do is write our paltry tales. Those women at Versailles, young, not special in any way—they were brave to share their stories.

Years after her death, when I saw her journals, I was not surprised at how often Shirley mulled over what might have happened in the gardens of Versailles on that hot August afternoon. What she loved most was how intensely the two schoolteachers were told: Go right. Avoid that path. Take this.

There is never any proof. I suppose I will come back to that. There's no one alive to confirm that what I'm writing down is true. That the celebrated novelist Shirley Jackson, age forty-seven, and the pregnant nineteen-year-old Rose Klein Nemser, became the best of friends for one brief moment in time, a wormhole, a slip between one world and another. Is it possible to reserve one's cynicism? Stanley is about to return home, with my husband, Fred, at the end of an arduous day of adulation. Perhaps it is time to mix them their martinis.

"DID YOU TAKE HER TO THE DOCTOR?" Stanley asked me when both men had returned that evening. The younger son, Barry, had arrived earlier, disappearing first into the kitchen and then upstairs to his room. He'd stopped in to see Shirley but not stayed long. She was still hard at work, the typewriter keys clicking like hailstorms, lengthy bursts, some lasting several minutes or more, to be followed by bouts of silence, the grind of the paper roll, a ping or two, and then another long, emotional outpouring of *tap, tap, tap, tap, tap.* It seemed the household functioned around that sound, that it was the linchpin and the director of all activity: if she was typing, that took priority over anything else.

We never did get to campus that first day. I'd sat listening to Shirley's typewriter from the front parlor as I reclined on the clammy leather sofa. Both the armchairs seemed spoken for, even though no one else was in the house, an Agatha Christie opened on one and a set of marked-up galleys on the arm of the other. I had finished *An Adventure* and skimmed its pages again, and, as the early-September heat drifted in through the side windows, I let my eyelids drop and drifted off to sleep. Downstairs, the house seemed to let me sleep easily, without dreaming. Or perhaps it was the exhaustion from the previous night that caused it. In any case, the nausea of the past weeks had entirely left me, and I felt blissfully at peace. But at Stanley's question, I sat bolt upright, guilty as charged.

"Doctor?"

"She didn't tell you."

"No," I said, beginning to formulate an apologetic explanation. His eyebrows, dark and heavy, drew together; his scowl reminded me of my father's, and I had to remind myself that someone like Stanley Hyman was unlikely to use violence. "I didn't know—"

"Shirley," he said, raising his voice so that it carried before him as he entered the library. "You forgot Dr. Toolan."

A short silence.

"I was working," I heard her say. "Stan. I need another hour, I'm almost done. Can you send Barry down to the market, or ask . . . ask the girl, the new girl. Can you ask the little wife to go get us some chops? Rose. Can you ask Rose?"

Fred, who, arriving with Stanley, hadn't moved from the high-ceilinged hallway between the two rooms, nodded to me. "I'll go with you," he whispered. "Come on."

I stood obediently.

"We'll go," Fred told them. "We'll get whatever's needed."

That was fine with Stanley. He didn't care how things happened, so long as they did. Some of the new students were coming to dinner, as was their elder son with his wife and children. When we got to the market, Shirley had already called; the chops were cut and the string beans and potatoes had been set aside. We took a container of milk, and some apples, and a bag of farina, as she'd asked the grocer to tell us.

The chops alone were 89 cents a pound, and she'd ordered enough for twelve. I felt faint at the thought of what a household cost to run. Did they always live like this? There was an awkward moment when Fred pulled out his wallet, knowing he couldn't possibly have enough cash in there to pay, but Mr. Powers told us the Hymans had said to put it on their account, and he walked away before we could pretend to be disappointed. Later, knowing better, I admired the grocer for not taking any cash he could get for Hyman groceries as quickly as possible. He must have been a man most appreciative of the arts, to his own detriment.

We walked up the hill, Fred carrying the two sacks, one in either arm.

"Was it wonderful?" I asked him.

His cheeks flushed pink; I had not an inkling why.

"It was okay."

"Who did you meet? Do you have an office? Do you have a classroom? How was lunch? Is the pay enough? Will you like it? Will you have time to finish your thesis?"

"The pay's fine, Rosie. Nearly five thousand dollars."

For the first time ever, I imagined a life without worry.

"And we'll save most of it, staying here," he said. "They want us to. Stanley thinks you'll be good for Shirley."

"Me? How?"

"My office is next to his, it's huge. It's as big as the one I shared with those other fellows at Temple. Bookshelves and a desk and a view. And the campus is, well, it's like nothing we've ever seen.

Views in every direction, all woods and trees and a little pond with swans in it, and there's this field, in front of the main building. The Commons. And if you walk to the other end, they call it The End of the World, there's a wall and then the world drops off, and you're staring out at enormous green mountains in every direction."

"You like it?" I teased him.

"I like it," he answered seriously.

"Shirley told me about a Bennington student, a girl who disappeared into the mountains," I said then. "She went for a walk by herself one afternoon and never came back, no one ever found her. I'll show you her picture, the articles from the paper."

He shook his head; nobody had mentioned Paula Welden to him.

"Oh, it was years ago, Fred. Still, it makes you think, all those mountain trails leading god knows where. Nobody knows what happened to her." I sighed. "But Shirley says the students are pretty."

He shrugged. "They're okay."

I was still so happy. I had Fred. My world was safe. "Just okay?"

"Don't be ridiculous, Rose. I didn't do anything."

We were two houses away from the Hymans' place, and Fred started walking faster—striding, really—on his much longer legs. "I meant," I began to say, but didn't finish. He turned left, into their driveway, and I paused, watching him, but then I kept walking straight, without him, up the hill another few houses, and through the back gate to the college, so that I could see for myself what my husband had enjoyed that day. When the road split, one large building off to the side and the main campus before me, I thought about my direction. Right turns were the order of the day, I told myself, and strolled past a big barn and over a footpath to the little duck pond and then down into the thick of the dormitories.

Someone had told me—I think Barry the night before—how the Bennington College campus was purposely designed so that no building was easily accessible from another. Entryways did not line up; paths were deliberately several degrees off the direct route— the idea was that nothing would ever be too easy, no excursion possible without conscious thought.

On the face of it, the dormitory buildings appeared to my inexperienced mind to represent simple privilege in its most concrete form. One pretty colonial mansion after another, a parade of Taras down a well-maintained, nicely landscaped drive. And the girls, blowing cigarette rings as they walked, their kohl-outlined eyes and lean dancers' bodies and cleverly embroidered coats and bright stockings and cheerful knitted caps. Bohemian entitlement embodied by one after the other. We were the same age, those girls and I, but it didn't feel that way to me. We were the same age, but none of them knew what it was to be poor, nineteen, and pregnant. They were too bright, too hip, too extraordinary to be tethered to so banal a fate.

Nobody on the dormitory road said hello to me, not the girls arm-in-arm chattering loudly, nor the ones pointedly strolling alone in poetic abstraction, nor the ones paired off with portly professorial types, chins stretched upward like birds hoping to catch morsels of predigested worm. In this world, I was invisible. If I stuck out, it was as someone not worth remembering.

Nonetheless, I moved slowly past each building on the campus, looking for some particular sign, some marker I would know when I saw it. Eventually, I gave up and headed back down the hill, but I told myself I would return soon, look around again. I am not the smartest woman, far from it, and yet I have a certain instinct for danger.

Five

THE BOY WAS WAITING in my room when I went up at the end of the evening. Exhaustion had pulled me from the lively conversation on the porch; my limbs felt heavy and tired as I climbed the stairs. He was propped against my pillows in the dark, playing his guitar.

Soft lemon light from the hallway dappled the floor. He sat up as I entered, lowered his feet off the bed, lifting the guitar with him so that he could continue strumming. Piles of our not-yet-stowed clothing sat on the single armchair. He nodded with a friendly, egalitarian air. "I wanted to ask. I bet you sing."

"I'm very tired, Barry."

"We play, we have a band, and Sally sings. We bet you do, too. We're pretty good, it's cool, Laurie jams with us when he comes up on weekends."

"I don't sing," I said, jaw clenching.

"D'you play?" He had such an open face; no one had wounded him. In this bustling house, he knew only love.

"You should be in bed." I knew my tone was cold. I placed a hand on the doorknob, pulled the door open wider.

"It's fun. Think about it," he said, standing, the guitar neck held easily in his right hand. He loped down the long, book-lined hallway to his room, the one nearest his parents' domain at the front of the house. Oh, I envied him, with his safe bedroom and his long book-lined hallway and the dragonflies that blinked at his windows while crickets nattered outside—someone had taught him to play, not just guitar but with all of life's niceties. I shoved the door shut with my hip, felt the definitive click as the knob settled into place, leaving me apart and separate.

As I got into bed, I felt the bedroom walls press in on me ever so slightly, like the light, loving palms I used to stroke my pregnant belly. God, I envied those children—but at least the house approved of me.

Six

Ten days later, we could still be found at the Hymans' house. The semester was in full swing and our daily habits had become, in their odd way, ordered and predictable.

Breakfast. Two shifts. First twelve-year-old Barry and the two professors, soft-boiled eggs and hot cereal, lightly browned toast spread with butter and marmalade. Shirley presided infrequently; it seemed to be a meal that made itself, although all detritus was the responsibility of the ladies left behind after the last door slam. By eight-thirty, the house was awash in a thick, peaceful silence, the only sounds the light pattersteps of Shirley's cats, the ticking of the hall and kitchen clocks, and the low humming the icebox emitted.

I stayed in bed as long as I could. It was only September, but there was already a morning chill in the house that lingered until long after the sun began to glimmer at the mottled windowpanes. As I dozed, I would feel the way life purred through the house even in the stillness. With my head snug on a pillow against the wall, the house's soul breathed with me, and through me, seeping into the baby's rhythms and my own. I was sleeping better; I felt prepared for the eerie dreams when they came—I felt the house was talking to me, that it liked me and wanted me to know. And because the house liked me, because the house and Shirley liked me, I felt calm and appreciated, safe as I had never imagined I could be.

From the bed, I glimpsed the first reddish leaves drifting slowly through the air; the crisp scent of transformation had never before been so intense, so pleasant. Coffee had begun to taste good to me again; when I smelled the fresh pot, I tossed back the quilt and pulled on my robe. Downstairs, Shirley might already be at work, but if not we would sit and talk in morning murmurs, as if the baby inside me were asleep and not to be awakened. It was evident now, a taut panel across my belly, and I found it soothing to run my hands over it. The gesture invited every stranger to recognize my condition, and I liked that; I was less shy on the baby's behalf already than I was on my own. I liked even more the way it felt to sit with Shirley, in silence, and wait—me for my baby to grow, and she for the abrupt jolt of inspiration that almost always began her workday.

When it came, whether she was at the dishes or staring out the window, cigarette in hand, or beginning to disjoint a raw chicken, she would matter-of-factly cease the activity—turn off the faucets, push back her chair, drop the knife on the counter—and leave the room. It was as if she were called, each morning, by a voice: *Now, now . . . here we go . . .*

I finished the kitchen chore she'd begun and headed upstairs to wash and dress. Fred's gray argyle sweater was my outfit of choice on most mornings, worn over a light wool skirt that I told myself still looked okay, even though I could no longer pull the zipper all the way up or clasp the hook and eye at the waistband. Often, after dressing, I would fall asleep for another hour. I had never been so tired, so absolutely to-the-bone tired, in my entire life, I would think, as I rested against the pillows. I never had to wait for sleep. But after that second drowsing, my energy was high. It was time to walk into town and do the grocery shopping. The baby would be stroked by a number of friendly hands; I didn't mind this invasive gesture, the depersonalization of me in service of the personalization of the life I carried. In fact, I found it comforting, a confirmation that my baby would matter in the world. And by extension, perhaps I would as well.

Funny how it was the life growing inside me that for the first time let me feel as if the story I was living was my own. Sometimes, watching Fred while he pored over student papers, red pen in hand, I would wonder if he had ever felt himself a hero. Even his scent was a gentle one; the slight musk at his neck in the morning was sweet to my nose. And the thoughtfulness with which he listened, the simplicity of his kindness: In his life, with Lou always present as the acerbic, confident twin, had my husband ever felt himself the star of his own story? I never asked him. The question seemed a cruel one, and he was so very kind to me. Perhaps I was wrong to be silent. But that's easy to say now.

In truth, I thought about my own mother more than my husband. I was consumed with two ideas. The first was a determination to be a far, far better mother than she had ever been to me. No screaming fights with my child's father that had the neighbors hanging out their windows. No petty theft. No standing on the street watching while a landlord tossed shabby jackets and damp towels from a third-story window, so that everyone on the block knew precisely how paltry our belongings were, far more humiliating than that we couldn't pay our rent.

I was going to show up for every teacher appointment, help with every science project. I was going to make sure my child had laundered clothes. I was going to clean his ears with a damp washcloth, and teach him which fork to use and how to set a table (as soon as I was certain of those rules myself).

And on the other hand, my pregnancy taught me something else. I became certain that my poor, pathetic mother loved me. To the best of her abilities and at superhuman cost. For all her failures, and they were many, I found it in myself to forgive her nearly everything. I thought about writing to her almost every day. She should know that I loved her, too.

I wanted to explain all this to Shirley. She, too, had a difficult mother—hers a judgmental, conventional socialite who was embarrassed by Shirley's writings, Shirley's weight, Shirley's Jewish husband. I thought Shirley lucky, however; she'd been born into comfort and had the choice to rebel. Did she understand what a luxury that was? Working side by side with her, dusting and changing beds and folding laundry, I had the sense she knew where I'd come from, how frightened I had always been. Sometimes I believed she was the mother who was raising me all over again—to be self-confident and proud, fearless in my speech—and I was the daughter who treated her with honor, never moody or argumentative, always helpful. I knew myself to be less educated, slower on my verbal feet than Jannie and Sally, but I was certain I had them beat for domesticity.

. . .

IN THE AFTERNOONS, before I began to make dinner, I would amuse myself in the Hymans' library, taking down one book after another to feel the nub of the leather against my palms. Stanley told Fred there were thirty thousand volumes on their shelves. Given the floor-to-ceiling bookshelves in every downstairs room and along the hallways, I did not doubt him. There were books everywhere, piled on the side tables and by everybody's beds and even stacked haphazardly on the floors. Sometimes Fred and I would find ourselves in front of a bookcase, stunned silent at the expanse of volumes. "How can I pick just one?" I asked Shirley one afternoon. She'd come in from a visit to Jannie's dorm room to drop off clean sheets and towels, and her cheeks were unusually pink from the crisp September air. Dropping the bulging pillowcase of dirty clothes on a chair near the filigreed mirror in the front hall, she came into the library, perched on the sofa arm right by where I sat cross-legged on the floor, books scattered on the edges of my skirt. "Whatever I pick there'll never be time to read them all!"

"How can you pick just one?" she echoed, selecting the nearest book. She still had her gloves on, but she opened it anyway, and began riffling the deckle-edged pages. "Pick it up and start reading. If you like it, keep it. If you don't, pick another."

"But what will I like?" I asked. When she was cheerful and chatty, like this, I twirled up on the inside as if I were made of the dust bunnies I'd startled when I sat down. All I wanted was to keep her with me, grinning and friendly.

"Try this one," she said. "Maybe you were meant to be a witch."

"Me? I don't think so!" It was an oversized black book with gold lettering, the size of a photo album. *The Discoverie of Witchcraft.* "You don't actually believe this, do you? I mean, it's more of a joke, isn't it?"

Shirley pulled a few more witchcraft titles off a shelf and handed them to me. *"For a charm of powerful trouble, like a hell-broth boil and bubble."*

"Shakespeare," I said, triumphant.

She paid no attention, as if such a realization were so fundamental as to be unworthy of notice. I opened the first book, felt the coarse weave of the ancient pages. "I'll read it, I'll join your—what do they call it?—your coven."

She looked delighted. "We'll make a spell for an easy childbirth." For a moment I imagined she might really have her own club of witches, hold meetings out in the backyard where the old elm stump could serve as a perfect altar. I'd been told it was the bar for impromptu summer parties, but I liked this idea far better.

I laughed out loud, charmed, wishing this were possible. "A coven of housewives," Shirley murmured, and I could see she'd begun to mull with the intensity that meant she'd slipped into her writer's mind. "Methinks we've stumbled onto a rather intriguing idea," she said, drawing the pencil from her bun so that hair spilled to her shoulders lankly as she crossed over to her desk.

The second book was foxed and worn along the spine, caramelized tape at the top where the leather had split. I opened it carefully: published in 1931, its glossy pages were crumbling at the edges. *Witchcraft, Magic & Alchemy.* I would have asked her where it came from and what she'd learned from it, but she was busy adjusting a piece of yellow typing paper against the paper table, and I knew there was no point.

The typewriter's clacking began almost immediately. I sighed, closed the book, but not before I saw that there were pages of beautiful prints inside, of fiends sculpted onto the face of churches, oily creases along cheeks and foreheads, demons engraved or painted or drawn by hand. Would that I were an artist and could create such images. To make something beautiful: oh, that seemed the epitome of accomplishment! I ran a hand around the curve of my belly.

As I straightened the stacks of books, I imagined the house watching over us—Shirley still wearing her buffalo plaid jacket, a cigarette in hand as she hunched at the typewriter; and me, cross-legged, using books like children's blocks to erect a circle of guardians around me. I leaned back against the shelves, watched the rosy beige of the wall as it peeked out between the rows of African masks across from me. I swear the walls glowed approvingly as I lingered there, *Witchcraft, Magic & Alchemy* on my lap.

I could learn witchcraft, I told myself, with a delicious rebellious thrill. Fred intended to provide our baby with material comforts, a settled place in the world. I'd not need magic, of course, any more than Shirley did. But what power it could give me. I opened the book, began to read in earnest.

I REMEMBER ONE MORNING, early that October, when Stanley returned home around ten or ten-thirty in order to pick up some books he needed for the reading seminar that afternoon. Shirley was in the library, deep into a nearly constant clickety-clackety typing. The ideas were flowing. She'd exited the kitchen an hour before, without warning, when I'd picked up someone's half-eaten toast and begun to chew it with ashamed enthusiasm, saying, "I always believe in eating when I can."

Her smile widened—I felt thrilled when I amused her so—and she nodded, and then removed her apron, repeating, "I always believe in eating when I can." "I'm silly," I said, and she answered, "You're a funny child." I was inexplicably happy as I washed the dishes and dried them, replacing the bowls and plates on the shelves in their harum-scarum arrangement.

Stanley's breath was warm against my hair; he'd come up behind me, and I jumped, cheerfully exclaiming in surprise.

"Shh," he said. "She's hard at it."

He placed his fingers lightly on either of my forearms. Shaving cream had dried in a dot just below his right eyebrow, and I could see the black of the pores in his wide, ruddy face. I wanted to wipe my damp hands on the dish towel I held, but I did not want to know if he would grasp me harder if I moved, and so I remained as still as I could while his eyes grazed over the surface of my face.

"Beautiful Rosie," Stanley said. I suppose that women who are often called beautiful have no idea what the rest of us feel like when we hear it, but there are no other syllables so charged. Beautiful. That word easily makes a woman so.

The typing paused. Stanley let go, moved easily past me to the kitchen counter and the pile of books he'd left there earlier.

Shirley's fingers began to tap at the typewriter once again.

"You're good for her," he said.

"I am?"

He opened the topmost book, flipped the pages with great attention. "Last year," he said, placing a finger on the text to mark his place, "she couldn't leave the house. At all."

"Why? What happened? She seems so—she seems fine. To me. I mean."

"She was frightened. Of the women in the village, of the students. She was ill. That's what it was. Dr. Toolan thinks she was depressed. But she's much better since you came here."

"I haven't done anything," I said.

"You give her someone safe to talk to." I didn't respond. Stanley raised an eyebrow at my expression, went on to explain himself. "Someone who isn't thinking about the gossip here. Gossip at the college or in the village."

"Gossip?" I asked.

He put his books under his arms and gave me a sweet, self-deprecating smile. In that moment, I could see again how a woman might find him handsome. "There's never smoke without fire, as the old saw goes."

I waited, trying to ignore the tight way my throat closed.

"But we're fine now. It's over."

Shirley's typing slowed, and he glanced toward the door, more alert to that sound than any other. "Thank you, Rose," he said. And that was it. When the door slammed behind him, Shirley's typing took up its earlier pace. I think she typed straight through until about three o'clock, stopping only when she needed to insert a fresh sheet of paper. Later, as I was about to start dinner, I went to the study door and she was deep in thought, a pencil in hand, poring over a small stack of yellow pages. She looked exhausted but not worn. Happiness in the set of her shoulders, the tilt of her glasses, the bend of her neck. I decided not to ask her my question, just to use the potatoes and leave rice for the next evening.

ALREADY MY RELATIONSHIP with Fred was free of that adolescent engrossment that had marked our first months. Our connection felt matter-of-fact and permanent; he was safety. But he and Stanley didn't interest me that much. And that's what we'd become: me and Shirley; he and Stanley. They talked and talked and talked. To be honest, I felt bewildered at the way they thought about literature. I thought of myself as someone who loved to read. But when I listened to Fred and Stanley, I was confused by what they found in books. They rootled around so deep inside what they called "text" that all the story seemed to disappear. Everything I enjoyed was gone. And, though I never said this aloud, it seemed to me that whatever they were doing to stories was unkind and put a distance between what I believed any writer intended—entertainment— and the reader lucky enough to find that particular book.

Fred and Stanley often stayed up so late, talking, that I didn't even hear my husband come to bed. In our room, I found his scrawled-on yellow legal pads, half the pages written on and turned over, page after page of Stanley's thoughts and Fred's thoughts about them, the outpouring of feverishly connected minds. I never tried to decipher the scrawls. Not only was I not interested, I also felt that what they were doing had some unpleasant effect on the child inside me, as if their diligent dissection might distract the nascent being, turn it from a path of pleasure and fantasy to one of surgical analysis.

I heard them talking Shakespeare. Also Freud and Darwin, sometimes Nathanael West and Flannery O'Connor, but always coming back to Iago. Iago, Iago, Iago, until the thought of Shakespeare's villain brought Stanley's affable face to mind.

They sat at the dining room table—long after the rest of us had moved on, to the dishes, to the porch, or off to homework (Barry) or murder mysteries (Shirley)—discussing Darwin and Freud and Shakespeare. Stanley remained troubled by Iago, about how best to interpret his motivation. They returned to this subject again and again, so that even I began to understand what it was that they pondered so deeply. They were enamored of the notion of pluralist criticism, had concluded it was unethical, if not impossible, to consider a text simply from one critical point of view. The core of *Othello* is the question of Iago's motivation: Why does he lie about Desdemona's faithfulness? What is his purpose? The whole play hinges on this question. So how to read him?

Stanley: "Is Iago a stage villain? The devil? An artist? A Machiavellian? A latent homosexual in love with his best friend and leader?"

Fred: "He's all of them, isn't that what you said?"

Shirley, calling from the living room, standing as she did so, this argument interesting enough to call her from *Cat Among the Pigeons*: "He's the devil."

Stanley: "You dub him the Elizabethan era's James Harris?"

Shirley: "Most certainly."

Me, dishcloth in hand, from the kitchen doorway: "Why?"

She: "Because that's the way Shakespeare wrote him. *So will I turn her virtue into pitch.*"

It seemed Shirley and Stanley had every line of every work of literature locked accurately in memory. Usually both of them re-called identically, but when there was disagreement, Stanley turned out to be the one with the more precise recollection. He was also, and this is not meant as a criticism of Fred, the one most inventive with the question of how to dissect text. Iago, in Stanley's view, could be understood only if one used a plurality of critical tech-niques. Fred soaked in Stanley's words, nodding over and over as Iago's motivation was re-dissected through the psychoanalytic view, through symbolism and theology, and through the history of the play itself and of the folklore roots of the fundamental story. Fred, who was already growing a scrubby beard just like Stanley's, would sit at the table, scribbling down sentences as fast as Stanley spewed them. They drank copious amounts of Scotch, and occasionally—without warning—began to spout dirty limericks until they laughed so hard that Stanley started pounding the table.

Shirley always liked those moments the most. She would put her Agatha Christie or P. D. James down on the chair arm and head back into the dining room, pouring herself another Scotch as if the glass with the melted cubes she'd left in the living room weren't hers. She was happiest, I thought, when she could let words patter down around her, landing and glancing off her upturned face. If he could make her laugh, keep her entertained, Stanley would push himself to greater effort, saliva glistening on his tongue and lips, red-faced. And when the guffaws died, he was always the one to give that last wistful chuckle, as if he already missed how happy he'd been. "Scotch, Shirley! *It wad frae mony a blunder free us,* Shoil, if only we had more of it!" And he would pour into whichever glass he could reach, liquor splashing on the tablecloth. And then he'd sigh, longing for more afterglow before raising the refilled glass to his lips.

Both the Hymans could drink a hell of a lot more than anyone else I knew. She popped pills, too, Dexies to wake up and something else to fall asleep, and there were candy dishes with pills in them in the kitchen and by her bedside. Once or twice, I'd heard her offer a Dexedrine to one of the girls, to help with focus when studying for a test.

But she never, ever seemed out of it. Never drunk, never high. He ranged across so many enthused states of an evening that it was dizzying, but not her. Once in a great while, she got angry and left the room, but she did it quietly, in a kind of grand, noble gesture. For a big and untidy woman, she could be most regal.

This brings us to an evening in mid-October. It had to be a weeknight, because Jannie was on campus and Sally back at her boarding school in Boston. Twelve-year-old Barry was upstairs, supposedly doing homework, but I could hear the vibrato of guitar strings as I walked past his room on my way back downstairs after using the bathroom.

The phone had rung several times during dinner, as often happened. No one answered it. This was also a normal occurrence. But tonight, perhaps because it was chilly and the wind was high, there had seemed to be a greater level of tension about this than usual.

As I held the banister in my right hand, heading down the

stairs, I heard the ringing start again. Shirley was already in the parlor, the men were still at the table, still arguing the logic without end of their eternal debate. The phone rang and rang, perhaps ten rings, and then stopped. In a moment, it started again.

Stanley and Fred continued talking, raising their voices above the ringing phone without paying the slightest attention. I walked past the open door and into the parlor, where Shirley sat stiffly in her chair, head cocked to the side.

"He might as well take the call."

"Excuse me?"

She cracked the back of her mystery and opened it up. "He might as well take her call."

I said, "Who is it?"

She studied me as if I were either very stupid or extremely naïve.

"I'm sorry. I don't understand."

"You don't," she said. "And it's delightful, in its way." She opened her book. It seemed she had begun to read, but then she closed it, sighed, and asked if I felt like taking a walk.

She was often out of breath from the simple act of climbing the stairs, so this surprised me. I nodded, yes, and offered to get both our coats. Shirley's was a well-worn but still luxurious mink; I liked to bury my face in it whenever I went to the closet. She treasured it, I know, perhaps as much I did my fine blue wool. We went out the front. Somehow she was always able to open that sticky door; I never could, and always used the kitchen entrance when I was alone.

I had not walked on the long paths through the campus at night before. The air pocketed in the dips on either side of the tarred road, along the swathes of field that I could sense only in the darkness. One who has never walked on unlit, untraveled roads in the dense, nearly crushing cushion of night air can't possibly know how brilliantly, exhaustingly, each footstep echoes. There's a tautness to it, a tension, and I have never felt so brave as out of doors in such drenched dark, finding my way through the impenetrable air.

Shirley was furious. No fear in her, simply the stiff thudding of her robust frame, her thick-soled shoes. Her breath came quickly; as my eyes adjusted, I could see dense, foggy bursts of it. I tried to match my footsteps to her own; she was not a graceful woman, her rhythms unpredictable at best.

"I suppose," she said suddenly, "that you presume fidelity to be an outmoded and unnecessary feature of marital union?"

"Me?"

"Obviously." Sarcastic.

"You mean cheating? Do I think it's okay to cheat?"

"That is the question on the table, Counselor."

"Well, no," I said. "I hadn't thought. We've never talked about it, but why would one marry and not be faithful? Why make those promises and not mean them? I don't understand."

"We're not supposed to own one another. Or to treat love as if it gives one the right to possession."

I listened to my own footsteps, the hesitance of my treads just a half- or quarter-beat behind each of hers.

I said, "I don't think I would want . . . I mean, marriage is possession, isn't it? Isn't that what you're doing, giving yourself to the other person?"

"I don't know," she said, and all the familiar Shirley—witty, ironic—seemed to have drained from her voice.

"Is Stanley—" I couldn't finish.

"Is Stanley ever not?" she said bitterly.

I had read about open marriages. Somehow I assumed the people involved would be more attractive than Shirley and Stanley. They were old, and flabby, and sloppy, and although they had eyes lit by extraordinary intelligence, I didn't want to touch or be touched by them. Stanley exuded something animal, something charged, but it didn't work in a sexual way on me. Yes, he was attractive, but no, I was not attracted. I didn't feel I should have to make that clear. I was married. That settled the matter. I was out of bounds.

How innocent I was! Some of the least attractive people I know have done some monumental extramarital fornicating, bragged about it, left long marriages because of it. But I honestly couldn't picture either of the Hymans *in flagrante.* They weren't physical beings; even the effort to clear the table or carry a load of books from one room to another seemed demanding. And the notion of sexual pleasure, well, somehow it had always been connected to beauty for me. It was the beauty of Fred's chest and stomach, the muscularity of his organ and the lean of his thighs—that was what made me yearn for him. Not what made me love him, but what made me want to make love to him. And the idea of Stanley, the idea of his penis as an object to emerge, erect, from the nest of that belly, from behind the zipper of those crumpled trousers—well, I did not relish the thought.

And she was certainly no Lady Chatterley. I hated to let my mind draw the pictures it was drawing.

"In the beginning," she said softly, "in the beginning, it was fine. It was part of what made him Stanley, part of what made us special. Unique. More original than anyone else."

Ahead of us, car headlights appeared around a curve and began to bear down the road. We stopped in the grass, waving cheerfully as the white sedan passed us and headed toward the back gates, brake lights winking over the bump before the stone columns.

"But you would think that after twenty-five years, you would begin to think that he would either settle into our life or leave it, not hang like this. Me or them. There is a never-ending supply of them."

"The students."

She nodded.

"That's terrible," I said.

"They are so impressed by Stanley's mind." Again, the sour, sarcastic tone.

I hadn't pictured such a danger until this moment. I had been so tightly focused on our new friends, on the baby alive inside me, on the newness of all of it—I had assumed, I had simply assumed, that the language of marriage we all spoke was a common one.

"Not Fred," I said. "Fred wouldn't."

She snorted. It was not a pleasant sound.

I had never before noticed a creakiness in my hip and thigh, but suddenly I felt pain sear my leg, up into the muscle at my groin. I doubled over. Shirley patted my back.

"I'm not upset," I told her. "I'm fine, it's my leg, the baby moved in a funny way. Fred would never."

"The devil is a most extraordinary teacher." I never could equate plump Stanley with the tall blue-suited devil of Shirley's fiction. I suppose she made her devil thin and blond simply to confuse—

"Why would you say that?" Yes, I could hear the whiny aggrievedness in my voice, could hear but not control it. "Why would you stay? Why ever would you stay with him?"

She turned back in the direction of the house, walking with stiff purpose. I kept up with her. The movement helped the pain. And I had never been the sort of woman who storms off confidently in a fit of fear, or fury.

"I keep trying to understand why I would leave," she said. "Or who I would be, without him. Or what I would want or think or do. Don't get me wrong, silly Rose, I do know I am most to blame if I stay. I fully understand. But I have no idea who I would be."

I took her hand. It lay soft and slightly cold between my own.

She said, "We were your age when we began. Students at Syracuse. Children, I suppose. And now, after all this time, no matter who he . . . screws . . . no matter who he beds, I don't have the slightest idea how I could go. Where I could go. I know why, I fully understand why. I just don't know what life I would make."

"I've always believed in fighting for yourself," I said.

She burst out laughing. "You, little Rose? You?"

At that age, at that time, I felt wise as often as I felt foolish. And every time I was reminded of how little I knew I found it painful and surprising, as if my own frailty had once again crept up to tease me. It doesn't change. The Me I think of, the Me I know, may never outgrow her teenage self, shy and self-effacing.

I can imagine my own daughter will one day seem older than me; she has a sterner core.

Perhaps that's why it is so easy for me to recall the way it felt when Shirley called me Little Rose. And how the night smelled, the odor of cold that one smells only in New England—apples and oak leaves and freezing water, and the day's sun caught in the grass, a blanket of fog around my shoes. I was gratified by her affection, gratified, as if the insult of it was a form of kindness.

I knew so little of love or what it felt like. I could only assume the guises it would take from the novels I had read. And Shirley herself, part creation and part creator, was wisdom and art made manifest. She put an arm around me and leaned some portion of her weight against my shoulders, and I bore it for her. We walked in silence down the long drive, out of the campus and back to the house. Upstairs, Barry's guitar was louder; he was singing. His voice was lovely. The men's debate, at the table, had continued— so many words respoken I could no longer parse the sentences: motivation, pluralism, unconscious, melodrama, complexity, revelation, damnation, imagination, hierarchical, democracy, weakness, temptation. They had not noticed our absence.

The phone rang as I hung our coats in the closet. Shirley, fresh Scotch in hand, paused at the door to the parlor. She did not look at me, nor back at the dining room. The phone rang, five, six times, and then stopped.

"For whom the bell tolls," she said. I wasn't sure how to answer. "Perhaps we must create a spell to silence a most insistent pest."

"I'll help you," I said earnestly. "There has to be a spell for getting rid of someone like her." I tried to imagine who the woman might be. Was she someone I'd seen in the village or on campus? My mind could not create a more compelling woman than the one in front of me, the one Stanley already had.

She leaned in so close that I could feel the chill still clinging to her hair. "Sometimes," she said, "one has to dispense with spells. Be pragmatic. Take action."

"Take action?"

"Yes, action. One has to be practical." Her eyes were unaccountably dark, her mouth taut. I would not want her to be angry with me, not ever, I thought. I felt a tingling pulse through my fingertips and along the curve of my ears, where the heat of the house was challenging the cold I'd brought in with me. "Some situations demand spells, but others, well . . ." She paused, studying me, as if deciding how much she was willing to say. "I am not afraid to take matters into my own hands."

I nodded.

"Not when the situation demands it."

I opened my mouth and closed it, without uttering a word. "Good night, little Rose," she said abruptly, and she winked. I have never forgotten this. She winked.

She was joking, of course. She was the kind of woman who would laugh when things were most tragic. As much as I admired her stories and her novels, I admired this even more. "Sleep well," I told her, but then I was the one who went upstairs.

Later, when Fred came to bed, I did not mention that I'd gone out for a walk. I let him feel the baby kicking—this had just started and was fascinating to me—then I kissed him, turned on my side, and went to sleep.

Seven

"I'LL HELP WITH THAT," Shirley said. I was melting wax off the candlesticks—the Hymans had a motley collection of them, formal cut glass, silver flutes, shabby braided brass, and sturdy pottery. To my mind, she treasured them beyond their value. She generally preferred that I use chipped saucers and juice glasses and rinsed-out jam jars for the sturdy candles whose light we nightly dined by. When we set the table with some of the good sets of candlesticks, we were en route to a more celebratory evening.

After those raucous evenings when our customary numbers were enlarged and the table vibrated with sparring and laughter and liquor, I always spent a good morning hour returning the candlesticks to pristine condition. I loved this task. I loved the melted wax odor, slightly sweet yet redolent of flame. A better smell to me than the cat, cigarette, and pipe residue that laid flat stale prints on every surface in the house from day to day.

This was a few weeks later; perhaps November had begun. I moved over to make room for Shirley at the sink. She chose one of the sterling silver bouquets, elegant draped petals in which the taper would form pistil and stamen, and began to peel the warmed wax with her fingers, working intently, as if there were no higher calling.

"You stopped early," I said.

"I smelled fire."

Observations like this one did not surprise me, not anymore, and I calmly asked if she'd called the fire department. "Oh, no," she said matter-of-factly. "It was a fire from the past, a big one, and I could smell how the wind carrying the screams and falling ash had come from far away. Far away and years past. Who would I call upon for help?"

I bent my head over the sink. The squat blue candleholder I was denuding was from a local potter who'd come to dinner one night; thinking about her elfin chin and yellowing smile, the long gray ponytail slung like a squirrel's tail over her right shoulder, was more pleasurable to imagine than the memories I was now suppressing. Thoughts of my father were ones I never wanted to have. I gritted my teeth. The baby kicked inside me, suddenly alert.

"Rosie," Shirley said. "We all have pasts that shame us."

I held my breath.

"We all do."

I shook my head, re-dipped the candlestick into the bowl of steaming water.

"Fire consumes whatever's in its path, life or structure or forest. Some say the world will end that way." She looked at me quizzically; I didn't know what she meant. "There's no greater force with which to reckon."

"We moved so much," I said. "If only there were a spell for keeping people in one place."

She rested the silver candlestick on the drainboard, wiped her hands on her skirt. With glasses off, her eyelashes were pale as an infant's, her wide face guileless. I bent back over the steaming water. "The experience that makes you who you are. Would you genuinely want to change that?"

"Yes," I said, surprising even myself with the force of the single syllable. I would have, I would have given almost anything to begin as a different person in a different family, with fires only in fireplaces and a mother who dressed me in the morning and was there for me in the afternoon. A snack on the table, and questions about what I'd learned in school. I'd been at friends' apartments when their mothers asked such things, and, oh, envy was the word for what I felt.

"You can tell me anything," Shirley said, picking at the wax with her misshapen fingers.

"There's nothing to tell." A childhood like mine is a cancer; you know it will spread and alter everything it touches, and when you want to preserve the good things, you would be foolish to let them near such poison.

"I won't breathe a word, if it helps you to bare the tale, as Dr. Toolan encourages me to do, well, I'd be honored to receive your confidences."

"I don't want to." I would not tell another soul, I thought. Not ever. And then I made my mind go blank. I am *not* Eleanor, I thought, and grabbed onto the sink edge, abruptly afraid that I might fall. I am *not*.

Shirley looked so sad; faint lines across her forehead, damp on her cheeks. A clicking began in the hot-water pipes beneath the sink. I had the sense the house was impatient, that it wanted me to tell, and I imagined the way the pipes that carried heat and water up its veins were like a lifeblood, I the child inside these walls, a Russian doll nesting in its fecund iterations. "I have to sit." It didn't help; my heart was pounding.

Shirley placed the second silver candlestick in the bowl of hot water, dried her hands by patting them on the dish towel on the table. Her hand on my shoulder was warm; she grasped me firmly; in a moment, I could feel the pulsing of the blood in her fingertips, and it did what she intended—it slowed my heart, it calmed me down.

"We're not so very different," she said softly. "We hoard secrets of the prison house and could such tales unfold. Why, poor Dr. Toolan tries to inspect the palatine bones with his fat butcher's fingers; no matter how enthusiastically he stimulates the maxilla and mandible, there are certain matters I hold entirely to myself. God knows my mother doubts that. She thinks I reveal far too much, but mostly that's because the way I write embarrasses her country club soul. Even so. There are some things I don't like to let myself think about. Secrets even from myself? I wonder sometimes . . ." Her voice trailed away.

I stood and returned to my task, did not look at her—I did not want to see her face. Whatever she thought she'd suffered as a child, it was nothing compared to what I'd endured. Peeling the last resistant hunk of opaque wax from the base of the candlestick, I let my fingers caress the smooth glazed surface, brushed the water from the porous underside.

"Will your parents visit? Do they ever come to stay?" I asked deliberately.

"Why, Rosie," she said. "You have a cruel streak." It amused her, I could tell. She thought I was too small a presence to inflict real injury. She picked at the wax on her candleholder a moment longer, a more deliberate rhythm now, as if she had already returned to the typewriter in her mind.

She was right, of course, but wrong. It was a diversionary tactic. I did not want to confess my father's sins to her, and so, though she knew the what of it—could smell the rain-drenched ash and melted roof shingles in the history of my skin, clinging to the memory of the clothing I'd worn when, as a tiny girl, I accompanied him on his business—I would not deliver the how or the why. Just think what subject matter I might have been.

They did what they had to do, my parents. They did what they chose to do: lord knows I cannot justify any of it, and she might have been able to, Shirley. I could have told her. Could have seen my life created in her words, become a creature settled for posterity in black and white. But I wanted to be her friend, you see. And I was certain no one likes the spawn of petty criminals. Except a man like Fred Nemser, that is, and even his affection I did not actually understand.

STANLEY HAD AN ODDLY EVOCATIVE VOICE. Shirley couldn't carry a tune, but Stanley could perform vague mimicry, so that listening to him sing, while not entirely tuneful, left one thinking about the artist he was imitating, and in a not-unpleasant way. The balladeers of the Appalachians, for example, were well served by the reedy nasality of his singing. I remember the way he would sing some of the morning's intended classroom offerings, out on the porch, his breath visible smoke trailing up into the slatted ceiling. When Fred sang to me, his mouth close to my ear as we huddled under our quilts in the cold bedroom, it was language lulling me to sleep. When Stanley sang, it was a story, complete in detail from start to finish, as if the characters were people he himself knew and wanted others to be introduced to. They were his friends, James Harris and Barbara Allen alike, close to him and real to him.

I was often jealous as Stanley swung his briefcase around the corner and disappeared behind a snowdrift. If I were someone else, another girl, from another world, I would be able to follow him up that hill, onto the campus, and sit in the lecture hall and soak up all the infinite variety of his thoughts. I envied my own husband when he set off, minutes later, his long legs enabling him to catch up to Stanley with ease.

"Remember everything," I would call. "Tell me later."

And Fred would nod, his eyes on the path where Stanley had been last seen, waving a gloved hand in high salute before he, too, disappeared behind the towering snowdrifts. I would head back into the kitchen, humming the ballad Stanley had sung, and once in a while Shirley would tilt her head at me quizzically as we dried the dishes and I would immediately stop. Soon enough, when she began to sing, I would become lost in her storytelling and forgive the inconsistencies of tune:

They had not saild a league, a league,
A league but barely three,
Until she espied his cloven foot,

And she wept right bitterlie
"O yon is the mountain of hell," he cried,
"Where you and I will go."

This particular ballad, the one both Stanley and Shirley loved so much, was called "The Demon Lover." James Harris and Jane Reynolds have destroyed each other through some hundred variations of this ancient song. The basic story is that they plight their troth but the man is pressed into service on a merchant vessel and disappears. Soon Jane learns that the ship has sunk and she is heartbroken. Time goes by, her grief lessens, and eventually she marries a ship's carpenter and has children with him. When James Harris reappears, she does not recognize that he is a devil, fails to notice his cloven hoof. He convinces her to leave her husband and children, and go off to sea with him, her true love. Once their boat disappears over the horizon, the ship's carpenter hangs himself.

Usually James Harris ends up destroying both himself and his beloved Jane. That was the part that Shirley loved.

Folklore is as different from literature as can be: there's no author. And the form is meant to change, whether slowly over time or in a moment as a singer or storyteller perceives a new angle. It is the collective vision that forms a folktale. Stanley concerned himself not only with the unique and evolving structure of the ballad form but also with the psychological and societal needs the stories were intended to fulfill. I can see that "The Demon Lover" supports the notion that marital fidelity is safe, that the devil is the man who lures a woman from her home. But it is also the story of a first love so unforgettable that a woman is willing to risk losing all in order to regain it.

Nowhere in the song, not in a single variant that I have seen, does the balladeer focus on the fates of the abandoned children. Their mother kisses them good-bye and sails off to what she believes will be happiness. What happens to the kids, especially in the versions where the carpenter hangs himself? How do they survive without a father? Do they do better than my sister Helen and me? And why did Shirley love this story so?

A mystery to confuse us all: that loving someone, no matter how deeply, gives just one window into who that other is. Devil or carpenter? Love only gives us faith. We show our love through labor. Yes, even Shirley. The housework and the writing were acts of love.

Shirley and I, both part of what Stanley called the ancient anonymous collective, small voices in the historical agglomeration of ritual and understanding that becomes our folk culture. I am an archetype. My roots go back to the great mother, Gaia, and beyond, into whatever past predates her.

Slipping through time. The very first conversation I had with Shirley, the first one I remember in detail, was about the two maiden schoolteachers who believed themselves to have slipped into the days before the French Revolution, at Marie Antoinette's farm on the grounds of Versailles. Those women believed themselves to have crossed through a hole in the fabric of time. But what if they had the entire notion wrong? Not a slip in time, but an omnipresent self?

Look at me.

I myself am the slip Shirley was so fascinated by, and yet I am hardly fascinating at all. I could have been alive in ancient Rome, beating togas clean in the waters of the Tiber. Or in the Yucatán, pounding corn into grain on the grounds of Chichén Itzá. Centuries from now, there will be someone just like me, shortening the hems on a space-fiber airproof gown, perhaps using only thoughts to do the job. I am the constant, throughout time and place, through history. Put me at Versailles, in the garden, during the last days before the French Revolution, and I will make sure the dauphin cleans his teeth before he goes to bed, will check his spelling lists to make certain he has memorized his assigned words. When it rains, I bring the chairs indoors. When it is sunny, I suggest a picnic.

No wonder those maiden teachers visiting Versailles were concerned with whether they should turn left or right. In the absence of the extraordinary, we become excessively concerned with the mundane. Or perhaps it is that some of us find the mundane so very beautiful. I can't tell. I am overwhelmed with a sense of shame at how little I have been, how little I have mattered in the scheme of things. And yet, I think of Shirley Jackson and Stanley Edgar Hyman, once the Jester Royalty of my world, and they are dead and perhaps quite forgotten. Were they ever that much larger, in the eyes of history, than I?

At some point, in some day of some week of some year, the particulars eventually determined by the fact of the occurrence, each of us is dead and gone. Time fills in our afterimage, puddle water swirling over a thrown pebble.

Eight

In January, about a month before the baby was due, I was in the
library listening to seal-plump Mrs. Morse, the village's library director, a widow who used the position of her desk—overlooking
the quaint triangular square—to monitor all visible activity, and
used the position of her job—overseeing the exchange of written
information—to monitor all thought. It was Mrs. Morse who told
me everyone knew those bohemians from the college thought they
were better than the regular folks, better than us. She thought I
was the Hymans' hired girl. Fred was rarely in the village, except in
Stanley's company, and perhaps it hadn't occurred to her that I was
old enough for marriage. I didn't really look it, except for the indis-
putable fact of my pregnancy. Mrs. Morse seemed to assume I was
an unfortunate from upstate that Mrs. Hyman had taken in, most
likely to practice witchcraft on. Mrs. Morse definitely kept a protec-
tive eye out for me.

It was Mrs. Morse who nodded discreetly toward a well-dressed
blond dropping books at the return desk. "That's her, Professor
Hyman's friend."

"His what?"

"His lady friend." She sniffed. "Not that a married man should . . . but one has to pity him, saddled with that strange, strange woman."

And that was how I learned the most fundamental fact of the Hyman household, that Stanley had fallen in love a couple of years earlier, with a local woman, a bright, attractive woman in her mid-thirties, utterly suitable were he not a married man. Theirs had been a love affair, not a rapid-fire set of encounters, not fucking on his office couch or in her dorm room. She had a home. He wanted to live there. Shirley, on finding out, had nearly died. She had just published *We Have Always Lived in the Castle*, the story of two oddly intertwined sisters who live on a grand but decaying estate on the outskirts of a town just like North Bennington. The elder sister has been found innocent of the poisoning murder of the rest of their family; the girls and their uncle were the only survivors.

Much of the novel has to do with the way the villagers hold the sisters in deferential hostility. The penultimate scene, in which the villagers actually attack the castle, was one I thought of the day we left Bennington forever. Riddled illusions, riddled dreams. I was so far past crying by then, so done with admiration, so exhausted by devotion that my fealty to the Hymans had charred and gone brittle: it, too, had transmuted into resentful fury.

Such fancies were what Shirley Jackson could and did spend her best time cultivating. *We Have Always Lived in the Castle* is both beautiful and terrifying. Still, every imagined work is based in truth: Shirley's hostility to her fellow villagers was exposed in the writing of this novel, and when it was done, she felt not relief but fear. For many months, she did not leave the house, except to visit the psychiatrist Stanley convinced her to see.

Mrs. Morse knew all the details. One had to admire the depth of her research. She nodded proprietorially at the woman, who had stopped to pull her gloves on, while I shook my head doubtfully.

"But she's so, she's so . . ."

"Pretty."

I had to agree. The woman was graceful, blond, conservatively bloused beneath her beige car coat. But stranger than her quiet, pulled-together appearance was the carefully composed nature of her face. Shirley's eyes, even deflected through the thick panes of her cat's-eye glasses, were bright and inquisitive, always darting. Even when she was at her stillest, after several Scotches or first thing in the morning, those eyes never stopped searching: they read moods and weather, tracked a cat across the living room rug, found Barry's friend—the one she'd nicknamed Mealtime because of his unerring instinct for arriving as the dishes were placed at the table—peering in a window, knew where the scissors had been left, surmised what the postman's wife had fed him for lunch. And this woman—I think, but am not sure, that her name was Caroline— deposited her books in the return bin and left the library without once scanning the room for stories or signs, for usable details.

"She doesn't seem at all like his wife," I said. "Like Shirley."

Mrs. Morse made a sound that I can only term a ladylike version of a snort. "Nobody's like that one. Not here or anywhere."

"She's a good woman."

The librarian shrugged, opened the copy of Mary Stewart's *This Rough Magic* I'd selected, and inserted a circulation card. "*Odd* is the word I'd use. Not like the rest of us, doesn't get along."

I thought about explaining that a woman like Shirley didn't have to get along, that it wasn't necessary to belong if you were special. I even opened my mouth to do so.

Mrs. Morse seemed to know what I was about to say. "She's a strange writer, my word, those things she writes. Some of us call it mean-spirited. We know who she means, no matter what names she picks. A decent woman doesn't write about her own neighbors, does she?"

I stammered. "I don't know."

She closed my book with a snap, handed it to me. "He seems like a nice man."

"He is," I said.

"She's a nice lady," Mrs. Morse said, tilting her head toward the door through which Stanley's mistress had exited.

God, I was young. I genuinely believed that moral people lived in small towns, that this was the reason they ran from the Sodom of cities. I didn't understand how weighing one point against the other is a little bit like the geometry of a triangle, perfect in the abstract and impossible in reality. I still believed that people who cheated looked different. Mistresses were large-breasted and blousy, with crayon-red lips. Men who cheated had tired eyes and ran tongues across yellow teeth, leered at random women.

Even worse, I didn't understand that gossip is as dangerous in the country as the urban variant I'd known. Here, too, it alters with repeating and retelling. It is those people who like to clean a story up, improve it—those who know the power of a good read—who are the most dangerous, perhaps. Stories in their hands are altered and reshaped, are thrown and centered, drawn up high and pulled wide like potter's clay. They teach the material of life to conform, that's what they do; it is, and I now know this for certain, an inherently immoral act.

That afternoon, after I placed the chops in the icebox and arranged the Scotch and red wine along the sideboard in the dining room, I stretched out on the misshapen leather couch near the front parlor bookcases and let the baby's insistent kicking keep me from falling asleep. I'd had no idea I could serve as a panacea, but now I knew I'd been one. This household had needed me, and I'd arrived. I'd been more useful here than I'd ever been before, to anyone.

I did not pick up the book about the ladies from Versailles, but it was as if I had, as if my drowsy state freed me from the swollen grounding of my pregnancy and let my thoughts roam, pernicious, up the walls and under floorboards, wafting up the radiator pipes and out in bursts of steam, inspecting the bedrooms and the bathrooms, the long hallway that ran the length of the house from Shirley's room in front to mine at the very back, the closed trunks in the attic with their mantles of accumulated dust and the pile of discarded trousers and sweaters on the floor of Barry's room—I would get to his laundry, I told myself, and felt the baby thump competitively against my ribs. I had taken on the laundry for the family without demur; I was so grateful and it was such an easy thing to do.

. . .

SHIRLEY WAS ASLEEP on their bed, wearing a gray velvet dress, a sheen of sleep heat dampening the broad planes of her cheeks, her pages from the morning at her side. Pencil clutched in clenched palm. She slept so heavily it was difficult to see her breath moving through her body; yet as I floated I saw for the first time the pictures her mind made: a demon dancing and yet it looked like me, a cat curled across my shoulders, candles aflame and violin strings plucked in single-minded cacophony. I saw the book of spells she'd shown me—leather-bound and ancient gray, its pages flipping in midair—and when I opened my eyes I was still on the couch, my hands crossed over my pregnant belly, one leg firmly on the floor. The floorboards emitted that series of light, cheerful creaks that confirmed no one was walking anywhere, that I was alone.

I turned my head, wiped the sleep spittle from my mouth, gazed drowsily at the bookshelves. The book of spells lay on its side, on the floor, as if it had willed itself off the shelf. *A spell for making Stanley faithful,* I told myself. *Or one to make a missing mother return.* Did I want her back? Or would I rather Shirley was happy? I pulled myself up from the couch with a groan and retrieved the book but did not open it. I wanted my mother, yes. But I wanted her to be a person she could never be. Was there any spell inside these musty pages that could turn such a flawed being into someone I'd be proud to call my mother? I didn't think so. When I closed my eyes, I could think only of Shirley, and how even she, worthy as she was, was forced to suffer such pain. I suppose I drifted off again, because I saw Shirley clamber out of bed, retrieve her cardigan, and button it slowly, as if there were something very much on her mind, something that had been decided.

Next I was with her as she strode down the high hill of Prospect Street and up the matching slope on the other side of the village green. She seemed to know precisely where she was going, pale cheeks flushed, boots crunching the sugary layer of frost—was it morning? The sky was pinkish, the view mottled with that gray-blue steam that floats above the valley as the fog rolls off the cold mountains and down, onto the paved, inhabited parts of town. We had not walked in this direction before.

We knocked briskly on a front door, ignoring the politer possibility of the doorbell. And when she answered, I already knew who she would be: Caroline, Stanley's putative lover, no house slippers or ragtag writing cardigan for her. Of course, her loafers were polished, bright copper pennies in the slots. She was too well bred to blink at the sight of her unexpected caller, merely crossed her arms beneath her correctly sized chest and shifted a thigh to prop the front door ajar. She did not invite Shirley inside.

I knew I was asleep; I knew where I was, propped against the pillows on the couch in the Hymans' library, pale afternoon light streaming through the ancient windows and across my legs. And yet it was morning, it was cold, and I was outside, adrift, like a balloon that had lost its tether but not its purpose, and I could see Shirley's mouth moving as she spoke, the way her tongue lifted against her teeth and then drew back, the way her words were steam clouds rising against the warmer inner surface of the open storm door.

I want to say I heard what they said to each other. I didn't. But I knew. I knew Shirley told her not to call again.

Caroline's knuckles tightened; I could see it, hidden as they were beneath the crossing of her upper arms, the cabled wool of her navy sweater. She said, "I haven't telephoned. I am not that type of person." Offended but reserved, that careful near-smile playing on her lips.

"You would bore him. In a week, you would bore him to death."

Caroline's chin lifted. "I would comfort him."

"As if he needs that. He is expert at finding a willing pair of legs to open wide enough. For *comfort*."

"You're cruel."

"Merely honest."

Shirley's open jacket brushed the gray flannel of Caroline's trousers, that's how close she stepped. "He'll never leave, and I can tell you why. He depends on me. For everything, from the first thought he has in the morning until the last sip of Scotch he downs at night. He trusts me. Whatever *comfort* you provide, you'll never take my place." She tapped Caroline's wrist with an arthritic finger. Tapped it again, so lightly. I swear she barely touched her. But Caroline recoiled—grabbed that forearm with the other hand, pressed fingers around the bare flesh with her breath held; she was too well bred to show how much it hurt. "Stay away from me." Her gentle voice gone stiff and, if it was possible, even more formal.

"I have no interest in being near you."

"You'd die without him, that's the only reason, that's why he stays."

"So he tells his doxies."

When Caroline shut the front door in her face, Shirley seemed delighted. She was in no hurry to close the storm door. I watched her gaze triumphantly at the white-painted surface, at the burnished brass knocker, at the silly decorative window too small and high to allow a visitor—at least one as short as the current one—a view inside. Shirley's breath came quickly, steam rolling over steam, the fingers of her right hand so awkwardly misshapen, the nails short, tips grimed as always with pencil dust. I breathed with her; her lungs were mine, and then I opened my eyes, heard her typing in the next room, and fell back asleep again, but this time without dreams.

At least when I awoke a half-hour later, I felt somewhat rested. It was warm in the house, and her pile of pages had mounted while I napped. She was cheerful as we began the dinner preparations. I remember that we talked about the baby's practical needs, that Shirley promised she would dig out the rest of her children's old clothes from the attic for me. I wondered why Laurie's wife had not received them and felt victorious.

THAT NIGHT, AT DINNER, Stanley and Shirley were in particularly fine form. In the late-afternoon post, she'd received an invitation to come back to Syracuse, their alma mater, to receive an award, and she was immensely flattered. "Redemption is mine," she proclaimed, raising her wineglass to ours.

"Redemption is thine, and mine as well," Stanley said, and she began to bemoan the work it would take to get there, the organization involved, the packing and planning for the family's well-being in her absence. He corrected her, arguing there was little involved. "Man's work is from sun to sun—" she began, and he interrupted,

"And Shirley's novel is never done," and I remember the way their eyes met, how very, very married they seemed to be. I was happy. I liked the way Barry watched his parents; I liked the way Fred grinned into his napkin, as if pleasure had spilled over, soiled his face. That librarian was a jealous liar, I told myself. The beef stew on my plate was rich with tomatoes and wine; Shirley had taken kitchen duty tonight, and it was one of those occasions that her concoction turned out to be masterly. I hated that librarian. I hated the idea that there were currents I could not detect, that one could be pulled under, even here.

I slipped a foot out of my shoe and put it gently on top of Fred's oxford, tickling his ankle with my toes. He blinked and swallowed, choking slightly on a too-large piece of carrot. I surprised myself almost as much as I surprised him. It had been weeks since I had done more than tolerate his touch; I was uncomfortable about my size and clumsiness, embarrassed at the presence of the baby, as if the sounds of our lovemaking, even restrained, would impede its growth in some unknowable fashion.

I yawned, putting everything I had into showily smothering it.

Fred said, "You're tired. I'll bring you upstairs." Stanley paused, mid-sentence, and muttered something about Iago being a patient fellow, willing to wait until after dinner. Even Barry bade me a cheerful good night. And Shirley told me to leave my plate. As I rose from the table, and Fred slid a hand under my elbow, Shirley grinned. A lusty, friendly grin. And then she asked Barry whether he'd read Sally's letter from Boston, and the attention of the family shifted.

Upstairs, we were intent and serious. When the bedsprings

began to squeak, Fred lifted and shifted my hips, maneuvering me off the high bed and carefully lowering us both onto the bare wood floor. He finished more quickly than I'd expected him to, and I clenched his naked bottom, not letting him free until I, too, was done. Then he brought me a damp cloth from the bathroom and I cleaned myself. He lay beside me on the bed for quite some time, his breathing matching mine, until I think he decided I had fallen asleep. He pulled his trousers back on, and his sweater, and closed the door with one soft, experienced click. His footsteps on the creaky stairs demonstrated both dexterity and knowledge. Had satiety done its usual trick, I doubt I would have known he'd left.

No mind. A roseate glow polished the tall windows that faced the bed, myopically resisting the dark world outside. I was warm, and had been loved, and the baby's heart pulsed within me. I couldn't tell if it was raining or if the pattering I heard was the constant ticking of the water as it rose within the radiator pipes. A veritable nesting doll of nurture—house, me, baby—in sweet placental drift.

Nine

A FEW AFTERNOONS LATER, I was once again deep in sleep on a couch, this time in the front parlor, when I was awakened by Stanley's hands on my shoulders—he was shaking me, although I don't believe he meant to be so rough: "Where is she? Why weren't you watching?"

He still had his coat on; as the flaps splayed open, I glimpsed dry bits of whatever casserole they'd served for lunch on campus; some dotted his beard as well. The room was cold; he'd left the front door open in his hurry. I tried to remember when I'd last heard typing, that soothing rhythm that lulled me through the days.

"She's gone?" I said stupidly.

He ran up the stairs without answering; I heard his footsteps in the wide hallway, the sound of their door opening, the squeak and thud of a cat unceremoniously rejected. And then the bedsprings as he sat heavily on their bed. I could picture the way his hands cradled his drooped head, the slump of his belly and the gapping of his shabby, speckled shirtfront. I'd been so deeply asleep that my arms and legs were numb and heavy. Only the baby's undulations had the forthright confidence of waking. My eyes were open, but I could barely shift my gaze. Perhaps that's why I heard her footsteps crunching ice on the pavement, heard her turn through the trees into the yard and up the porch.

We had barely a moment before Stanley heard her, just enough for me to see the splash of a handprint along her cheek, the mud on her leg and on the mended pocket of the buffalo plaid jacket some unknown guest had abandoned at the house long before my time, the one we each grabbed when in a hurry. "Where have you been? What happened?"

"I fell." Her voice was matter-of-fact as she brushed at a still-damp splodge on her calf. Stanley thudded down the stairs.

"You left!" He steered her into the kitchen.

"I slipped," she said, the words trailing down the hall as if she wanted me to hear. It did not take a genius to know that she was lying. "I went for a walk and I slipped." Such satisfaction in her tone; she was delighted to have worried him.

I sat up, held my breath so I could hear better. He said, "I told you I talked to her, I told you. I don't lie to you, I never have."

Her voice was too quiet for me to catch her response.

"You didn't have to," he began loudly, and then he, too, began to whisper furiously. One of the gray cats leapt onto my legs and turned, winding down into sleep with an insistent purr. I let her stay, ran my fingers through the soft of her fur. I even admired their battles. Nothing thrown, no neighbors gathering to gape and gossip. Whatever else they were—and I had not forgotten my walk with Shirley in the dark, or any of Mrs. Morse's aspersions—they were so very good at being married. I listened to their voices edge and parry; soon enough I heard her laugh and his accompanying chuckle. They'd settled it, whatever it was. Then the clatter of the plates being drawn from the shelves and the clink of silver.

She was cheerful and he sober as we laid the table, folded the well-laundered napkins. It did not appear to be an effort; rather, they seemed mutually satisfied with whatever they'd agreed to. Later, at dinner, Stanley brought up Spinoza and proceeded to explain why the mind and body are of the same essence, for the benefit of Barry and poor Mealtime, who seemed to be paying an extraordinary price for pot roast, delicious as it was.

THE FOLLOWING WEEK, it was a Tuesday, Mrs. Morse at the library jumped up as I entered. "Did you hear?" she asked. The downy hair on her lined cheeks caught the light from the hanging brass fixtures over the reading table. To be that old was unimaginable to me.

"Hear what?" I asked, looking forward to the gossip.

"What she did? The lady of the house?" Mrs. Morse placed both hands on the oak reading table and took a gaspy breath, as if her heart were racing.

"Who?"

"Your Mrs. Hyman!"

"What did she do?"

"Oh my, oh my word, she went to visit the professor's lady friend. Everyone knows about it, everyone. Scared her half out of her wits, the things she said, her witch's threats. Told her to get out of town. That's what I heard. Everyone knows it. Everyone in town. Mrs. Hyman left a mark on her arm like Satan had burned her to the flesh!" Mrs. Morse's rheumy eyes were open so wide her crow's-feet had stretched flat. "And now, I think she's gone! Run away! I haven't seen her since before the weekend, when she came in to drop off her books." A sob of excitement. "She took out *Herzog*."

"It's a big book," I said mildly.

When Mrs. Morse shook her head, her tightly set bob barely shifted. It was only Tuesday, after all; by Friday, her gray hair would droop loosely in a multiplicity of directions and she'd have her fingers in it whenever she remembered, trying to twist the curl back to its original enthusiasm. "She's always here on Mondays, to read the Sunday *New York Times*. Like clockwork, every week. Something's wrong."

"I'm sure it's not." I tried to hand over my books, but Mrs. Morse was too excited to see the proffered stack.

"I tell you, that Shirley Jackson, she did something. She's not right, I tell you. Her and her witching ways. If that lovely woman, if something has happened to her, it's your lady did it. I promise you that."

I didn't know what to say, and so I repeated myself, said firmly that I was sure the woman would turn up. I wanted to say Shirley never went anywhere without me, I almost said it, but it wasn't true. Had she left the house once that week, or was it twice? When were the dreams true? Never? Ever? I had no idea.

"Do you remember a woman named Paula Welden?" I asked impulsively. "A student years ago? Who disappeared?"

Mrs. Morse's rheumy eyes went wide. "She did that, too, did she? Another friend of Professor Hyman's, I suppose. Well, I must say—"

"That's not what I meant," I said. "What do you remember about her—that's what I wanted to know."

Mrs. Morse leaned closer, with a fierce twist of the lips. "No smoke without fire, isn't that what they say?"

"No, that's not what I meant!" But it was as if I'd plugged some eccentric machine into a wall socket; she was off to her desk, gathering up her ring of keys to go to the file room where old newspapers were stored. Aghast, I left my books on the returns desk and slipped out the door.

Later, as I unpacked the groceries from Powers Market, as I placed the potatoes in the bin and the leg of lamb in the refrigerator, I did not recount the day's gossip but pretended I'd not been in the mood to collect any stories—such vagaries a pregnant lady is allowed. I did not want Shirley to know what others were saying or, worse, what I myself had done. Or perhaps it was that I did not want to see her face as I exposed her. I did not want to know the truth.

Ten

But late in the evening, long after the dishes were done and perhaps because she looked so relaxed in her armchair, one leg tucked underneath her skirt, ice cubes melting in a glass of white wine as she turned the pages of yet another Agatha Christie, I had to ask.

"If you *did* do something, something practical, to make things different—"

"To assert my claim?" Eyebrows raised along with the glass; was she amused or merely pretending to be?

I folded my own legs beneath me, took the crocheted blanket off the back of the leather couch. The men's voices from the dining room a waterfall of tenor and bass, and from outside, the chill stroking of the February gusts against the windowpanes. On the one hand, I was hoping for a story, a fire-in-the-fireplace, brandy-in-the-glass kind of tale. On the other, I wondered if she would confide in me. If there was actually something to confide.

"Shoving down the stairs and poisoned mushrooms have been my characters' choices," she said, tilting her wineglass to catch the light from the brass standing lamp behind her chair. The little glimmer of the liquid-drenched ice cubes seemed to take all her attention. "And of course a little fire-setting here and there."

My own throat felt very dry.

"But as I've gotten older—wiser—I've begun to realize how potent a weapon simple fear can be." She sipped her wine, glanced at me as if we were strangers, and picked up her book again. I admit she frightened me just then, more than a little. But it did not reduce in the slightest or alter by degree my love for her.

Eleven

MY PREGNANCY IS WELL ADVANCED. We have begun to joke about names at the dinner table: Dulcinea, Thor, Prufrock. It has snowed so deeply that there are full days when Shirley and I do not go out of the house, trusting to Mr. Powers at the market to get our chickens to us, our flour, our coffee, our cans of peaches in syrup. Her writing project consumes her. She is happy.

One morning, Stanley asks me what I have read of it. Shirley's typewriter is already clacking away in the parlor, and Stanley's eggs are my responsibility by default. I sigh as I stand over the frying pan, one hand on my back, hair curling over my damp forehead. Slattern in training. Fred has already left for the college; he had a student to see.

"Read of Shirley's novel? Nothing, not really," I say, although in fact I have glanced at the newest pages by the typewriter on several occasions. I don't want either of them to know. I love the bits I've read. The woman in her book is a middle-aged runaway, a widow who discards her entire life to begin again in some anonymous town, with a new name and no history. She is a psychic, or so she claims. I think she is Shirley, or Shirley is she. But could it be that

Shirley always becomes her characters, that when she wrote a schizophrenic, she became one, and that when she wrote an agoraphobic, she became unable to leave the house? In any case, Angela Motorman seems to please her.

"It's good, though, she says," Stanley announces, and the way he studies my face, I see that he is certain I know precisely what the material contains.

"Don't you read her work?"

He sips his coffee, flicks through the pile of papers he has brought to breakfast, but does not pick up his red pencil and begin making teacherly comments. "I always read her work in progress," he says, and then he sips again.

"Well, then."

"She doesn't want me to read this," he says.

I flip the eggs over, for just a moment, so that the glossy yolks begin to lose their sheen, then slide them sunny-side up onto his plate. He takes two pieces of toast, rye, with butter. No juice, just the endless cups of coffee. He has not shaved yet this morning, although he is fully dressed. Perhaps he will go off to work this way.

Even with my slippers on, the chill of the floor creeps into the soles of my feet. As I bring the frying pan to the sink, I shiver involuntarily. When I turn around, having soaked the pan, Stanley has already finished his eggs. A few dark crumbs speckle the front of his sweater, and I think there is a dab of egg at the side of his lip. I don't tell him. After more than five months sharing his home, a part of me remains wary of Stanley's potential for anger, for violence, for passion. Fathers, I know, are unpredictable at best.

He brings his yellow-streaked plate to the sink, layering it into the soapy water I've just left in the frying pan. "Do you sew?"

I nod yes.

"I need a button," he says, and he thrusts his shirt collar toward me between pinched thumb and forefinger. He smells of cigarette smoke and something I can only call the odor of sleep, and his nose is close to my neck. I am big with child, huge with my husband Fred's child, and I am very young but I am certain there is something charged between me and Stanley Hyman. I look through my lashes rather than directly meet his eyes.

"I'll get a needle and thread." On the pantry shelf there is a tiny basket with the basics: white, blue, and black thread; several needles stuck into a wine cork; a small scissors; and a thimble. I unwind a length of white thread, try to get it through the eye of the largest of the three needles. My hand trembles.

He stands in the doorway, pleased with what he has created. I tap the thread end against the needle again and again; every so often it slides partly in and then out, and I am holding my breath. Suddenly my legs feel damp, and I have peed on the Chinese slippers Shirley gave me at Christmas. Those embroidered red silk shoes my first Christmas present ever.

Stanley chuckles.

I have never been so ashamed in my life; I did not feel a muscle letting go.

"Your water," he says.

A small clear puddle between my feet.

"The baby," Stanley says. "Shirley!" he calls, and the typewriter pauses. "It's time for her to go, our little Rose. The baby's coming! I'll go up to campus and get Fred. You drive her to the hospital."

In the bustle that begins then, Shirley's pale cheeks are rosy with officious pleasure. Later I suppose I wonder if she anticipates how badly this will hurt, if she both envies me and is delighted that this pain is coming to another. Stanley moves quickly; they both do. I am in the car, my suitcase at my booted feet—ungainly Shirley knelt to do them—before I actually comprehend what has begun to happen.

Shirley grinds the gears, trying to head safely down the hill. The Morris Minor slides and shifts, and I should be worried we will go off the road, but I am somewhere else, somewhere deep inside where muscles knot and pain feels oddly distant even as its waves rise and surround. Natalie is about to arrive, although I still don't know it will be her. At this moment, just before, she is a perfect stranger I would not recognize were I to stumble upon her unexpectedly.

I remember the whole beginning as a succession of flights and drops, a little see-saw of the right throbs and the wrong.

Henry James's words, the opening of *The Turn of the Screw*, and that sentence is more perfect than any other description I might give: my daughter, perfect manifestation of the imperfection of love, will shift my understanding in precisely this way.

Twelve

Two weeks later, winter was even more harshly set into the Vermont landscape, snow banked deeply on every road, so that the pavement was reduced to a slippery ribbon on which only one vehicle could pass at a time. The Jackson-Hyman home was halfway up the hill beneath the Bennington campus, and neither direction was passable for a new mother and fragile infant. Natalie, wrapped in several blankets, was carried out onto the snow-strewn porch twice a day, mostly so that I could smell the icy fresh air. Motherhood did not come to me easily. My breasts were enormous; I could not stop sweating; I resented my daughter's endless needs and struggled to find the determination to mother her that I had been so wedded to just weeks before. The house and its denizens had begun to irritate me. No one made the slightest attempt to coddle me, to celebrate my accomplishment. If anything, now I was reduced in status, relegated only to the chores of maternity.

Shirley, who had gone back to cooking—her version, which involved astonishing messes and haphazard cleanup, and was often inspired but sometimes failed disastrously—while I was in the hospital, was eager to get back to work on her book. It was impossible to misunderstand this; she avoided the kitchen so assiduously that I had to imagine she was storing her lunch in her desk. The second day after my return she had Fred come ask me what to order for dinner. I believe I roasted two chickens, and listened as the Hymans and my husband cheerfully decimated them down to the bones, while I tried to soothe cranky Natalie in the hallway.

I thought perhaps we would be stuck indoors for eternity, the smells of Natalie's diapers just another stale note to add to the odors of pipe and cigarette tobacco, spilled liquor, food remnants, cat, and mothballs. I was shaky on the stairs—the birth had shocked me profoundly, I admit, and though I was consumed by the person it had produced, there was an *Et tu, Brute?* quality to the way my body had betrayed me I would not soon forget. Sleep was a constant thought—wanting it, falling into it, existing on the edge of it. I thought about my bed in the way I used to think about having money to buy clothing or makeup, as if those few square feet of mattress were the key to happiness.

When Natalie slipped into sleep, I followed her. When she awakened, I did, too. If Fred was home and interested, I would hand him the baby and hope to have enough free time to take a shower and brush through my hair. It was falling out in handfuls, and Shirley told me that constant brushing had allowed her to hold on to her locks after each of her four childbirths. For me, not blessed with Shirley's sharp tongue or her talent, my beautiful hair was one of the things that defined me, that allowed me to feel valuable. I kept a brush in my skirt pocket. Any few seconds I could grab, I would pull it out and try to cosset my cherished hair.

One morning, when the house was quiet—this about a month after Natalie's birth—Shirley brought a stack of laundered diapers into my room. The baby and I were drowsily lounging on the barely made bed, and I'd been studying, not for the first time, the formal prettiness of the missing Bennington student Paula Welden in the newspaper photo I'd excised from the article about her disappearance. Shirley glanced at the wrinkled photo, startled. "You held on to this?"

"Yes," I said. "I worry about her."

"It's late for that," she answered.

"You knew her, didn't you?" Despite her earlier denial, I was certain of it. I don't know why. There was an uncomfortable silence. She was so rarely at a loss, it made me feel sorry for her. And that, for whatever reason, made me think of my mother.

"Were there any letters?" I asked.

"Just Geraldine. So that kills the workday."

One had to be cautious when Shirley's mother was named; the only time I'd seen her cry all winter was while reading a letter Geraldine had sent from the West Coast. The arrival of these missives always gave rise to something—dramatic readings of the contents, even more alcohol than usual, sour mornings-after. Shirley, for all her derision of Geraldine, never failed to write back immediately, sitting over her typewriter to pound out the pages with the same fervor she devoted to her fiction. "If I sent my parents my most recent short story, it would have as much truth in it," she said once, as she unwound the final sheet of a letter from the typewriter. "There. A letter to Mother that's good enough to print in *Ladies' Home*

Journal. Not a curse or a hair out of place, nor a complaining child. Not even an unwashed dish. That's going to please Geraldine."

Shirley picked sleeping Natalie up from the bed with expert efficiency, the sateen edge of the baby's blanket swishing dust motes from the wood floor. "You must always tell the truth," she sing-songed against Natalie's scalp. Her skin, like Natalie's, was pale, thickly dimpled, comforting to the touch. She was better than a mother to me. And when she held my baby, I did feel linked to my own history, my past and future. Love, not of the body but of the ineffable—the love of self that also means the love of others, the love of self not from the swollen, satisfied connection of organ to organ but something slighter and more true, the pull forward and backward of the atoms of our being. "Nattie, Nattie, little one, you will always tell the truth." And witches' curses (fairy godmothers' gifts) come to pass, in stories and in life.

How strange a wish, wasn't it? Shirley lied as a professional duty. But of course she somehow created truth. She chose the best side of the story, shaped and polished it, not so it was perfect, but so it was real. She told me once: "Things have to be true in the world of one's characters, they have to be true in that world, have to happen there." She did not work for the census or take legal depositions, but she ferreted out useful truths all the same. In a story of hers called "The Summer People," Shirley wrote about an elderly couple who is treated royally by all the citizens of their summer community until that one year when they decide to stay on after the holiday season. What follows is terrifying, and a reminder about how situational graciousness can be. Sometimes when I think about how much I loved Shirley, how good she was to me, I try to quell the nagging idea that all of it was conditional, an accident of timing, of mutual need.

Natalie began to fret, and I sat up to take her back. The baby's body folded into my crooked elbow, and I was flooded with a sense of relief I did not yet understand. Owning Natalie made me feel safe. She needed me so much. I was already wary of the day when I would be insufficient and she ashamed. Our heritage requires it, the grim memory of my childhood is written in my soul; I cannot move fast enough to outwit my past. I could sniff her shame arriving on the wind. Would that I could avoid it.

I opened my blouse and my brassiere in order to nurse the baby. Natalie latched on, pulling at my nipple, and I sighed with the pleasure of it. Of mattering so. And Shirley sat on the bed and leaned against me, close to my breast, so that I could feel the brush of her breath against my skin. I have never been so close to another human, not ever, as the three of us were at that moment.

JUST A FEW YEARS AGO, I mentioned to the mother of one of Natalie's friends that I had known Shirley Jackson, and she lit up with a kind of savage delight: "That dyke," she said. "Poor woman, to have to pass as straight all those years. What a life she must have had."

"Dyke?"

She nodded, leaning back against the park bench with an ostentatious thud. "Oh, yes, everyone knows Shirley Jackson was gay," she told me. "Think of her writings, those novels, the way women were always . . . ever so close. You know."

"I knew her," I protested. "There's not a chance."

"Innocent Rosie," she said, as if I weren't nearly thirty, an adult in my own right. "That's the way women handled it, back then."

We slip, we careen through time. We slide, we lurch back to our beginnings.

"She liked men, I know it," I said, remembering the way Shirley looked at Stanley, wanting to entertain him, fascinated by him, enmeshed in him.

"Nobody likes men," the woman said, waving her daughter over to tie an errant shoelace. "Nobody likes men," she repeated, as the child scampered back to the swings.

"Hah." I thought it had to be a joke.

"Men don't like men. Women don't like men. They're many things, but they aren't likable. Men aren't for liking. Women are for liking. Men are for, well, other things."

I laughed out loud.

"It's not funny," she said. "It's true."

I looked around the playground. It was a pretty fall afternoon. None of the other mothers were paying attention to us, pairs of heads tandemed one toward the other, bench after bench of coupled souls confiding, while children ran and scuffled dirt and leaves or jounced on the teeter-totter. Was it possible that men weren't friends with us? I wasn't sure. I never was sure. No matter what Fred and I did to each other, I loved him. I mostly felt more connected to him than to anybody else, except my daughter. But I didn't always tell him what I felt. I treated him with a certain wary consideration, but it was born of knowledge and respect, not fear or sense of danger. He was my friend. I was kind to him. And I liked him. I really think I did.

SHIRLEY AND I LOVED ONE ANOTHER, I admit, and we were close, but if anything, what lingers for me now is a sense of being part of her, and her a part of me. A sense of being seen. But I do recall something else she said that wintry morning, something that perhaps explains her better than anyone ever could. I remember the quiet envy in her voice when she watched me grip baby Natalie against my bare skin. She said, "You love her, don't you?"

And I shrugged, and maybe laughed lightly. Of course I did. My daughter taught me that love was not a choice.

"I loved mine," she said. "As best I could. I do love them."

"Of course you do." Remarkable, given where I came from, how easy this was for me to know.

"My mother. So young when I was born. Do you know, they tried to abort me?"

"What?" Geraldine had told Shirley that?

Shirley nodded, her cheek still gentle against the skin above my breast, her breath mingling with the baby's.

"Why would anyone say that to a child?"

"She wanted me to know. What a sacrifice she'd made for me. That was what she wanted me to know."

My own mother, who stole for me, neglected me, and then disappeared from my life—a pathetic, self-pitying being who would have squeezed a corpse to see if there was something liquid left in it, something she could make use of—even she knew what love was. I can bring to mind the aromas of coffee and cloying musk cologne, the silky slide of her face powder and the brittle ends of her hair-sprayed do, and it adds up to my mother as she leans down to kiss me good night. I am young, perhaps four years old, and I have been alone in some apartment all evening while the others were god knows where. At least my father wasn't home. My mother loves me. Whatever else she is, and not much of it is good, she is a woman who loves her little girls.

"That's horrible, that's vicious," I told Shirley, lifting Natalie off the breast, breaking our momentary trinity. I burped the baby. She was half asleep, and I placed her in the bassinet, tucked her blanket tight, and watched to make sure the drift into sleep was real.

Shirley tapped a finger on the photo of Paula Welden. She shrugged her fleshy shoulders, not meeting my eyes. "We do what we do," she said, mockery rippling through the words.

"Yes," I said uncertainly.

"Do you want me to put the clean diapers away?"

I did. Shirley opened the second dresser drawer and placed the baby's things inside.

"What do you think happened to her?" I asked. "To Paula? After she left the campus? After she hitched the ride to Glastenbury Mountain?" Shirley pushed the drawer shut with a bang, rattling everything on the dresser top: my hairbrush and Fred's shaving things, the baby's talcum powder.

"I've told you, no one knows," she said irritably. That I had elicited an edge was slightly thrilling. I tucked the baby's blanket more tightly.

"She ran away for love, that's the story I prefer," Shirley said slowly, selecting her words. "Paula Welden, that is. She ran from what was stultifying to what would allow her to feel alive."

"Did you know her?" I could not help myself.

Shirley paused. "Rose."

My throat was tight with the danger of it.

"I told you before," she said. "I never knew the girl." That flat delivery. *I never knew the girl,* and yet I'd heard that note before, that rigid, rejecting tone: *Don't ask,* it said to me. *Whatever you do, don't ask.*

And then, out of the blue, she said, "Think what she did to her mother, disappearing. It is our children who betray us. Not we who betray them."

Was she right? Perhaps I had betrayed my mother, not understanding who she was. But I could not believe that. I had seen my mother clearly and never failed to love her. If Natalie does that for me, I'll be satisfied. Of course she'll leave us, won't she? Growing up requires it. At first it will seem a condemnation of every happy moment that has gone before. But I'll come to terms with it. I'll grow to like the new arrangement, the shift in power, the sense of freedom. I expect the pleasure comes later, a chatty letter filled with good news when all you'd been expecting were bills.

"I want to see it," I said. "The place where Paula Welden disappeared." I grabbed a sweater, drew it over my head.

"I have to write my letter."

"I want to see it."

"Well, then, we'll go," she answered, giving in with surprising ease, as if she understood how desperately I needed to see the mountain trail where Paula Welden had gone. I'd find a clue there, in the underbrush, that all the others had missed. I knew it. One left for me, a sign to tell me once and for all how it was possible to be from an honest-to-god family, a picture-perfect family like Paula Welden had, and still want to leave. As I was thinking this, Shirley pulled the baby's sweater off the bed. "Come on." Was she resigned or mischievous? What was she thinking? I don't have any idea.

So shirley did not work that day, a rarity. Instead, we placed the baby in her blanket on the seat between us, and Shirley piloted the Morris Minor to Glastenbury Mountain. She drove with confidence, a perilous cigarette ash hovering over Natalie's swaddled form. It was a gray morning, one of those Vermont mysteries when the sky above and old snow on the ground muddle together to eliminate any sense of horizon, and trees and bushes become eerie iced sentinels along the road. I'd never taken an adventure with Shirley; each of our journeys had been purposeful—to visit her doctor or mine, to pick up a visitor at the train or a large package at the post office or Barry from school on one occasion when he wasn't feeling well. I'd sat in the back after Barry came to the car that afternoon; I preferred not to engage with the children, who by now preferred not to see me at all, as if I were the hired nurse sent to mind their mother. I'd made it clear that I was indifferent to them, and they'd eventually responded in kind. Even Sally, who'd at first been eager to be friends, to share novels she was reading or inquire solicitously about my pregnancy, now met my glance with a sullen indifference. The satisfaction was mine. The fervency with which they loved their mother—and she them—was one of the few thorns in the hide of my happiness.

I can't blame the kids, in hindsight; nor did I blame them then. It had been my choice, from the start. They would have befriended me, had I allowed it.

(Sally, outside the bathroom door, my second morning there, a folded green towel in her arms. "I warmed it. That belly of yours deserves bunting. Here."

"Thanks," I said, lifting it from her proffered hands, imagining she saw herself in me, wanted friendship. "Thank your mother for me."

And the flicker across her face, as if she wasn't sure whether to be amused or offended. She wanted to be fond of me. How Shirley-like she was, her bright, inquisitive gaze, the mobile stretch of her mouth, the vigor of her speech.)

One of the ways I could see how much the kids adored Shirley was physical; they touched her and rubbed against her like cats, sought her ample lap and her shoulder, jockeyed to sit close when they shared their schoolwork with her. Sally was the writer, the one Shirley seemed most drawn to. If Sally snapped at her mother defensively, Shirley would grow distracted and strange, unable to focus. She couldn't fake it when Sally upset her. But for her part, Shirley was often snippish with Jannie. Jannie seemed to tolerate gibes with an ease I admired. I barely knew Laurie, the elder son. Barry I saw the most of, and I envied him the most. She loved him simply. He was an easy, friendly boy—puppyish in his affection, but smart and funny—and Shirley would drop her chopping knife into the onions on the counter so that she could grab him and ruffle his hair at the end of the school day. He'd nod at me politely, but he never said more than hello, rarely looked me in the eye. I'd have understood myself to be invisible, were it not for the way he sometimes jostled me roughly as he headed for his mother's hug. His shoves were purposeful, I could tell, the same way he'd leave the door to Fred's and my bedroom open and his book on the bed some afternoons. Shadows of his body creasing the white coverlet, a flaunted crime scene. The point was that if I would not be his friend, I was invisible.

But today I was alone with Shirley, no children vying for her attention. She was in a good mood. She seemed to like driving in the snow, the way the tires slid on icy snowpack and the engine strained in the effort to tackle the steepening slope. "We're going to Glastenbury, where she really disappeared," she said, "not Baldy, not Bald Mountain, even though that's the one I used when I wrote about her."

"You wrote about Paula Welden?"

Shirley's chin jutted all the way to the steering wheel; she was having trouble seeing the road, what with all the gray slosh the tires churned up and spat onto the window. "Of course," she said. "I'm a practical housewife. I put every part of the chicken to use." She paused, as if the icy road were suddenly more demanding. "My novel *Hangsaman*, well, I thought about her with that. And the story I mentioned. I called it Bad Mountain instead of Glastenbury. Short and to the point."

"I feel funny about her, ever since you told me," I admitted. "As if I could have been Paula, really."

"You?"

I held Natalie tighter. "At least she had that father doing his best to find her."

"You would never be like her," Shirley said, in that same flat tone I'd heard before, when she denied knowing the girl.

"What was she like?" I asked carefully.

Shirley turned left, onto a wide, uneven road, so few tire tracks that each was visible in the plowed-down layer of snow. "I wouldn't know, Rose. How often must I remind you? I did not know the girl."

"Did Stanley?"

"In those days, I knew all of Stanley's students," she said evenly. Caught on some errant splash of icy muck, the windshield wipers screeched against the glass before settling back into a more easy-going *swish, swish.*

"I don't know why the story makes me feel so scared," I whispered, as if Natalie in my lap might understand my weakness. "Even though she was the one who chose, you say it was her choice to go there. Disappearing, there is nothing worse than the idea of it."

"Yes," Shirley said, agreeing. "But you have Fred. He would make sure that you were found."

"That's why you had to write her, to make her last." And in that moment of understanding, despite what I was wondering—what *was* I wondering? What did I suspect? Certain that she was lying, although I did not know why—we were safer together than we might either ever hope to be, apart.

And then she said, "You can't let anything go to waste."

"What story was it, the one you wrote?"

"'The Missing Girl.' Have you gotten to it yet?" I was systematically reading through all the stories in Shirley's files, published and unpublished. On Shirley's dark days, and she still had them with relative frequency, I would look in on her mid-afternoon to discover she'd retreated to their bedroom, where she would hide under the covers until she could convince herself to emerge. With the vestige of tears visible still on her cheeks and along the bosom of one of the velvet dresses she favored, she'd not meet my gaze when she entered the kitchen to join me in the chopping of vegetables for the evening stew. We'd been trying to cook with more consideration for Stanley's heart condition, cutting butter and potatoes, and she would ask a question about what I'd done to brown the mushrooms or I'd ask whether baked squash would please that particular evening's company. She'd open the cupboard door and pull down plates, and we'd continue on as if the day had been a usual one. I'd not tell her my day had been spent reading her old stories and thumbing through witchcraft textbooks, imagining I'd find a spell to cheer her up. But of course she knew.

"It's in the recent files," she said. "An amusing trifle, as Stanley would say."

The narrow highway wound treacherously, so that an oncoming truck threatened to take ownership of our lane. Off Route 9, we turned onto an icy side road; I think it was called Woodford. The car skidded to the right, and I placed my hand firmly on Natalie's sleeping thigh. Shirley steadied the car with a similar maternal insistence. I hadn't realized I'd been holding my breath until I let it out with a long huff. She glanced at me, one brow lifted.

"We witches generally don't perish in snowdrifts," she said.

"Houses drop on you."

"We float proudly above the jeering mob before we plunge and perish in flames."

I pulled Natalie onto my lap, where she gurgled peaceably and turned her head to nuzzle my waist. The blanket was too close to her mouth. I tucked it under and wiped a little bubble of saliva from her lips. Cold as the car was, it smelled of damp books and cigarette smoke, just like the rest of the rooms in the Hyman universe. It occurred to me that Natalie would always recognize this smell and call it home. Lucky girl.

"Ah, here's the entrance to the trail," Shirley said, pulling around the ice-mudded parking circle. It was surrounded by a berm and a ring of skeletal bushes, and beyond that a stand of snow-hooded beeches. At the edge, brook water trickled over sharded boulders of ice, and in the distance I could hear the louder thundering of water in the river. I shivered, thinking about the forest where Hawthorne's Goodman Brown spies his neighbors (and perhaps his own new bride) en route to their coven meeting, and loses his love of life. Did I want to cross into such a dark, forbidding forest? What might become of me if I did?

"I meet my shadow in the deepening shade; I hear my echo in the echoing wood," Shirley said, her voice harsh. I should have known she would love Roethke as much as I. I'd studied him back at Temple University, and thought he spoke to me and for me like no one else I'd yet read. Anyone whose parents have failed them loves Roethke more than any other poet, I suppose. She reached for Natalie, and took my daughter to the breast of her fur coat. "Poor Paula Welden," Shirley said, opening her car door, ancient metal

creaking in the sub-freezing air. "Deserved or not, she met her shadow here."

"It's too cold for Natalie. She isn't dressed properly." She wasn't, I'd not taken time to put on the sweater Shirley'd handed me, just grabbed the blanket from the crib and wrapped it around the baby, thinking there was no way in the world we'd be getting out of the car.

"It's fine. Cold air is good for babies!" Shirley tucked my blanketed infant inside the flaps of her open coat and tilted her head. "Come on."

"Give her back, it's way too cold," I said. "Give me the baby."

"Don't be a silly girl, get out of the car."

"No."

"We can go to where Paula was last seen, one of the shelters. Just a short distance up the path. It's for hunters and summer hikers, and someone saw her there that afternoon. Come on, I want to see it." The trail had been recently used, I could tell. Boot prints hardened to ice prints, several sets of them, as well as the wide swath of ice crumbs churned by snowshoes. But the icicles hanging from tree branches looked as fragile as cheap jewelry. It wasn't safe to take the baby up there.

"She'll catch a chill. Give her to me." I could hear how tight and high my voice was; it hurt my own ears to speak so firmly. All I wanted was to have Natalie back, and yet I didn't open the car door and go around to get her. Instead, I leaned across the seat and held out my hands. "Give me Natalie," I said.

"Case in point. Here you're given choice and you select the only direction that means staying still."

"Give me my baby."

Shirley seemed amused. "Our Rose has thorns." But she bent down to hand me my daughter.

She left the door open, however, so that no matter how tightly I snuggled Natalie, she would be exposed to the same freezing temperatures in or out. Shirley pointed up the trail, and asked me if I could see the beginnings of the ridge. I shook my head no.

"Someone saw her up there, she went up the path and to the right, she made the right turn, Rose, and she argued with a man. That's what the newspapers said. She was seen up there."

"We should go home."

"But someone else saw her at the bus station in Bennington, buying a ticket to Canada, if I remember correctly, and somebody else saw her on a train heading south. Her parents broadcast a radio message asking her to return, no matter what." She paused. "Come to think of it, I wrote a story about that, too."

"It's too cold."

"'Louisa, Please Come Home,' I called it. It's a good one."

I'd already read that one. She was right. It was my favorite of her stories. "Get in the car. It's too cold."

For such a large woman, she drifted with delicacy, seeming to undulate over a snowdrift, undeterred by the frozen tire tracks that dimpled the unplowed lot. An imaginary creature has that freedom to move without regard to bulk or height; she was real, but sometimes I wondered. She called loudly, "You get used to the cold once you're out in it. See those berries? I'm going to get a branch." A trio of trees, just off the parking area but ten feet or more from the path, so that she had to step deep into a crusted bank of snow. Her slight

Chinese slippers went dark; her stockings gleamed with damp; she seemed not to care at all. Turning to smile at me as she wrestled a branch heavy with red berries, her glasses glinting opaquely. Coat wide open, the pale skin of her plump cheeks barely flushed, I thought the whole heavy bulk of her might fall into the snowbank, and I held my breath. At the ready, even if it meant leaving Natalie on the seat and digging into the snow with cold hands to lift her. My treasured navy winter coat ruined in the effort, my shoes permanently stained and gritty. I opened the car door, clutching Natalie inside my coat—she would have been far more cozy had I let Shirley swathe her in the folds of her fur—and picked my way across the snow wash, furious at having compromised. Unwilling to do otherwise.

"Rowanberries, look! Ah, Rose, a rowan tree's a rosebush with a noble heart. It saves the red foxes in winter, welcomes the birds back for spring. First sign that winter's over is robins snacking on them. I like to have a branch on my desk, it's good protection, or so we witches say." She twisted the thin branch left to right and back again, forcing the fibers to tear until the laden bough came off with a snap.

"Protection from what?"

"Lovers find one another, evil's vanquished. Rowanberries attract love and repel wrongdoing. Roses, Rose! I'll bite into one. Give me rowanberry lips, although my eyes aren't blue enough for Robert Graves." She popped a berry in her mouth, winced at the flavor. "Bitter berries, but small price to pay."

"Stanley will hate it if you catch cold," I said.

She considered this with a certain detachment, but it was just for show. Already, she was returning to the car obediently. I followed, huddling over Natalie. We sat quietly for a minute or so, trying to warm up. I watched the icicles dance at the ends of the tree branches and imagined I could hear the tinkling sound they made, such delicate wind chimes capping the brutish beech tree limbs.

"Whatever happened to her, really, isn't as important as what we remember," she said. That idea was so large and complicated I could hardly imagine all its permutations, and so sat silent as our breath fogged the inside of the windshield.

"The worst part is how people forget," she said eventually. Natalie gurgled something plaintive in her sleep. I stroked a chilled baby cheek with the pads of my cold fingers. "They just forget, that's what I wanted to say in the story I wrote. That it's easier to forget than to endure the pain of remembering."

"Yes."

"And feeling what you lost, and imagining what could be the truth. I hate the notion of what-if. And yet I believe it better to be missed than to be forgotten."

"Yes," I said again. I hugged Natalie even tighter, until her eyes opened in surprise and she gave a wail. I would be a mother worthy of missing. I would.

Shirley sniffed suddenly, and then again, with the intensity of a hunting dog.

"What is it?"

"Fire."

No, I thought. *He'll never leave me alone.* But I kept my face still and calm, hoping that for once Shirley would not guess the images in my mind. Wherever in the world he'd landed and whether he was alive or dead, it seemed my father wanted to be caught, and caught by her.

"Where?" I asked.

"A long, long time ago," she said. She closed her eyes, breathed in deeply. "But coming again."

I was silent. My damned father. His scent clung to my soul.

A fire coming could mean only that he would whisk me off, the only times I knew him cheerful and full of stories of the old country, of his mother's cooking or the way light lingered in the mornings in the rocky hills behind the village—hills that had protected them all when they were forced to run. And I'd be adoring him, and proud to be descended from this infinite and never-ending line of sturdy survivors. Loving and admiring, and then the car he'd borrowed would pull up behind a row of buildings in some random town and he'd say, "Sit here," if I was lucky. Because sometimes he wanted me to pour the kerosene with him; it went faster that way, and I'd be dizzy with the smell and with the honor—he never took my sister with him—and I'd be proud when he praised the splashing pattern I created in the narrow hallway at the back, where the stock of toys or insurance files or ladies' undergarments were stored away from customers' view. Fire. He always made me leave before he set it, but there was the sound of lost oxygen in the darkness nonetheless. A siren in the distance, and he would pound the wheel, push the car a little harder. "Sleep, Rose," he'd order. I'd lie down on the seat, close my eyes. A heart pounding so hard takes a long time to slow. I sniffed my fingers; no kerosene touched them, and yet the scent clung. Smelled it for days, no matter the soapy diligence with which I washed my hands. Remembering, I smell it now.

"Who is Graves with the rowanberry lips?" I smoothed the blankets around Natalie; her lips were dark red, even more beautiful than the succulent berries clumped limply on the branch on the seat next to me, droplets of snowmelt glistening. I wanted to read whatever Shirley read. I wanted to know enough to keep up with her, with all of them. If I took a book from the Hyman library each time I finished one, I'd not make a dent in what they had. But I wanted to, desperately. Already, I had read Horace's odes and Emerson's essays, Poe's stories and Hawthorne's, anything to keep up with them at table. To laugh along with the way they spoke to each other, catching reference after reference without effort. Ah, me, I hoped to master being one of them. Or at a minimum, to have their respect.

"Don't worry. We won't be around to see the fires," Shirley said. She smoothed her skirt, straightened her blouse, gave a halfhearted swipe to a damp spot on her skirt.

"We won't?"

"Some might call it fortunate."

"How do you know, how do you do it?"

To her credit, she did not pretend to misunderstand. "I've always been able to." She laughed. "I know what cats think."

"I can only guess what that is."

"They're more interesting than you'd suppose."

I nodded, inexplicably charmed at the notion of all Shirley's cats competing for her attention, even slyer and more insistent than the children.

"There was a camp here, a little cottage. Years ago, when Paula disappeared. It burned down, though. I remember when it burned."

She pointed behind us, and I turned in the seat and for the first time saw the low white ranch house perched in the snow at the very far end of the parking circle, the barbed wire and wood paddock that held four horses, the two dingy windows. Inside, a small child peered at us, as if perched backward on a couch. "Do you know them?" I asked.

She shrugged. "Probably. They bought the place after the fire here."

I said, "How did the fire start?"

She studied me. "You're made of good, aren't you, Rose? You aren't like other girls your age." I sat taller, hugging the baby inside my coat.

Potency surged through me: I was a mother now, with a perfect husband and such an extraordinary friend, I thought that anything was possible. "I want to be important" burst out of my mouth, stark truth. The words hung in the frosty air as if they might etch letters into the ice sheen on the inside of the windshield.

"No, you don't." How dry her tone.

"I do. Maybe I could write. I love books. Perhaps you'll teach me, to hear what cats think and imagine that dead people are still alive. And parents miss you when you disappear. I want to believe what you believe." Slipping so quickly from eager to desperate: I would take the fatness, and the cheating husband, and the messy house and the cats and the depression and all the rest. I really would. If I could know the world the way she did, render it amusing and sardonic and ever so smart, well, then, anything would be worth it. Any suffering, any past, any difficulty. "You'll always matter, you'll never be forgotten." I was breathless with the thought of it. "You'll live forever," I told her. "You'll live in books."

She turned the key to the engine with an angry slip of the wrist. It sputtered reluctantly, and its struggles made Natalie cry. I'd said something wrong. It seemed so unfair, when I'd been trying to tell her that I loved her. She was my hero, and she hated the idea that I admired her. Did worship look so much like its envious twin?

"It takes more than wanting," she said cruelly. "You don't have the language. You don't want to share. You hoard your past. You clean it up. Withhold the details that make you what you don't want to be."

"That's mean."

"You lack courage, Rose. You aren't brave."

"All I am is brave," I said hotly. "You have no idea, you have no idea what I lived through, what my life was like. And you change your stories all the time—you do, you've told me so yourself!"

"I clean them up to make them read better. I don't care what the hell I look like, or anybody else." I found that hard to believe. Her chin trembled—anger or self-pity made manifest—and I told myself it was a kindness not to respond. But honestly, I couldn't speak. I felt that sick, sad nausea that comes when you've told your truest truth and gotten no more notice than if you'd asked to borrow a stamp or whether a hemline was even. Mostly, I did not want to cry.

"I regret nothing," she said then, quietly. I pretended not to know what she imagined my accusation to be.

We returned to the house in silence. As we headed toward town I wished I were Shirley or any other woman in the world. Not

Paula Welden, of course. But with Natalie's gaze steadfastly fixed on mine, I wanted more. I wanted to be worthy.

BACK AT THE HOUSE, Sally was reading in the parlor, sprawled across the long, shabby sofa as if she'd been there all week. For me, it was the first indication that Friday afternoon had arrived. Sally's presence always signaled the end of the workweek. Natalie another week older and Sally installed back at the dining room table, where her banter with the writers and artists and critics who lounged there put my feeble efforts to shame. Yes, I admit it; my heart did the proverbial sink into the pit of the stomach. As usual, she did no more than lift her eyebrows at the sight of me. We were at war, unspoken, but war all the same.

I brought the laundry into the living room and began to pair socks while Sally and Shirley hashed over the week's events. Sally had brought a story to share with her mother, something she'd written for school, and I was pleased when Shirley began to criticize it. "You trivialize your gift," she told her daughter, and I had to suppress a little smile of satisfaction. If I ever wrote anything, I'd wait until it was perfect before I showed it to Shirley. I wouldn't waste her time.

Stanley came home next, and was pleased to hear that we'd been out, even more so because we'd been to Glastenbury Mountain. "Always the best place to ferret out the next piece of the plot," he said approvingly.

"We weren't working," Shirley said, defiant and a little excited. Challenging him to tell her no, to say that a day without writing disappointed him or even that it pleased him—daring him to tell her what to do.

Was I the only one to breathe in sharply? Bright-eyed, observant Sally watched them both as well. Only I saw something darker there, I thought, the result of knowing Shirley best.

"Your girls always go to the mountains, don't they?" Stanley said finally. It took me a moment to realize it was Shirley's characters he meant.

"I suppose they do." Dry Shirley, giving him nothing, and yet she was flirting.

"What does Natalie say? Not Rosie's baby but yours—the girl in *Hangsaman*?"

"Remind me," she said, delighted.

"Oh, what was it?" He shook his head from side to side, amused, thoughtful. A game, of course; it was Stanley, and so he remembered precisely, he always did. *"'A tree is not a human thing, with its feet in the ground and its back hard against the sky; it cannot tolerate the small human tendernesses moving beneath . . .'"*

"I thought you would do the part before that, when they're in the woods and she's scared." She had sat up, straighter, and her cheeks were flushed with pleasure.

He nodded. "I can do that, too, Shirl."

She waited. I watched her watch him as he examined the voluminous storage depot that was his memory, and saw them both grin, relieved, when he nodded to himself, having accessed precisely the snippet of her prose he wanted to recall: *"'Or choose perhaps a throne higher than the moon, on a black rock, where sitting we can rule the world, where the stars are around our feet and the sun rises when we glance down and beckon'"*—he cleared his throat—*"'where far below there are contests to make us laugh and above us there is nothing but our own crowns and sitting there forever we can watch and end eternity with a gesture of our finger . . .'"*

"A veritable steel trap, that brain of yours, S. Edgar."

They were both so pleased with themselves I was startled when Stanley went to the sideboard and poured their evening drinks. Somehow I expected to keep talking about Shirley's novel *Hangsaman* a bit longer; they seemed to be having such a good time. As I continued with the laundry, I thought about the book, Shirley's second novel. It had been written at Bennington, but Natalie was hardly the well-bred Connecticut girl I imagined Paula Welden to be. I'd forgotten her when we picked the baby's name. No one had mentioned it, either. Maybe every girl has a little bit of Natalie in her. And a little Paula Welden, too.

"Lost girls go to the mountains," Shirley said lightly, sipping her drink, and we laughed together; even Sally and I momentarily joined in the sheer pleasure of knowing that in this often confounding world, there was a clear destination for the sorrowful, the angry, and the confused. Someplace far from this house, from this lovely nest of brilliant, fascinating people. Glastenbury Mountain. Now that I knew the mountain's dark secret, I need never visit her slopes again.

Before Fred returned from the college, I had all the laundry folded. As I hoisted the basket to the stairs, it seemed that the very walls smiled from behind the watercolor paintings by Shirley and the children's school photographs. Thrummed in approbation, approval of my industry and dedication. I went from room to room, stowing clean laundry in the correct drawers, proud and cheerful. In our room, Natalie snored gently, one fist curled by her plump cheek. I tucked her blanket around her feet, and took the back stairs down, empty laundry basket in hand. Shirley and Sally sounded happy in the kitchen, where they were finishing up dinner preparations, stewed peaches and a lamb stew. When Sally laughed loudly, I smiled agreeably so as not to set my teeth on edge. And when Fred came home, I hugged and hugged and hugged him until he practically had to peel my arms off his shoulders. He was my family, after all, and he had promised to love me forever. We went upstairs. I told him everything, repeating everything I'd learned about Paula Welden, about the mysterious way she'd disappeared. Almost everything. I did not say anything about Shirley, about how strange her voice had been when she'd said she'd never met the girl. And I did not tell him that Paula Welden reminded me of me, of how invisible one can be and still be somewhere on this earth.

I nursed the baby while he put his books and papers on the desk. I changed Natalie's diaper. He told me about the inspired discussion his class had had about the Book of Genesis and harvest rituals. Confidence made him even handsomer, and I clung to him as we made our way down the stairs as the first dinner guests arrived. I was so proud to be his wife. How could anybody be dissatisfied to have what I had?

Thirteen

IT WAS PART OF THE PECULIARITY of Shirley and Stanley that the visit from Fred's parents was not a disaster. You would think that a couple that had entertained Dylan Thomas—held a raucous party in his honor that spilled out into the snowy yard and permanently offended the neighbors—would have little interest in an elderly candy store owner and his delicately tyrannical wife. But the Hymans behaved so graciously with Selma and Marvin Nemser that I believe when they climbed back up the steps of the train that Sunday morning in March, both Fred's parents were congratulating themselves on their son's good fortune. Mrs. Nemser even patted my cheeks after she leaned over to give her new granddaughter one last kiss.

"I got my figure back quickly, just like you," she said. "Twins, and I was back in my own clothes before the month was out." We were related by blood now. She was trying to like me, to make the best of things.

So cold it was, that day and every other until the very end of the month. It made us plan all outings as if we were off to climb Everest. Mrs. Nemser had borrowed gloves from Shirley, and I hoped no one would have to remind her to give them back. It would have been easy to assume the Hymans were rich, to think the gloves wouldn't matter. I hated to think I might have to say something. I remember the puff of fog that wafted from Fred's mother's mouth, the way her teeth gleamed slightly yellow behind it. She had outlined her lips with red lipstick, the way she did for only the most elegant occasions, and in the harsh March light the flat paint drew attention to the gray hairs that sprouted along her upper lip. I would never let myself go to seed that way, I thought. I had created life and I was no longer afraid of Selma.

"Have you seen my mother?" I asked, stepping closer in the hope that Selma would answer in a whisper.

"No. She hasn't come around." She was stripping Shirley's soft leather gloves down her fingers, regret at imminent loss already apparent, her face concentrated in longing.

"I wrote to her. About the baby. But the letter came back, and I'm worried. I phoned Mrs. Cartwright in Wayne, the lady my sister Helen keeps house for. She said Helen left. Where could they have gone?"

Shirley, chuckling at something Fred or Marvin had said, paid no attention to Selma's proffering of the gloves. Instead, I ended up holding them, clutched under Natalie. "I wouldn't know about your mother. I'm sorry, Rose."

"If you hear anything, you'll tell me, won't you?"

Selma Nemser leaned down again, kissed Natalie's hatted head. "Of course, dear. But sometimes—" She stopped. I know she meant to say that some relatives were a blessing to lose. I could not agree. I don't think anyone who has ever loved someone like my mother would. Because while we pretend we have choice about who we love, it isn't actually true.

I EXPECTED THAT after the Nemsers left we would laugh about them, just a little. Chuckle at the undue respect they showed the gold-rimmed china, despite its chipped edges and scratched paint. Marvel at the way Mr. Nemser cleared his throat, pushed his glasses up on his nose, and fiddled with the top button on his shirt whenever he began to speak about Fred's twin brother, Lou. As if acknowledging that Fred's being doubled somewhere, out in the world, was an uncomfortable fact, vividly tied to a sense of guilt.

At dinner, over Shirley's chicken with artichoke hearts—one of her fallback entertaining dishes—Marvin had told us about Lou's recent promotion at the *Examiner*. "Weekends to begin, but Lou says after six months if he don't start splitting with the other two news editors straight down the biscuit they'll be some surprise in store."

"He'd leave?" Fred asked.

"Never." Selma's certainty would have ended all discussion under normal circumstances, but Shirley put her fork down and took a sip of wine.

"Why not?" she asked. "Move for the opportunity? Try another city? He's a boy who likes to stay close to home?"

Selma nodded proudly.

"Does he look like our Fred?"

"Identical," their mother said.

"No," I said.

At either end of the table, Stanley and Shirley raised their wine-glasses in unison, drank deeply, and picked up their forks. Jannie, the elder daughter, the only one of the kids home that evening, studied us with a grave consideration that bordered on sympathy. She was the one at school at Bennington. I never could decide if she, with her placid authority, was the bigger threat to my relationship with Shirley or if Sally—bracingly intelligent and wickedly fun— was Shirley's favorite. Barry was a most adorable pet but far too young to be real competition: it was the girls who most concerned me, although I never let them see it. Even now, as Jannie watched me, I let my eyes brush over her as if she weren't present.

"Which is it?" Stanley asked, calmly. Fred's loafer touched my calf, ever so lightly, and I could not tell whether it was reproach or encouragement. I focused on the pale, lemony swirls of chicken broth that coated my plate, even after I had reduced the breast and vegetables to a pile of frail bones.

Every so often, a swish of cold air drifted over my legs and feet, as if the ghosts of cats long dead sought table scraps. I shivered, my thoughts on Natalie, who was soundly asleep upstairs under a heap of blankets.

"They're identical," said Marvin, and Selma nodded.

"We were," Fred said. "As kids, nobody could tell us apart, but now it's easier."

"Not with that beard of yours, just the way your brother wears his. Such handsome faces you both have, I don't understand why you want to cover them up."

"Fred's taller," I said.

"Less than an inch." Selma shrugged dismissively.

Shirley dotted her lips with one of the napkins I'd ironed, offered to pass the chicken again, then signaled to Jannie that it was time to clear. When I stood, Shirley told me to stay where I was. I sat. I would have liked Fred's mother to know I pulled my weight in the household, that I was no freeloader. But I sat all the same.

"Is he married?" Shirley asked. "Does he have a girl?"

Selma sat up taller. "He's young yet. There's no hurry. Not everyone's in such a rush."

Shirley's glance was delighted. Sympathetic, amused, delighted.

"Help me in the kitchen," she said, and I pushed back my chair willingly. It turned out what she wanted was just that, kitchen help, and she set me to whisking cream for the pie while she pulled down dessert plates and glasses for port. She hummed cheerfully, keeping time to the Glenn Miller record Stanley had put on. I whipped and whipped, until my right arm grew sore. The cold of the bowl cut through the wool of my sweater. At the same time, I felt warm, a trickle of sweat chilling the skin at my neck.

Down the hall, Selma began to giggle, the sound strangled, high and overripe, pleasure on the edge. I heard something knock into a wall, Stanley's laugh, an alarmed, amused warning from Fred. They were dancing.

"Shirl! Come quick! Let Freddy give you a turn!"

Stanley was most definitely drunk.

"Someone's at the door," I said. I felt the pounding move the floor and walls, rather than heard it, the music was so loud. At first I'd thought it was the reverberation of drums and cymbals on Stanley's record.

Shirley put down the pie knife. "Stan! Someone! Get the door!"

"I have arrived, in all my glory!" It was Kenneth Burke, Stanley's mentor, a much older visiting professor in the English department. With him came a blast of freezing air, the stamping of frozen feet, and a call for Scotch. Shirley drew down a stack of glasses, turned to me with sparkling eyes.

"Let's see how Burke does with Selma," she whispered.

"I'll finish in here."

She was already gone, eager to see what chemical reaction this combination might create. I finished whipping the cream, put the bowl and plates on a tray, and took a deep breath, wishing I could stay in the kitchen by myself all night. If Natalie woke, reprieve would come; I let my mind drift up the stairs, willing her to do so, but as usual, she did what she wanted. In this case, it was to sleep through it all.

Burke and Selma were dancing. I could see a certain beauty in her. I had never seen her happier, her marcelled gray bob tilted so that the ends brushed against the pale blue of her new sweater. Her mouth was wide, her chest high, her matronly belly pulled in and shoulders back. Despite her sensible shoes, she moved like a lithe, much younger woman. Normally, she watched with such stern judgmental coldness that the prettiness of her bones was virtually invisible. Burke seemed to like her.

Marvin and Stanley leaned against the bookcases, gazing at the dancers like doting parents, watching how Burke dipped her just a little too far. He was shorter than she, and Selma was not a tall woman—no more than five feet, four inches, either of them. Compact and vibrant, Burke radiated openness. Where Stanley charmed by looking closely at you, so that you felt seen, kind Burke took in the entire universe at a glance. I have never known a man more appreciative, more understanding, more certain of the goodness of others. And yet his wit was astounding. Selma's color was high. "Oh my! Oh my!" she said as I entered the room. "Time for a younger woman to dance!"

"No," Shirley said blithely. She and Fred, drinks in hand, had taken up observational positions on the couch. "Look at you, Selma! You're grooving!"

"Dance with me," Marvin asked her.

Shirley joined him with alacrity. Neither Marvin nor Shirley moved with the grace of Selma and Burke, but they stepped and dipped and turned. I offered Stanley a Scotch. He took it. As he sipped, he called across the room to Fred, loudly. "You know what I think? You know what I think? I think Salinger's a phony and a fake."

Burke twirled Selma. The edge of the rug had lifted slightly. I wanted to warn him to watch where he stepped. Shirley and Marvin landed by the liquor cart and poured themselves fresh drinks.

"Why'd you bring up Salinger?" I asked.

Shirley said, "Burke's a better dancer."

Stanley ignored both of us.

"Salinger's a fake," Stanley said again, even louder this time.

Burke winked at me.

"He's a phony, Burke, for all he says he hates phonies, that's what he is. Shallow. Wouldn't know the Tao from a towel rack, if he walked right past both of them."

Shirley hoisted her glass of port, entering the fray. "Stan's right," she proclaimed. "Hiding up there in New Hampshire as if he needs solitude. He's afraid of being seen. He's afraid, that's all."

Burke led Selma easily, without watching her movements. He was a dapper man, even when drunk. Never a hair out of place or his shirt collar imperfectly pressed. He always looked as if he were amused, and tonight was no exception. He held on to Selma's hand and waist though he'd stopped dancing. "Salinger's hardly a fearful man, Stan, simply a private one."

"He's a know-nothing, Kenneth, it's undeniable. Yes, he's the fashion, the spurious fashion. Salinger's Big Religious Package, that's what I call it. A jumble of religions."

"That's right," Shirley said, emphatically. "The Upanishads, the Sutras, Meister Eckhart—"

Stanley took over. "Buddhism, Jesus, the Old Testament, Lao Tse, Sri Ramakrishna, Chuang-Tzu, Suzuki, Epictetus. I could go on for ten minutes, listing all the goulash he's put together. It makes no sense, not for Zooey, not for anyone. A lot of mumbo jumbo, and it's supposed to add up to what?"

"I like Salinger," Fred said quietly.

"Shhh," Selma said. Marvin was plopped in Stanley's armchair, thumbing through one of Shirley's mystery stories, drink in hand. Strands of his comb-over had flipped backward, a slick gray waterfall.

Burke dropped Selma's hands, walked over to the tray, and poured himself a Scotch.

"They're all sacred symbols. Related by intent."

Stanley's face had grown very red; he was angrier than made

sense. "Decorative symbols. Related by their inorganic connection to the story."

"What story are we talking about?" Selma asked, from the abandoned dance floor. Posture erect, one foot pointed and chest lifted, her breathing still slightly labored. Her right hand curved, waiting for another palm to meet it. Marvin turned a page, ran his fingers through his hair, inadvertently rectifying the comb-over situation.

"A story called 'Zooey,' Momma. By a man named Salinger."

Burke said, "I detect a certain measured whistling in the dark, Stan. Salinger has his strengths."

"You defend him because you like him."

"He has considerable talent."

"He won't last," Stanley said. "Flannery will. Baldwin will. Faulkner. Nabokov, yes. Not Bellow. And most definitively not Salinger."

"On what basis do you speculate?"

"I've told you. He's a fake, Burke. That's all he is."

"Ah Stanley, thou shalt not presume to know what history has not yet determined. Only time can tell," Burke said evenly.

Stanley swept an arm across his waist and bowed. "I'm not you, Burke, I admit it. Merely a lowly courtier."

"Don't try so hard, Stan," Burke said. Genial but cutting.

"A novel should require knowledge, should challenge the reader."

"Why?"

"Because otherwise it's cheap and tawdry, a dumbed-down affair. Do I display my member to an idiot? Then why the product of my brain, the most precious essence I produce?"

"For pleasure," I wished to say. He would have been amused, I suppose.

Shirley offered Burke a piece of the apple pie. He took it.

Stanley changed the record, put on Benny Goodman, then seized Selma Nemser with his pudgy hands. "Dance with me," he said, pulling her in just a little too close. Selma's smile tightened, but she acceded politely, her plump jaw resting uncomfortably just below Stan's collarbone.

I touched Fred on the shoulder. I think he was about to cut in on Stan and his mother, but Shirley called from across the room, "Stan. It's time for dessert."

He didn't seem to hear her.

"Stan."

His eyes were closed, his arm crossing Selma's broad back; he hummed along with the music. Burke lounged near Marvin's chair. I think Burke was reading over Marvin's shoulder; it was an Agatha Christie mystery, though I'm not sure which one. Fred and I waited near the couch, as if we both knew something was about to happen. I remember standing very still.

Shirley picked up the pie dish and dropped it, quite deliberately, porcelain shards and slippery apple slices scattering along the oak floor, tangling in the fringe of the Oriental rug. A single crash, no reverberation, its futility rendered even sadder by what followed.

Marvin read. Burke sipped his Scotch. And Selma and Stanley kept dancing. Shirley stood stiffly, her smile fixed and miserable, eyes bright with fury or unshed tears, one of the more awful sights I have ever seen. A streak of soggy apple clung to the bosom of her wrinkled green blouse, as if someone had thrown it at her.

"*Not waving*," she whispered. It was a line from a poem of Stevie Smith's that Shirley had shown me a few mornings before. It broke my heart when I heard it first, and then again that evening.

Nobody heard him, the dead man, and still he lay moaning: I was much further out than you thought and not waving but drowning.

"*Too cold always*," I whispered, a line from the next stanza. Shirley said nothing, but I could tell that she was grateful.

After a time, I knelt and began to pick up the larger pieces of broken china.

In the morning, at breakfast, the Nemsers emerged packed and cheerful, ate their eggs with gusto, and pronounced the visit, and their granddaughter, a grand success. We walked them down the hill and up the main road to the train station. The good-byes were enthusiastic, future visits promised, inside jokes alluded to, hugs exchanged.

Trudging back to the house, ahead of the men (Fred trailed behind, holding Natalie, as if afraid I might slip carrying her), squeezed close by the high snowdrifts on either edge of the sidewalk, Shirley congratulated me on my good fortune. "They're nice, Fred's parents. They won't do anything to hurt you."

I wanted to say I didn't agree, but it seemed ungracious.

"Lou actually has a girlfriend. I don't know why she didn't want to tell you," was what I said instead.

"Does she know?"

"Definitely. In fact, she's thrilled about it. Usually she can't stop bragging, how Lillian's father is a lawyer. And Lillian's house has two spare bedrooms. And Lillian's mother and her sister inherited an apartment on the boardwalk in Atlantic City. Selma's dream bride for Lou."

Shirley's cheeks were mottled pink, the texture slightly roughened by the cold.

"You should speak out more," she said. "Say what you think."

"No," I told her. "Why make them angry with me? What good would it do? They already think I'm—they already think he married beneath himself."

"Impossible," she said. "Who wouldn't love you?"

"Oh, so many people. So very many people," I said, thrilled at the thought.

She raised a pale eyebrow. "But why? What have you ever done?"

"I want to be somebody," I told her fiercely, forgetting that she'd rejected this notion already. Rather, not forgetting, simply hoping that a second try might reveal an open doorway I'd not seen before. "Like you."

"Like me?" Shirley's smile was small and odd.

"Of course."

The men, behind us, began chuckling about something, a low rumble of approval. Stanley declaimed, *"Is this a dagger which I see before me?"* When I glanced back, the blanket had slipped from over Natalie's mouth and she, too, looked amused.

"I'm not somebody at all," Shirley said. She took my elbow, as if for balance on the ice-streaked sidewalk.

"I want to be important, to matter. I want never to worry about money. I want to be free, and happy, and comfortable in myself, and not ashamed."

"Perhaps you want a magic wand as well."

"You think I'm silly."

Shirley shook her head no. "I think you're young. I forget, sometimes, you're as young as my own children.

"Rose," she said, "Fred loves you because you make the past better. You don't go where it's uncomfortable. Like his mother, you see the good side of things."

"I don't want to be like Selma. I want to be like you."

Her smile was small, her eyes so sad no sunlight glinted in them. The snow slushed with sucking sounds in the spots that weren't too icy to tread on.

"Be happy, Rose. What I do is the devil's work. You wouldn't like it." I didn't answer. I fancied myself cruel enough to see the world like she did.

"Don't live in your head," she said. "It doesn't suit you."

I didn't know what to say. I was hurt that she did not see herself in me. I hadn't really imagined myself a writer; rather, I'd imagined myself her perfect daughter, the heir to her craft. Perhaps I didn't write—not yet—but I was living a writer's life. I lived Shirley's life. Right at her side.

"And one more thing," she said harshly, as we turned in to their driveway. "Don't expect fulfillment to seek you out. It won't find you if you hide up there in the back bedroom, waiting. If you want to be someone, do something. Whatever it is. Stop hiding behind

me, or Fred or anyone. Find what you love. Go out into the world
and do it."

She worked the sticky doorknob up and left, pushing the old
door open with an expert jounce of the hip. "Don't stay so still," she
added, her voice softening. "Left or right's no matter, Rosie, just the
fact of turning."

Fourteen

MY MOTHER. A slivered moon night, that part of winter before the snow has fallen, cold hits the body like a shock and we are outside, my fingers frozen, and those are her limbs by the crumbling stucco wall: her arms, her legs swept into a pile by some insane and diligent gardener. Her eyes are closed; her mouth is peaceful. I want to wake up, I admit it, I'm not ashamed. *Wake up. Wake up!* I tell the truth, confess it here: *Momma, I saved myself instead of you.*

Fifteen

OKAY THEN, I thought. I would try. I had my pencil, and the yellow pad I'd taken from Fred's briefcase. *Okay, then.*
Begin at the beginning.

stanley will be home at any moment.

yes. stanley will be home, and should he catch me at these ramblings, he would not call me cynara, he would pompate until my ears went numb. and numb they are, no funds to pay for heating oil and stanley up at the college and laurie and jannie safe upstairs napping under piles of blankets. camping in, i told them, and laurie said he was a pie-near and then jannie seemed to want to be one, too, although with her only identifiable words being *balana* and *momma*, it is not an entirely foolproof interpretation. i left them up there, buried under mounds of covers, laurie taking firm positions for both of them about which one would drive the horses first—a spackled one and a shiny black one for a knight, they seem agreed on that—and which would be the indian prisoner in back. the top of the stairs hidden underneath a stack of resentful dirty clothes, and laurie's baby overalls need the hems taken up if jannie is not to fall down said stairs with her first unskilled steps, and still the shopping to do but if i walk down the hill to powers market everyone will be talking about that girl, that poor girl, and if she is still alive.

I write in lowercase, no capitals, just as Shirley does. It helps me think like her.

the reward her parents offered is enough to keep us in heating fuel for seven years.

weak-eyed stanley too blind to join the search party and me scared unto death about what might be out there. last night in bed, stanley said how could i be frightened? the dark i said and what they might have done to her. who, he said? out there in the mountains, i told him. did he know her? he said no, she was not in his class, and i wondered if he would have liked her. if she is—was—one of those girls who sit slack-jawed in the front row, admiring the professorial pearls he spits at them. would he have had her in for office hours? stanley i said, i can close my eyes and see her, the pretty blond girl from the pictures in the paper. paula, paula welden, of some place in connecticut. the father a businessman and she the oldest of four sisters, the first to leave the family home. lord knows there must be white columns and an imposing porch and a long, rolling lawn with hedges maintained like stanley's beard.

Shirley

Ah, me, I have it, don't I? I know Shirley. Does she know how well I know her?

girls like me, girls like us, we don't run away. we want to, oh lord, we grow so weary of the unending crusades against lank hair or for trim waistlines; how we straighten our spines, how nicely we shake hands with the fellow's parents. before they arrive, we enjoy a quick scotch with father, a private treat in the side parlor before mother comes back to take me in, to introduce me to mike or dick or some other suitable boy who smiles correctly and puts a hand under my elbow to guide me to the door. all four parents grin at us and pretend they are not already assessing how we will do together in life, what progeny we will produce, how well i will manage the staff, whether he will keep me in the style to which i have been raised. they know what clubs we will join, where we will sail, how i will allow him to win at chess, to teach me golf. i am tipsy, and i let him help me into the passenger seat of his neat roadster, but i am tricked up to be this girl. oh stanley, i cannot remember my lines, cannot stick to the part. never could, and as a result, here we are.

She will be proud of me.

a girl of eighteen knows so much, and is only eighteen, only eighteen. i am going to be thirty years old in a week, wife, mother, writer, a person of some considerable accomplishment and yet. ten years older than paula welden and we are both such fools. such mortals . . .

Are ye James Herries, my first true-love, come back to Scotland again?

   paula did not like potatoes, the way the starch left her hands sticky, and mrs. cummings did not like paula, and so she had to peel not one basinful but two before she was released from waitress duty for the afternoon. elisabeth had a boy in the room, no one paula knew. not that elisabeth was a tramp, precisely, but it did seem unfair that paula was always the one who found the sock on the doorknob. she should go in and get a heavier coat, push the door open and grab her jacket, but elisabeth twisted things so she would end up being the one to say she was sorry and if there was one thing paula did not want to do today, it was apologize to anybody. sallie ann's coat hung over one of the sconces in the common room, where it had been on and off since the rain began the previous week, but paula did not take it. her father believed neither in borrowing nor in lending, and he was going to be angry about economics—and her other grades— and was it paula's fault that the professor didn't like her. didn't see her, paula fumed, stuffing her cold hands into the pockets of her light jacket, didn't see her; was she invisible?

Not true, not true, not true . . .

paula did change her clothes. she never touched potatoes. she served the other students and ate her own lunch, and went back to her dorm where elisabeth was studying. she put on jeans and a red parka and took off, on a walk. she liked to walk. she liked to walk alone.

at the end of the campus driveway, paula dashed across route 9, trudged along the southern directed lane and within minutes, a truck pulled over and waited, frozen rain raising trills of steam on rusted metal.

"need a ride? it's cold to walk." the man's face was kindly, his work-worn hands awkward against the fine black circle of the steering wheel.

she thanked him, slid up onto the front seat. he's going far as town, he said. she aimed to hike the trails on glastenbury mountain, she told him, and he said maybe it's late to be heading up into the hills, half past three already and the weather so bad all week.

"could be mudslides, and the sun'll seem like she's set e'en earlier than usual."

the girl shrugged. he will remember later, he will tell the chief on tuesday afternoon when he hears she's gone missing, he will remember how skinny her shoulders hid inside the red parka. she was from good people, he thought, or looked like, but the way her eyes kept darting around and her fingers tangled over one another, she gave him the willies. she wiped her nose on the skin back of her wrist; he recalled that later, crushing his cap between his hands, shoulders hunched in his good green coat. he sat at sheriff peck's desk at the station, trying not to think about the other time he'd been here, back when mavis and he were new-married and maybe once't a while he'd had too much to drink. that one time, he'd let his feelings get the upper hand, the way she harped and picked at him about the fencing, as if she'd known aces about how to run a farm. and here now, mavis gone near three years and he would give a month of sunday mornings to tell her how much quiet she'd left be-hind. when they folded up the hospital cot and cleaned her medicine bottles out of the icebox, that was the first time since 1918 he'd felt alone and it turned out not to be what he'd looked forward to all those years.

never been a man of much imagination, had he? but now he pictured that poor unhappy girl, her stuffed nose and her reddened eyes, and the way her dirty-blond hair curled out from under the lip of her hat. and the jittering of her knee under her clasped hands. mavis would have asked her was she all right. maybe offered her a drink of water or brewed up a fresh pot of coffee once they'd tumbled down the rut-ted drive to the farm. but he'd only nodded and showed her the entrance to the trail, said she'd got no more'n an hour to walk before she should climb down the mountain.

"you get the notion she was meeting someone?" clyde peck's idea was the girl had a boyfriend she intended to catch up with, that no girl would hike that trail alone on a sunday afternoon in the rain, so close to sunset. had to be a boy involved, sheriff peck said.

"i hadn't thought it," he admitted. mavis would say he never thought about matters like this, the way he should have. fool woman wanted him asking and asking about her feelings all day long, as if they ever changed. proof of love was he never hit her but the once. he worked the farm no matter how much his back ached. no matter the weather. no matter the year. when she got sick, he took care of her, didn't he? why'd he have to ask her all those questions on top of it?

"if we'd had a child, after—"

"the one you lost," sheriff peck agreed, moving forms and papers around on his desk, looking for his cigarette lighter.

"if we'd had a child, i might have thought. but i don't know girls, see? girls like that, from the college."

"she was pretty," sheriff said, not looking up to meet his eyes.

he nodded, not saying he'd not realized it. he'd not paid enough attention.

I have it, Shirley. This is a story, one you would write.

where is paula? today some of the students and her professors took off up the long trail, along with the police and other locals who know the mountain well. gone to meet her lover, i imagine.

he is dark-haired and dark-eyed, and she has never been alone with him before. no. she knows him from home. he is . . . he is the gardener. no. he is her childhood best friend, the boy from next door, who their crowd all thought was destined for her. after the last basketball game, senior year, sitting in his father's steamed-up pontiac parked down the street and around the corner from both their houses, he tells her, he is going away.

her cheek against the stuff of his letter sweater, breathing in the effort of the game, the nutmeg scent of his skin, the steady gait of his heart, she turns her mouth toward his, expecting the brush of his lips. she opens her eyes. his elbow rests along the rolled-down window. he watches the dark eddy around the mortons' house, the bulwiches' and mrs. gavin's newly shabby colonial. "where," she whispers to the glimmer of skin at his neck, "where will you go?"

how seriously he clears his throat.

"james harris," she teases, "how can you leave your one true love?"

"i could never leave you, not ever, not dead nor alive," he tells her, lifting her blond hair out of the neck of her jacket. "i will be back if it takes seven years."

"i'll wait for you," she promises. "i'll never love another."

that night, pressed between the cold seat of his father's car and the warmth of his bare chest, paula plights her troth and is undone with love of him. when he walks her to her door, he rebuttons her blouse correctly, and tells her to wait for him. "no matter what," he says, and when he swings off the porch, he runs between the hedge and she sees the lights turn off at his house. only then does she go inside and stare at herself in the bathroom mirror, thinking, *now i know what it is to be loved.* she had wanted him to leave her his varsity jacket, but he did not hear her when she asked.

in any case, he will need a warm jacket, won't he?

in the morning, he is gone, leaving nothing behind for her, no note, no letter, no flowers to press gently between the fragile pages of a book.

when the harris parents ask her, she tells them what she knows. it sounds like so little. "he wants to try his luck," she says, stumbling lamely over the words.

"where, though? where has he gone?"

mr. harris says, "stop bothering the poor girl, she doesn't know. he didn't even confide in walter. why would he tell her?"

mrs. harris takes paula to james's bedroom, and it is the first time she has been to this other sacred place where a piece of his soul is squirreled away.

mrs. harris walks unsteadily through the door and crumples onto james's bed, running a trembling hand over the thin ridges of his navy cotton bedspread. paula stands in the doorway, uncertain whether she is allowed inside. so many trophies james has accumulated, his baseball statues and his golden basketball hoops, and the ribbons of red and blue and gold along the underside of the bookcase, under his desk. a photo of his old dog, ginger, the yellow-haired girl who died before they entered junior high.

paula wants to tell her lover's mother. *we are betrothed to one another, he has vowed eternal love to me. where have you put my picture? where have you hidden me?*

"you knew his friends, didn't you?" mrs. harris asks, the handkerchief damp between her fingers.

paula nods.

"was there a girl, someone special? who we might talk to? his father and i, we would appreciate it if you would tell us, paula. his friends, joe and sid and walter, they are so certain there was no one girl, that he played the field. but if there's anything you girls know? anyone we should talk to?"

i am the girl, i am that girl, paula tells herself angrily. if mrs. harris would look up, the old cow, if she had ever opened her eyes. but joe? or walter? why would they lie? they must be protecting her, or james himself.

his letter jacket slung across the back of his desk chair. *i want that jacket, i will have it,* paula thinks. but when she reaches for it, mrs. harris reaches faster, snatching the coat onto her lap.

"no," she tells her lover's mother calmly. "i don't know of any girl."

"WHAT IS THIS?" Shirley asks. The sheaf of scrawled-on paper in one hand, a pile of folded baby clothes lodged in the crook of the other elbow. Natalie and I, dozing curled together on my bed. For a moment, I am bleary enough to believe I am dreaming, but no, she has found my dumb pages, the ones I'd been tinkering with before I drifted off. "You've been writing."

I do not answer.

"Are you writing *me*?"

Her laugh is not a pleasant one. It's hard to speak; my voice has not yet awakened. Even my limbs feel heavier than normal, thighs and knees weighed down as if I've been drugged. I cannot wriggle my toes and fingers, and still I want to move my tongue and lips, form the words, tell her I did not mean to steal. That was not ever my intention. More, it was a game: I wanted to *think* like her, to know what it felt to be her. I imagined that I knew.

"What were you trying to do?"

"Figure it out."

"Figure out what, precisely?" I have heard her use this voice with the children. It cuts.

I mumble that I don't know. Because even though I do, I don't.

Shirley sits on the bed, setting the resentful springs to tuneless song. Folded clothes clutched against her belly. "You think you know how my mind works, do you?" she says. "You have no idea. You have no idea what goes on in here"—her skull—"and never will." How dare she, when she moves around inside my thoughts as if I've sold her acreage?

"Writing is the devil's game, Rose. Must I continually remind you?" I open my mouth. She shakes her head; she isn't finished. "You start a fire, it goes where it will. But storytellers must stay with their blazes." I want to tell her something important, but words fail me. "No driving off to safety, no hiding from what you've done," she says. "You aren't willing to live in that other world and let this one muddle on."

"I am," I want to say.

"Acquire your own sins. This one is mine," she whispers sweetly. The words do not match the tone, and though I cannot hear the anger, I am certain it is there. I should respond. I blink, wiggle my fingers, begin to feel some movement in my calf muscles. "Don't get up," she orders gently, as if I am ill. "Stay there."

How many times have I heard her talking with others about their writing? Am I the only one unfit to enter this kingdom? I am so sleepy I can't make sense of it and so I drift.

Her hand gentle on my forearm, fingers light as dust; I know her touch, or do I dream it? Is this a spell? Delicious paralysis creeps like a blessing along the length of me. My eyelids drift downward. My own breath sinks my chest, spreads through the gullet with the warmth of Stanley's whiskey. So comfortable here under the covers, and I am so very, very tired. Natalie's dreaming whinny, softly audible as it climbs the incline of dented pillow to my cheek and ear, reminds me of the blissfulness of trust, of letting go.

Shirley's breath, spreading hot into the depths of my ear canal. "Be honest, little Rose. You didn't write the truth here, did you? You couldn't, could you? You couldn't write what you believe."

I swear she has not touched me, her hands are nowhere near my heart, and yet I feel the pressure of her palms, she is pressing down, she is pressing down, it hurts. It hurts so much, *stop,* I want to say, *stop! I will not see it. I will not see what you want me to, I will not see what you did!*

But of course I have to; it's what she wants. And now I see her with Paula, there is fire, I know fires when my father builds them, and now her careless feminine method: witch's luck in the way she piled wood on wood, her disdain for kerosene, her pyre hot enough to melt bone. Such fury at a woman who has taken Stanley's attention for a beat too long; why this one? Was she special? The luring, first with tea and then whiskey and then the walk up into the mountains. This second seduction, frame by frame, she shows me: famous writer, easily impressed young girl. Shirley has an eye to the long game; she knows how to plan. She blocks out her scenes. She draws the houses where her characters linger. She outlines and diagrams; she has a mind for order. She puts it all in place; events play out the way she wants them to.

I am her pawn.

She knows I know, doesn't she? And she knows I'd never say, not even in a story. My loyalty is my greatest virtue.

"Stay away from what's mine." Her voice is hard and soft at the same time; she wants me to hear and obey. "Stay away from what's mine."

I will, I think. *I will never disobey you.* I can breathe now, I can breathe again. She has given me so much, earned my perfect loyalty. And she has shown me that loyalty is the only possibility.

I nod with my eyelids, all I can move, no longer sure if I am dreaming or awake. "That's what friends do," she says. I blink again. Wanting her to know I am on her side, on her side more even than my own. That's what I feel—she and Natalie, they are the women I live between, the two whom I belong to, whom I protect and to whom I have sworn fealty. I sigh. I sleep. I slip. And when I awaken, when Natalie's hungry wail pulls me back to the world, the dimness of evening has begun to shade the floral wallpaper between the windows and I am as groggy as I have ever been. The walls hover on their axes, leaning microscopically closer so that I feel their concern. The house is worried when I have not rested well. It likes the baby calm; it wants me healthy. It has plans for me

I don't yet understand. My arm hurts; I will have a bruise there, I can tell. My body is sore and tight along the calves, as if in my dreams I have run for miles, trying to catch up with someone.

I never see my foolish pages again, nor does she mention them. I meant to honor her. I loved her, and I understood her, and I wanted her to know it. Maybe she did. But of course she knew precisely what I wondered, she saw the direction of my thoughts. Even now, when I re-create in my mind everything that followed, the question of whether her attitude to me changed after that afternoon remains.

Admit it, Rose. Yes. I might have been to blame for what came next. Such misunderstanding, when all I intended was to show I saw her clearly. "Don't whine about it," Fred would say. "Move on. Make things right by what you do the next time." I know, I know, I know. I'm stuck reliving all the idiocies of the past, a poor example to anyone who stumbles on these pages. But likely no one will. These are my secrets, awkward as they are. And they are safe with me.

Sixteen

How long can i avoid telling what Fred did, about that March afternoon when I walked the baby carriage up the slushy road and onto campus? I'm stalling. I admit it. Maybe you need to know him better first. But perhaps you aren't like me; perhaps forgiveness comes easily to you.

There is one other event I should mention, as it happened only days before.

My mother's whereabouts continued to worry me. I was desperate to reach her, honestly. I wanted her to know that I had made a life. I wanted her to see Natalie, to hold her. Somehow the birth would not be a complete truth until my mother had shared it.

I steeled my courage and called my sister Helen's employer, Mrs. Cartwright, in Wayne, one more time, the week following Marvin and Selma's visit. "Ah yes, Rose," she said, "I've had you on my mind. I've meant to write you a letter, but what with the holidays and the weather, I haven't got around to it yet."

"My sister Helen's come back?"

"I didn't want to tell you why we let Helen go, not while the children were home for the holidays."

This was mid-March. And her children, Bitsy and Midge, were in their late twenties, married, with children of their own. Like their mother, they were pompous, stiff-necked, and hardly as civil as they imagined.

"In any case, Helen and your mother were given permission to stay above the stables just before Christmas. Mr. Cartwright extended himself. I wasn't so certain, given your father's history, and of course Helen was always honest with me about your mother's proclivities—"

I swallowed. Helen looked so much like my mother, rail-thin and worry-lined, though she was barely four years my senior—she'd worked for Mrs. Cartwright since the day she turned fourteen, and she was scrupulously truthful, scrupulously good. Helen's sacrificial devotion to my mother was what freed me. I knew it and was grateful, although I never understood the why of it.

"So when the Rolex disappeared from Missy's room"—that's right. it was Missy, not Midge—"the one we'd given her when she left Foxcroft, we spoke to Helen. We told her there would be no further warning, that the next, well, event, would mean the police would be called."

"Yes," I said quietly.

"And the Rolex was returned, without another word," Mrs. Cartwright said smoothly. "I found it on Missy's shelf, where it belonged, the next morning."

"So that was that."

"It should have been."

Although I had been out to the Cartwrights' home only once, trailing my older sister as she walked the half-mile from the train station in order to help her carry home several bags filled with clothing Mrs. Cartwright no longer deemed worthy, I could picture her precisely. I can only imagine the undergarments needed to restrain her volume inside her tautly fitted sweaters. The day I met her, she bent over to pick up some imagined dust mote and I caught a glimpse of her ankles, swollen above the band of her pink-and-gray argyle socks. Cashmere and soggy floral perfume, stiff blond hair and perfectly pointed fingernails, pale blue eyes that seemed too weak to pick out others' failings and yet never failed to do so— she was a selfish, hateful woman.

That December afternoon, Mrs. Cartwright had piled a heap of old clothing on the breakfast table in the kitchen, bright tangled mounds of castoffs that, even well worn, were worlds better than any sweaters or slacks Helen and I owned. We were to donate them to our temple, Mrs. Cartwright instructed, to help the needy. Helen and I made no eye contact, but each of us was already imagining how to cut Mrs. Cartwright's trousers to fit our frames, how to narrow the shoulders of the blouses and take in the skirts. I could not help myself, I drew a dark navy coat from the pile and slid my arms into the sleeves, sighing at the warmth. Finally, a winter's walk without shivering! Mrs. Cartwright eyed the coat with her vacant gaze. "There's nothing wrong with that," she pronounced. I nodded, in blissful agreement.

Helen took a step backward, away from me.

"I'll keep that," Mrs. Cartwright said. "I'd forgotten how nicely it falls."

The phone rang; her eyes brightened as if whatever intrusion it might portend would be infinitely more worthy than the current one. Mrs. Cartwright left the room without another word, not even a dismissive one.

She was a hateful, selfish woman. Even her husband had sighed after he let me in the kitchen door, when he heard the sound of her sensible pumps clicking down the long main hall.

I'd not seen Mrs. Cartwright since the afternoon she took her coat from my hands and threw it over the back of a kitchen chair. I wanted that coat so badly. For a moment, it had belonged to me and my entire being had felt protected. Oh, I wanted that coat.

And then the phone rang, or her husband called for her. Something happened and she left the room. I remember how my breath caught when she left the room.

And I remember how we trudged to the train station with those bundles in our arms. Helen and I did not discuss Mrs. Cartwright and her navy coat, not that evening or ever. We had both learned very early how to avert our eyes, but usually Helen liked to correct me. She was the guiding angel of our family and she took obligation seriously. That day, however, my sister was more than kind.

"Did my mother . . . did something else happen?"

A pause. Even down the wire, I could hear Mrs. Cartwright pursing her lips in the hall mirror, perhaps shaking her head dismissively. The telephone table, under a grandiose mahogany-framed mirror across from the obscenely wide front staircase, was her station, I knew; there she sat, hour after hour, scratching names off lists as she telephoned on behalf of charitable causes, cajoling her friends and acquaintances into pledges in exchange for bits and dribs of gossip and syrupy-tongued slander. My mother was simply a story to her, but one with limitless possibilities for self-aggrandizement.

"I hate to be the one to tell you, my dear. I know how difficult it must be, how devastating it must be to hear—"

"It's fine," I said. "Please tell me."

She sighed. The same sort of suppressed heave Mr. Cartwright had made at the sound of her footfalls. "Ah, dear . . ." I wonder if she had forgotten my name in the excitement of imminent cruelty. "Your mother extracted a large sum of money from my desk. The Christmas bonuses were in envelopes, in the drawer here, the hall table drawer. And I had given out most of them, but not the gardener's, nor the mailman, and there was a special bonus I'd set aside, for Helen herself, as she had so graciously worked on Christmas Day. But your mother . . . ah, dear."

"She took my sister's bonus?" Even for my mother, this seemed surprising.

"She denied it. But of course there was no doubt once the envelope was found."

"With her things?"

"No. She'd dropped it on the path to the stables." Mrs. Cartwright's injury seemed compounded by my mother's disregard for order.

"The police? Were the police called?" I kept my voice as neutral as I could.

"We would never do that to poor Helen. Your sister has enough to bear."

"Thank you."

"Of course we had to let her go."

"But do you know where she went? Do you know where they are?"

Cold and clipped as the answer was, I could hear the pleasure it gave her. "No, my dear. I couldn't give her a reference. Not after the events. I would have no way of knowing where they are."

I swallowed. I had dreamed about my mother, hadn't I, just as I had dreamed of Shirley? It was this house, the way it played with my mind—such ideas had never washed through me before I arrived here. Were the images I dreamed creating truth? Or had Shirley's witchery infiltrated, made me able to divine the future?

"I'm sure you understand," Mrs. Cartwright said.

"I don't, actually," I told her. Sweat broke out across my brow and under my breasts. My voice stayed low and even, but I could have cracked the telephone receiver with the pressure of my fingers.

"Pardon me?"

"I don't. Helen worked ten years for you. You let her go without a reference. No proof my mother was the one who took the money. None. But you assume. She has the reputation, she must be guilty."

The silence was brief, shocked.

"You have no right to use that tone with me," she said.

"I do. I have rights. I have all the rights that you do."

"That will be all," she said firmly, and in my mind's eye, I could see the way she pressed a fat finger down, disconnecting us.

I was in the kitchen, on the downstairs telephone, the one bracketed to the wall to the left of the shelves where Shirley kept her potpourri of plates and bowls and cups. On that wall hung a framed Valentine's card Stanley had once given her:

Shirley

O, Shirley J, you are my darling,
You are my looking glass from night till morning,
I'd sooner have you without a farthing
Than Katie Keogh with her ass and garden.
    Love,
    Stanley E.

It was on a cut-out red paper heart, typed, and someone—Shirley? Stanley? Clever Sally?—had framed it against a square of black velvet. Oh, I envied Shirley.

I was alone in the house, as I had been careful to be, before picking up the telephone and dialing Mrs. Cartwright's number, a long-distance call being a matter for consideration and planning. Shirley was at the doctor; her son Laurie was visiting his in-laws and had come early to drive her there. Fred and Stanley were at the college. Upstairs, Natalie slept. There were dishes to do, and a meal to plan, and I began the task. I had been rude to someone impossible, and this act had not made me feel as brave as I had hoped it would. If anything, it left me even more disenfranchised. I kept my eyes low as I began the dishes. I did not want the house to feel my resentment, to recognize my loneliness.

And then I thought, *Oh, hell, get used to me, house. I'm here to stay.* And I added soap to the water. Fred and I, we were too polite, too eager to please, too aware of our own youth and inexperience. We needed to be tougher, I told myself, letting the tap water run warm across my fingers. I placed a damp palm on the wall to the right of the sink window, and watched my soapy print sink in. We needed to grow up. We needed to be rude.

I thought, *I will tell Mrs. Morse at the library that she is wrong about Shirley.* I turned the water off, took the roast from the refrigerator, removed the butcher's paper. *No,* I thought defiantly, *I will tell Mrs. Morse that she is right. I will tell Mrs. Morse how very right she is.* And I looked straight at the kitchen walls and I thought, *I wonder what Mrs. Morse knows about fires, I wonder if she remembers every single one?*

That night, Burke came to dinner, along with his wife and one of Stanley's students, a besotted young girl. I tried a recipe for pork roast stuffed with figs. Shirley had never made anything like it. Everybody said it was delicious.

Seventeen

MARCH IT IS, and march I must. Up to the campus, finally, with the baby well wrapped under blankets. It is a beautiful day, a veritable lamb of a day. We are aglow with the anticipation of spring. Warm enough to unbutton my navy winter coat for the first time, but I don't. There are two small patches of baby yurp on my blouse, and I don't want to think about them. I can never remember the name of the French writer who said every woman is as beautiful as some man thinks she is, but I know I have him in the back of my mind. I am taking my baby up the hill and onto campus, eager to display her—and myself—to make my husband proud. He loves us, and I am certain of it. One thing he often says is that we are the reason for all he does.

The sky is bright, the air is soft. I can see clear across the campus, through the still-bare trees, all around the bowl of the valley and up the mountains in every direction. Paula Welden was lost over there, to the southeast, on Glastenbury Mountain, and to the north is the pond where we will swim again, I hope, come summer. I push the carriage over the rutted, half-frozen muddy road, at one with the students—girls in open jackets, books hugged in crooked arms, braided hair, cheerful knitted scarves slung loosely. We greet the spring together, another ancient female rite.

My boots are smeared with mud thrown back by the baby carriage's wheels. It is close to noon, and Fred's morning class will let out just as I round the duck pond. With luck, we will catch him before he heads back to his office in the Barn Building. Squirrels dart across the path. I slide briefly on a patch of black ice, catch myself without losing control of Natalie in her carriage, and giggle. I feel life everywhere—sap slowly recalls the course through maple trees; sleepy fish nose the underside of the melting pond surface; long-limbed girls trot past me, calling to one another with insouciance born of anticipation—*Life! I'm in it!*

Gleefully, we round the bend past the student center. Pairs and groups of girls emerge from the science building, begin to run toward the Commons or back to dormitories. August professorial types stroll at more leisurely paces, attended by one or more adoring acolytes. I grin with pride. Which one is Fred?

There is no warning, and so you won't have one, either.

He stands in the middle of the road, his arms locked around a small, peacoated, red-hatted girl, her bookbag smartly slung around her back so that they can press as closely as possible. They are kissing.

They are kissing.

Fred is kissing someone else, passionately kissing another woman, out there in the clean, chill air, with the blue of the sky reflected across the roof of the new library and in the snow-dipped puddles all around his feet. Nobody seems to notice, or give him a second glance. Have they seen this so frequently it means nothing?

He kisses. She kisses.

She is blond, like me; I can see the little wisps of hair escaping from under her red beret. They cling to one another the way you cling when you already know the body of the other but aren't yet used to it.

They are no more than ten feet from me. My heart pounds. I open my mouth, I want to call to him, to scream at him, *Fred! What in God's name are you doing?*

I close my mouth.

And Natalie begins to cry.

Fred's lips pause and hold, his eyes flicker open, he twists—still clinging to her damn mouth with his—and even when he sees me, and pushes her away, he keeps one hand against the arch of her back. She does not know me, has no idea; her expression is forgivably mystified.

"Rose."

I stare. I want him not to say anything.

Natalie's wail grows thinner, becomes a screech cutting through the balmy air, my panic her knife. I bend to her. I feel something so enormously blank that it has size and shape and volume in its absence. When Natalie left my body, there was a moment, the moment after pain, an indescribable agony teetering on the edge between now and memory—but this is worse. This is the worst moment that has ever been.

"Rose," he says again. He lifts the baby, holds her against his coat. Where the girl was. He holds my baby against that same warm spot, against his heart, against the chest where my head has lain, where I supposed no other head would ever be.

"Give her back."

"Rose."

I feel but do not see that the girl has left, has scampered down some pathway to the dorms. For a moment, I track with her; I wonder if she knows about me. I wonder if she cares. I want to blame it all on her.

"Fred," I say. "Give my baby to me."

He shakes his head. "Our baby," he says.

I want to say, *How could you?* I want to say, *I can't believe you.*

"I'm sorry, Rosie, I didn't, it isn't. It really isn't—"

"Isn't what? Isn't what, Fred?" Grit marbles my voice. I'd set fire to anything, wouldn't I, if only to release this pain.

"Everyone—" he begins, and then stops.

"I thought you loved me, it was all for us. That's what you said."

His breath comes in little clouds. "I do. I do, Rosie. I swear. We can't talk here, we have to talk. Come to my office." He keeps the baby tight in his arms but lowers a hand as if to take mine. How can he? That same hand, it has been on that girl's back, and now he uses it to touch me?

"Get away from me."

"Rosie, not here. We need to talk."

I can't say whether the people moving past us in either direction are gawking. I don't care. Fred's eyes brim damply; he watches only me, determined not to see himself being seen.

I am afraid that if I grab the baby from him, I might throw her. Rage trembles all through me; I can't control what I am, I don't know. I don't know.

I do remember that I spat at him, saliva clinging to his stupid, foolish Stanley-worshipping beard. I turned. I ran. Just like one of those lucky students with their brilliant minds, I sprinted. Past the Barn Building, down the long front drive, and out the main gates of campus, without stopping.

If I was crying, it would have been difficult to tell, what with all the ice melt dripping from the high branches of the trees that lined the road.

I ran across the street, stopping short at a melting snowbank, and stuck out my thumb. Not three minutes passed before I was perched on the front seat of a truck, aimed toward the mountains, away from North Bennington, away from Fred and Natalie, away from Stanley and Shirley and all the tainted souls I had not been smart enough to fear.

"Where you heading?" the man asked me. He was a farmer; I had seen his haul of bundled hay and chicken feed jouncing on the truck bed as I stepped up into the cab.

I was not crying.

"You a student?" He was mid-fifties, grizzled, his jacket emitting a complex and not altogether pleasant aroma, like liver cooking. The pockets under his eyes were deeply etched, deckled with brown spots; his smile was kind. Flesh had embedded his wedding ring through the years. An enviable malformation.

"Yes," I told him. "Glastenbury Mountain. I want to hike the Long Trail."

He put on his blinker, turning right. "I live up that way. You'll have about a half-mile to go after my place."

Melting ice blobs, caught under the windshield wipers, streaked the window.

"Don't know what it is about you college girls and that trail. Half the time that's where you're headed, no matter the time of year."

"It's a good place to get away," I said.

"I guess there's other places I'd rather. My wife says it's dangerous up there, what with mountain lions and such, dangerous for you girls don't know how to handle yoursels. You know about that girl, don't you, the one that never came back?"

I nodded. My throat was tight. All I wanted was to be alone, alone, alone, away from Fred and all other people. There was no one to trust and never had been.

"The fella dropped her off up there, he never got over it. Neighbor of mine, passed on these ten years at least, and never did get over it. The wife wanted to sell his acreage, after he died, but Martha said no. South-facing and clear, we could have used it, but she wanted no truck with him."

"He had something to do with it, the girl?"

We came to a halt at the stop sign before the mountain turnoff. The man lowered his window, spat, placed his bent elbow against the frame. Cold air shushed brightly through the window, well worth breathing.

"You ask me, no. But once't something like that happens to you, folks never see you the same." He eyed me suspiciously. "So don't you go disappearing, hear me?"

"I won't," I said softly, but in truth, I think I was meaning to. Is it lost girls who go to mountains, or do girls go to mountains so that they can be lost?

"Boy troubles, innit? I ain't supposed to see you was crying, so

I'm going to act like I don't. Martha says it's always summat with boys. Up there, a girls' school, you rich girls on the hill, and allus trouble with boys."

"They have boys up there," I said. "Husbands and such."

We were silent for some miles, the truck straining on the rutted, partially paved incline. Muddy snow spat up under the tires so high it spackled my window; as warm as the sun made me, I would not roll the glass down. I loosened the buttons on my coat.

He said, "My Martha told me a story. 'Bout one of them professors up there at the college. Couldn't believe my ears. Made her tell it twice. She says one of them fellas fooled around with one of those girl students and got her in the family way. Martha says that teacher up and got the girl to come live with him, and his family, wife and children and all. Big old house near the campus. Acted like it was all right as rain. And when the wife found out, what did she do?"

"What?"

He tapped the brakes hard, twice, so that I had to hold on to the door handle to keep from flying forward.

"That lady, that wife, she killed herself. Yep. That's what Martha told me. Heard all about it at the library."

"And the girl? The pregnant girl?"

He shot me an evaluative look. "Lady took pills and kilt herself. That other one, the student? She up and married that professor, raised his kids. Added her baby to the stable like a new horse, shift the stalls and it's all good, and that was that."

I laughed. "That's a short story," I said. "A story by a writer named Joyce Carol Oates. It's not true."

He shrugged. "Martha ain't much for making up stories."

"She didn't," I said. "She read it in a magazine."

He said, "You're too young to know how evil folks can be. You get to my age, you'll have heard it all."

"People in the village, they don't like the college much, do they?"

"It's not that. I say live and let live. That fellow Martha heard about, though, maybe it's wrong for folks like him to be allowed to do what they do. Summat like that, a man like that, don't you think he should be punished?" His tone was dark.

"Yes," I said. "Men like that."

He circled the truck at the edge of the turnaround, angling the nose back to the road. "What with talking, I took you the whole way. That's the trailhead, right there. You be careful, miss. Sun goes early enough, this time of year."

"I'll be fine," I said. "Thank you for the ride." I scrambled down from the high cab and held the door open for just a moment.

"You know there's a feller up there teaches a class about folk songs? My own daddy coulda taught that. Good money your parents pay, for you to listen to some devil teach you all the same such songs my daddy taught me hisself, out in the barn milking cows."

I smiled. "That's funny," I said.

"Sad is what it is," he told me. "Now shut that door and walk away with your sorrows. My pap woulda told you that, and he couldn't read nor write to save his life. Called himself Jim Harris, had to use a thumbprint to sign his name."

"Jim Harris?"

"Yep," he said. "James Harris. Just like the song."

"Amazing," I told him. "Your father was one famous guy."

"Just like me," he said, and winked. "But I ain't never been the devil, nor intended to turn into one."

I patted the car door. "Nice to meet you, Jim Harris, even if it means I've lost my mind."

He chuckled. "You made my afternoon, missy. Be safe out there."

I'D BE LYING if I pretended the trail didn't scare me, not another set of human footprints in the mud, and deer and wild turkeys stopped still in their tracks, eyes wide and frightened, backs rigid, as I strode past them in the brush, partially hidden by leafless scraggy oaks. When a squirrel scampered across the path in front of me, my heart caught. I restrained a scream.

You wonder, what was going on in my head? Did I think about what I'd seen, my husband kissing another woman, a fresher, prettier woman than I could ever hope to be again? I wonder, too.

Pain has an element of blank; it cannot recollect when it began, or if there was a time when it was not.

I did not have to look up those lines of Emily Dickinson's. I already had this as my answer, always did. I was numb. I walked as quickly as I could, my boots making sucking sounds in the mud. My fingers rapidly grew cold; tears froze in my eyelashes. In the woods, it is never as warm as it is in town.

I stuck to the path. In the back of my mind was the thought that I would stumble across her, across Paula Welden, a pile of bones not found in all these years. I would lie next to them, perhaps caress them. I would fall asleep there, waiting for the sun to set, and nobody would find me, either. I fancied the thought that Fred and the girl would raise Natalie, that my name might never be spoken again, he Ethan Frome, or she the quiet replacement bride for Manderley, the new Mrs. de Winter. So what if I was no Rebecca; my curse would cling to him.

I had been angry before—oh, frequently—and I had known humiliation, but I had never considered the possibility of pain like this. He had said he loved me. He had said we were a family. He had said, god, he had said we belonged to each other, for richer and for poorer but mostly forever. The fury that roiled around me was grander for all that I had not expected it. I had ceased to fear betrayal, I had believed in him, and he had wounded me more completely than the woman who had given birth to me.

At least with her I had always known she was not to be trusted.

By now, it had to be at least three in the afternoon. The winter sun had shifted, signaling the slow turn into evening. I kept walking forward and higher, the path narrowing, my boots soaked through, my toes stiff with cold. I knew I should turn back, I told myself I would, and yet I kept marching on, my nose and cheeks stinging. I wanted to freeze to death, or so I believed. If an image of Natalie intruded into the dim netherworld of my thoughts, I dismissed it. She would have to grow up without me. He would never get over what he had done.

I would go back. I would pack my things, abandon them both. And Shirley and Stanley, I would speak not a word to them. I'd leave for Philadelphia. Return to my dreary job at the hotel. I'd make my way to California, become an actress. Or lead a women's group—they had made fun of women's groups, only last night, at dinner. *The Feminine Mystique* had been the subject of Stanley's rancor; Shirley had not yet read it, but she was going to, because Friedan had attacked her unfairly. Of all the writers to call domestic, they had said. "I'm no one's victim but my own," Shirley had claimed. I, on the other hand, fit Friedan's bill to a T. The child bride personified, Stanley had said. But I wasn't. I was just young. I was not in chains. I'd said that, at the table. They smiled sympathetically, had the courtesy not to chuckle.

What else had Shirley said? She'd quoted a poet, about the way that love always presents itself as a new idea to those who discover it. I have no memory of the exact words, the quote, who said it—all I remember is that we were so damn certain of ourselves.

And here, barely eighteen hours later, I was that other cliché: the betrayed wife. I imagined Shirley waiting for me, at the bottom of the slope, the engine of the Morris Minor running as she read— what was she reading?—I told myself she was reading Betty Friedan, as she had vowed to only a night earlier, that she would have found something in it, would say to me, "Enough, it is enough what our men have done."

Yes, I told myself, I would find Shirley waiting, reading Betty Friedan, surrounded by the detritus of her family's life—records, books and student papers, discarded sweaters and shoes, one sweat-stained sock, a black umbrella with a bent rib—squinting into the text as evening began to circle the one timid car light, hair lank around her coated shoulders, reading glasses as fogged as the windshield, the pause before she raised her eyes to make sure it was me tugging the passenger door open. It would be warmer in the car than out, but only slightly, and I'd rub my hands together and tuck them between my thighs. She'd light a second cigarette, pass it to me, silent. I'd hesitate. Automatically fearful of dropped ash, but oh, what could it matter, after all—I'd take the cigarette between thumb and middle finger, then switch, ladylike, to hold it between middle and index. We would smoke, watch a winter-skinny squirrel dart from birch tree branch to maple, then linger—tension throughout its entire frame—as if our alien presence was both no threat and the worst kind. Eventually, and quite calmly, Shirley would speak, her breath visible like so much smoke in the gloom. "We go," she'd say. "We simply go."

I wonder now how many women there were back then, women like me. Shirley and I were two poles so opposite we were the same. I'd never considered freedom; all I wanted was to be seen. Being limited, confined, was a form of love—therein lay safety. She'd had all the freedom possible and didn't want it. In hindsight, what passed for bold independence in the Hyman house was also insidious tyranny. All families have some form of it.

Women experienced in shame perhaps break differently than those who have been more simply loved. Nonetheless, even such as we had certain contractual obligations to our selves. I pictured all of it as I trudged: glee quivered through her voice, and defiance, and also intention. I yearned for those five words and the way she would say them, I would preserve them in the amber of my most jealously stockpiled dreams. The touchstone of the turn—

"We go," she would say. "We simply go."

If I had ever pitied her before, I would not have to now. She would leave behind Stanley, his sins and hers washed clean by separation. No longer would she have to walk into Powers Market and have the hens cluck at her, their red-painted beaks achatter with the tales of her transgressions. Away from here, she could be free of jealousy, of remorse. I did not care what she had done, what she had lived through, what she had avenged. I loved her that much, you see. I blamed her for none of it. "Where?" I asked aloud. Hopelessness gave way, it vanished: with Shirley as companion, there would be both journey and arrival.

Without her, I couldn't say the same. Women disappear.

Natalie, left behind, might learn to miss me. I'd meant to keep her safe forever, but I had already exposed her to love's treachery—her father's—and now mine would come as no surprise. My breasts, swollen and hot, ached with the milk I had not given her, but if I turned my thoughts away, did not allow myself her image, the discomfort lessened. I understood my mother better.

And yet still, I would say to Shirley, "Now, please, yes. Let's go." She'd set the car in gear, and off we'd go, slip-sliding on the evening dark refreezing road.

AH, IF ONLY I COULD SPIN such gold out of the straw of my afternoon. But no.

My fancies had left the mountain but my physical self had not. I was still stumbling up the path in the gloom, still alone and unloved. Shirley would not come for me. This was mine to solve, and abruptly I felt certain that I could. I was not going to be the wife who goes calmly to her death, setting aside all hope of a future without her man. I was going to return, and pack myself up, and leave him to stew in the poisonous mess he had created. I hated him beyond all reason, and I was done.

I turned, began trudging heavily down the slope. The trip in this direction was far faster, even though I slowed as I went, not quite brave enough to face what lay before me. My toes were cold and stiff with damp. It would be a long journey from the mountain back to North Bennington, and I girded myself to find the stamina. Hungry, cold, and tired, but self-righteousness propelled me.

As I emerged from the clearing, I saw her car parked at the sign by the entrance, its engine running, cold clouding the windows. I had imagined it, and made it happen, just as Shirley claimed to do.

In the moment of victory, I first thought of striding directly past the car, dignified and ripe with justifiable anger. I have always wanted to be that kind of bold, certain woman. But I'm me. I hated to think of Shirley alone out there, lost in her book, slowly getting colder and colder, and perhaps running out of gasoline, having wasted her artist's hours waiting for me.

I opened the passenger door, slid in, and said, "I'm not staying. I can't."

Eighteen

"You'll do what you have to do," he answered calmly.

It was Stanley, not Shirley. Reading Betty Friedan, as if he'd not dismissed her out of hand the night before. They'd all been furious at her for the way she classified Shirley as a writer who romanticized domesticity. "I am a housewife," Shirley had said irritably. "And I am a writer. I never 'deny the vision.'"

"What does that mean?" I'd asked.

"She says that because I write I'm dishonest. Because I write about domesticity, as if that's all I write about in any case, and as if I pretend there's no work involved in writing."

Stanley said, "She doesn't have the talent to shine your shoes."

"I'd have agreed with her about so much of it," Shirley said. "But to attack me?" She took a sip of wine, stirred the pea soup with the ladle and held out a hand for the bowls I was proffering. "I'm the one who's doing precisely what she wants women to do, and I'm the one upon whom she sets her doggish wit?"

Stanley said, "Her doggish visage. I'll review her."

Shirley said, "Keep your razor wit stropped for a more worthy battle, S. Edgar. The book's been out a year; it's time we all forgot it." She turned to Stanley's childhood friend, another writer, up for two days to give a lecture. They were all writers, weren't they? "What's the gossip from town, Frank? Are you in love? News! News, please!"

HE WAS FLIPPING THROUGH the pages of *The Feminine Mystique*, pen in hand. One thing I'll say for both Shirley and Stanley, their mutual support system was laudable. Nobody was allowed to go after Shirley, not without feeling Stanley's wrath. He closed the book, slid it onto the seat next to me. He looked amused—whether at Friedan or me, I cannot know, but then he almost always teetered on the knife edge between disdain and pleasure.

"I thought you didn't know how to drive."

"I don't. But it's much easier than I thought it would be." He placed a hand on my knee, rubbed it. "You look cold," he said.

I shivered. "How did you find me?"

"Girls always run to the mountains, don't you remember?"

"Did he tell you? Did Fred tell you what he did?" I wanted to cry again.

"News travels," Stanley said.

He rubbed differently, his fingers lightly moving along the inner angularity of my left thigh. "Don't," I told him.

"Ah, Rosie. You've had a difficult afternoon." I had. His fingers moved into the crease of my thigh, warming, circling back and down and again, my breath catching the pace, joining. I closed my eyes. He pressed, began to explore the zipper of my jeans.

"No," I said, but there was part of me—and he could hear it in

my voice—that wanted revenge, and wanted him. There had always been a part of me repelled, a part of me entranced. I could
almost hear our shared warm rising, the chill of my skin no longer
quite so forbidding. He sighed. I opened my eyes. His were closed,
and I had the sudden thought I could be anyone. Not Rosie. Not
Rose. But any girl.

"Did you know? Did you know that he was—did you know
what he was doing?"

"It's small-minded to consider them the same thing, sex and
love. Provincial."

"Conventional." I pushed his hand away. He tapped my thigh
delightedly, then slid it back.

"Yes."

"I never claimed to be anything else."

"Look at you, Rosie, those earnest eyes of yours, always watching all of us, drinking it all in, wondering and pondering. You are
hardly conventional."

"It's only a year we've been together. Only a little more than a
year! We're married! We have a baby!"

"Fred's a good man, and he loves you. Why doubt him?"

"Doubt him? I don't doubt what I saw, Stanley!"

"But what does it matter? What is it about The Act? Sex is a
form of exercise, a set of sensations, a way to find release. Nothing
more."

"So he's having sex with her? Not simply kissing her in public?"

"Perhaps not the finest location to choose."

"How long has he—" I couldn't say the words. "With her?"

"Who?"

"I don't know! I don't know who she is!"

"And nor do I. The students consider the professors to be unusually interesting. I'm not sure which particular young lady this might have been."

Even more sickening. How many "particular young ladies" had there been?

"Get out," I said. "Switch seats with me. I'll drive us back. It's better."

He shrugged, as if to say it was my loss, and opened his door. How could he not understand the insult inherent in the ease of this; my lack of acquiescence mattered so little? The engine had been on all along, no need to wait for it to warm. I slipped the shift into first gear, pressed foot to gas, and leveraged the car tires back onto the road.

I was exhausted. I was furious. At Fred. At Stanley. At myself. "Was Paula Welden your student?" I asked. I did not see his face, but I could hear the way his breath held, for just that moment.

"Who?"

"Paula Welden. The girl who went missing."

"I never knew her," he said, his tone utterly noncommittal. When I glanced over, he was stroking the cover of the Friedan book thoughtfully, his meaty palm obscuring the title, his fingers lazy on the spine.

"You remember her, though, don't you? You remember when she disappeared?"

I had never heard Stanley's voice so deliberate and calm, the way the hostage speaks when the bad guy has the gun to his head. "No," he said. "I don't recall." I knew he was lying. He knew I knew. I focused on the asphalt road ribboning before us in the dusk. I did not want to hit a deer.

The Morris Minor clambered over the refrozen ruts in the driveway. Icicles dripped from the porch eaves, glints of light in the late-evening gloom. My heart pounded as I turned off the engine. "I can't go in," I said, and Stanley paused, his hand already on the door handle.

I started to cry.

"You're young," he said, almost tenderly. "What hurts now will hardly matter, much sooner than you know."

"You don't understand!"

"But I do. I do, little Rosie. This, too, shall pass."

"You have no idea," I said fiercely. "It isn't fair, it isn't right."

"Ah. You're quoting Shirley."

Her words were the right ones; I had not meant to do that. "It's not okay," I said. "You can say so all you like; I won't ever believe you."

Sudden arc of bright light in the gloom. Shirley emerged from the house, coatless, and marched down the steps to the rutted drive. She pulled my door open, blocked me in. "Where did you take him?" she demanded. "You left your baby crying for her supper, took my husband off to nurse instead? How dare you? How dare you steal my car?" As if it were the missing car infuriating her.

"I didn't," I began.

"Oh yes, as if there's any other explanation. As if Stanley got in the goddamned car and drove it himself." Her glare so baleful it makes my heart hurt to picture it even now.

"You don't know what happened?" After Stanley's appearance

at the mountain, I assumed my humiliation had been broadcast by the village crier. If Stanley knew, how could Shirley not?

"I know what happened," she said harshly. "What happens every single time. Stanley's a veritable magician of the loins. Far more compelling than any friendship I might have to offer."

"I would never!" I began, while her words growled over mine: "But you obviously did."

"Shoil," Stanley said, "you haven't—"

"In the house," she snapped. "Get in there, Stan, we have dinner guests. You have multitudes to devastate before the port is passed."

"You're wrong," I tried to say, not wanting her to be. Wrong. Ever. Preferring almost to be at fault than to see her with this particular flaw. But then she said something I'd not imagined she ever would, words so horrible my own mother would never have uttered them, the worst words ever.

"And you, worse than a murderer, stay out of my house," she hissed. "I befriended you. Take your oh-so-tolerant husband and your crying baby and go. You are no longer welcome here." And then she slammed the door open, lumbered back up to the porch, and stood there, arms crossed against her ample chest. "I'll get Fred," Stanley said, wiping condensation off the windshield with a gloved hand.

"No, don't! I don't want to talk to him!"

My legs would not move. Of course Stanley would tell her the truth. He would explain, and she would come back out to me, she would help me. She would tell me what to do.

Stanley slammed his door, crunched over the lawn to the path, and stopped briefly at Shirley's side. She did not move, did not turn to look at him. In a moment, he went into the house. She remained on the porch; I remained in the car. I wanted her to come to me, to be the comfort and the wisdom that would guide me out.

It was colder in the car with the engine off, and my breath quickly fogged the windshield even further. Shirley stayed up on the front porch, watching me. She was not going to come, not going to help me. Stanley came to the door behind her and watched for a time, as if he, too, were confused. I saw Fred pass by the living room window, Natalie in his arms, and then the younger Hyman daughter, Sally, knelt on the couch to peer over its back and glare out at me.

Two coated figures scrambled past the Morris Minor, a woman and a man, each carrying a paper-sacked bottle of wine. They paused, the woman bussing Shirley's cheek. Words were exchanged, both dinner guests glanced curiously toward me and the car, then opened the front door and let themselves in.

My teeth would not stop chattering.

Stanley came to the front door, opened it, and spoke to Shirley. He had a drink in hand, offered it to her. She did not respond, remained unmoving, staring through the dark as if she could see me.

I did not know what I was supposed to do. Nor do I have any sense of how long we stayed this way.

Eventually, however, I was the one that broke, pushing my door open with an agonizing creak of metal and ice.

"Don't," she said cruelly, a single syllable in the dark.

"What?"

"Don't you dare come in this house."

"Shir—"

"You of all people should know, should know better. You are no longer welcome here."

"But I—"

"I thought we were friends," she said bitterly. "Of all the women in the world, you were the last one I'd imagined could do such a thing to me."

"But I didn't, I haven't! It was Fred! Fred and a student!"

Something flickered across her face. She knew I was telling the truth, I saw it, and then I saw her face harden again. Now, looking back on it, I'm fairly certain that she hated me for being her, just then. She couldn't bear to remember how awful she had felt, how rotten that very first betrayal had once been. She believed me, but it was not enough.

"I can't have you here, not anymore," she said coldly. "I can't ever trust you again."

She turned on her heel, entered the house, and locked the door loudly and with a flourish. I saw her in the living room, both hands extended to greet the couple she'd invited to dinner. Her hair glinted red under the electric lights. A smile on her face—not a false one but a determined one—and no one even glanced out the window toward where I stood, in the freezing night, utterly bereft.

I let myself back into the car and sat. What would my next move be? The first fury of the afternoon's discovery was now so compounded that confusion had replaced blood and breath inside me. Any action seemed more dangerous than simply sitting. Even if I froze to death.

I sat and sat. Breath fog filled the front seat. I could no longer feel my fingers or toes. I drifted, numb inside and out; perhaps I slept. I know I did, drifting into a dream of sitting in the car, destroyed by the day's events, and drifting back awake. I was no longer cold. I dreamed the car was moving, jouncing down the long hill away from campus, and along the big road heading south, and then I woke, drifting, and dreamed myself awake.

Fred was in the car, Natalie in the back, wrapped in blankets, and pinpoints of starlight speckled the dark, dark sky. Heat slowly warming me through, down to the ends of my fingers and toes, behind my knees, my bottom. I must have lifted my head.

Fred, seeing me awake, continued driving for a long moment, in silence, and when he spoke, his voice like a frog's croak, awkward and unused to language, he said, "I can't even begin to apologize. I can't."

I was crying again, silent tears seeping down my cheeks.

"Things happened up there, things on the campus. I got confused, I did things I shouldn't have, it was wrong, and I know it."

"I can't go back there."

"We've left. We've gone. We won't go back."

"Your class," I said.

"I won't go back."

For some time, he drove without speaking. I closed my eyes again, fell back to sleep. When I awakened, we were parked outside a motel in Williamstown, and he had opened my door. "We'll sleep here," he said. "We three. And in the morning we'll figure out what to do."

I let him guide me inside the drab little room, turn on the stall shower, unpeel damp clothes from my spent body. I stood under the hot pounding water until my toes began to burn. I was so tired that even now I can hardly recall what it felt like to slip under the covers, to feel his breathing body next to me, listen to the baby's gentle snores. I fell asleep without pondering the ethics of where I was. I fell asleep because I could no longer stay awake. I did not dream.

But in the morning, when I woke, all the memories of the day before were with me, under the covers, denting the pillows, glistening through the window glass. I could barely breathe; rage overwhelmed me. I nursed the baby, each pull at the nipple another theft. I am surprised now, remembering this, that I had milk enough to give her. Natalie fell back to sleep, sated, and I slid from her and Fred, as if their very ability to remain calm was a cushion that could smother me.

He had not packed an article of my clothing, merely baby things and a change of shirt and boxer shorts for himself. The keys to Shirley's Morris Minor sat on the pine-paneled dresser, next to a crumpled handkerchief, Fred's limp wallet, and a stack of three folded diapers. My jeans from the day before were almost dry, stiffening over the radiator. I pulled them on, took the keys, and left.

Our room was on the second floor. Looking over the railing, I saw that we were one of only two cars in the partially cleared lot. I tiptoed down the staircase, holding the railing to keep from slipping in patchy snow turned to ice by the shoddy work of whoever had hastily swept the stairs. It was barely morning, stars still flickering vaguely against the brightening sky. Shirley's car started easily. It knew me; I'd probably driven it more than anyone else these past seven months.

I followed the signs north to Vermont, and found myself back in the driveway of the Hymans' house a little after seven in the morning. The door was shut, the curtains drawn; the house was asleep. I tried the lift-and-turn ministration that worked for all the others but could not open the door. I stepped off the porch, and made my way around to the kitchen entrance, where I knew I would not be denied.

Lights were on there; the smells of coffee and toast drifted out as I turned the doorknob. Business as usual. I tiptoed to the kitchen. I would make her listen to me; once she heard my side, heard my story, she would be the one to apologize. I had not seen her do so before, with anyone, but I was certain she would want to, for me. In the light of day, we would both be kind.

It wasn't Shirley, but Sally. Was it the weekend? I had no idea what day it was. "Oh," she said. "You're back."

"I expected your mother."

"I'm sure."

"Have I offended you?"

"Me?" she said, turning the fried eggs for just a moment. They were for Stanley, then; he liked them just a flip of the spatula past sunny-side up. "I'm not interested enough to be offended."

I had earned her rudeness, and yet it was a victory as well, to know that I bothered her. I told myself I was not going to grapple with a child. I left, went up the stairs and to our bedroom, and began to assemble the clothing Fred had left behind. A moment later, Sally appeared in the doorway, a plate of eggs in her hand.

"You're practically my age," she said. "Thinking you're so tight with Shirley, so groovy, so above—"

I would have laughed if it hadn't been so sad. I wanted to apologize to her. Part of me wanted to ask her to the movies, or to walk into town with me, or whether we might exchange sweaters—we were close in size—but I was a mother, a wife, and now a woman scorned. She was a child by comparison.

"I'm packing up my things. I won't be bothering you much longer." And I opened the closet door and began to pile my few dresses on the bed, slipping the Hymans' hangers out as I did so. Sally left the plate of eggs on the dresser, picked up my good blue dress, the one with the four brass buttons, and folded it neatly. I did the same with the older blue dress, and she took the gray wool. Her hair smelled of baby powder, as if she'd borrowed Natalie's before I arrived. In less than five minutes, my clothing was packed. I looked at Fred's shirts, still on their hangers in the narrow closet, but left them.

I left behind all the Hyman children's old infant clothing, the soft, worn blankets and little sweaters. I loved those sweaters, bright oranges and soft creams, hand-knitted and uneven, the pills and pulls of their previous owners only adding to their value for me. "Take them," Sally said indifferently, but I couldn't. I was far too proud to sneak even an old burp cloth in among those items that clearly belonged to Natalie. I wanted Shirley to know I'd been honorable, not grasping, that I'd left her completely. Sally unearthed an old pillowcase and tossed the baby's few things inside. I hauled my stuffed suitcase, careful not to bump against the scarred mahogany stair railings. All of a sudden, I was terrified I might alert the others to my presence, come face-to-face with Stanley.

As usual, the front door would not unseal itself for me. Sally jiggled the knob as she pulled the door slightly up and open. Sally said, "How will you get to . . . to where you're going?"

"I'll get a taxi at the train station."

"Oh, then. Well, good-bye." She paused, flushing the same pinkish pale her mother did when moved. "You don't understand her," Sally said bluntly. "You think you do, I know you think so, but you don't."

"Yesterday—"

"This has nothing to do with yesterday, whatever you tried to make my father do—"

"I didn't!"

"I don't care. She's not ordinary, not an ordinary person. You don't see it."

"I do!"

"You used her. You took advantage." I had never heard a voice like that, so furious the rage had burnt itself to ice.

"I protected her! My god, I would have stopped her, none of you stop her, you all know what she's done, what she's capable of doing! You don't stop her!"

Sally began to close the door. Her face was white, eyes narrowed. The hand on the door trembled. If I had ever looked at her before, I had not noticed she was pretty, that her bones inside her body moved fluidly, that her frame was graceful. I would have liked her, I thought, but then her lips twisted cruelly. "That's not what friendship is. *You* wouldn't know. Well, congratulations. You don't know Thing One about my mother. That won't stop you, I'm sure. You can brag about her to every jackass you ever meet. Whoop-de-doo."

"She is my friend, she is!"

Sally shook her head dismissively. "Greedy, greedy Mrs. Nemser."

"I hate you," I said. "I hate you all."

They were easier to blame than Fred. I see that now.

As I walked past the living room, I could not see inside the windows; they'd gone opaque in resistance to the lemony sunrise. I thought, *The house has closed herself to me.*

I walked into town, past the library and grocery store and up the road, to the station. I waited until the train was due and the lone taxi arrived to troll for arriving passengers. "What will it cost to take me to Williamstown?" I asked.

The answer was twenty dollars. I didn't have it, but Fred did. I'd seen a little more than that in his wallet earlier. This was the end of Bennington College and the Hyman family, I vowed. No matter what they did, I would never see them again.

I opened the taxi door. The driver said, "Give us a minute, love. Maybe someone from the train'll need a ride our way." If I'd been someone else, he'd have hauled his bony frame out of the car and taken my bags to put them in the trunk. "Get in, then," he said, but I shook my head no, picturing Stanley's fat hand slithering up my leg. I'd wait in the cold.

"Get in, then," he said again. But I didn't. Did I know what was coming or was I so stubborn it made me stupid? If I had an answer then, I hardly remember now.

Nineteen

GOD, I WAS YOUNG. *In a minute there is time for decisions and revisions that a minute will reverse.*

I stood at the train station in the cold sunlight, shivering, trying to keep the bags I carried from sinking to the icy grime on the outdoor bench. When the train came near the station, the rails would begin to vibrate, first with a low, comforting hum that grew louder and more painful to the ear until the moment when it softened into the sweet exuberant rattle of arrival. My purse burned my forearm, so tightly had its strap wound around my flesh. I felt myself already a visitor to this place, not a familiar face in sight, and even if there were I could no longer claim to know anyone.

It was as the tracks began to resonate that I heard the chipper insistence of the Morris Minor's horn. I turned, uncertain what I would say to Stanley this time. Frost clouded the windshield. The taxi driver tilted his head with a demonic cheerfulness, didn't bother to castigate me for abandoning his vehicle. All's fair in love and trade, was what his eyes said. I remember his jacket was a worn corduroy, and that his knuckle skin was red and cracked where his fingers curled around the black plastic of the steering wheel. "Sorry," I murmured. He rolled up his window.

And as I opened the Morris Minor's passenger door, I suddenly knew that this time the driver would be Shirley, and though my breath caught at the thought of it, I slid in. Hands on my lap, purse clutched there, suitcase at my feet. And once again, I found myself in the front seat of the car, watching humidity bead down the inside of the frost-streaked windshield.

She uncranked her window. "Thanks, Mr. Donovan," she told the taxi man. "I almost forgot my own houseguest."

He waved in forgiveness, his grin an acknowledgment of both respect and amusement for the oddity that was Shirley Jackson. She cranked the window up and sat, rubbing her palms along the steering wheel, crooked fingers extended out as if at any moment she could begin to type a life in thin air.

"Don't say a word," she ordered. Was she still angry? I obeyed, allowing the expansive silence of companionship to lift me once again. I loved her enough that her wanting me at all was sufficient to impale the breastplate of my fury's armor. I forgave without a moment of wavering, even though I tried not to give in quite so easily. "Come back to the house. You're part of it, you're part of us."

I closed my eyes, savoring the thought.

"You want us to be perfect, but we're not. Not a one of us, Rose. Not a one. We all do things to one another, we all hurt one another; we're cruel or unkind or unforgivable in a multitude of other ways. Stanley, lord knows, Stanley has hurt me countless times." She paused. "And I him, albeit in my own fashion."

"I didn't do anything. I didn't do what you thought I did."

"No, Rose. You didn't."

"I'd never do such a thing to you. I thought you knew that. I thought you knew me."

Her face was tired. "Please come home."

"I've never told anyone," I said, straightening in the seat to gaze at the smattering of heavily scarved and hatted passengers alighting from the train, shabby suitcases clutched in gloved hands. Such lucky innocents—anticipating adventure or returning from it—while I, returned to the Eden of the Morris Minor, knew far too much for someone who had lived so little. I wanted Shirley to understand the full measure of my loyalty. "I've never even told Fred."

"Told him what?"

"I'm your friend, no matter what. I don't care what you did. I don't."

Cold as the air was in the car, I felt the warmth of her breathing and my own, the way our rhythms matched. She said, slowly and oh so carefully, as if this was what I'd meant, "Each marriage has its own mysteries, Rose. Yours will survive."

"I thought Fred was just like me, I thought he'd claimed me, I was his." My eyes filled again, how dull to cry so much.

"It changes nothing, really. We soldier on. Don't you see, Rose? You can't leave this life, not the baby, or even Fred."

"I've never hurt him," I said, sniffling, starting to love my tragedy a little now that I could share it. I'd have been a perfect woman for a man who beat me, I suppose; I should count myself lucky to have been courted by those of kinder cruelty. "What he did, what he did to me, to me and Natalie, it isn't fair."

"No."

"Then I can't stay, don't you see? I have to go."

"That's silly."

Her tone pragmatic, as if I were one of the daughters, as if my anger had been rebellious instead of righteous—as she spoke, I found myself increasingly relieved. Why? I can't say. I suppose because more than anything I wanted to find a reason to return.

And I did feel the pull not only to my husband and our daughter, but also toward the book-laden tables and the musty couches, the Asian masks and Shirley's odd figurative paintings on the walls, the dirty dishes accumulated on the window seats and atop the counters, the heady musk of tobacco and spilled bourbon and burnt chicken skin, the cats in mock sleep on stairs and desks, the spill of sweaters and jackets on the velvet loveseat in the front hall. I missed it all already, and it missed me. I imagined I could hear the walls heave a plaster sigh that ran from basement to attic, their cool surfaces undulating in relief that I had realized I was needed. Those maple floors needed my feet to soothe their anxious planes; those high-foreheaded windows depended on my vigilance to monitor the coven of evergreen trees that parleyed in swaybacked communion in the yard. Of course I would go back.

She put the car in gear, turning her thick neck to look over her shoulder as she reversed. Her skin pulled with her head's movement, gauzy fabric wringing and unwringing as the car straightened and we began to drive toward the house. I don't know what I was thinking; I remember I felt calm and safe again, as if Shirley would make things right.

And then she said, very thoughtfully, "If anybody's a child bride, it's you, Rosie. And Friedan's wrong, because you aren't helpless at all."

I wasn't?

Twenty

I DID NOT GO TO RETRIEVE Natalie and Fred from the motel in Williamstown. Shirley dropped me off at the house and left almost immediately. She took Stanley with her, but it would have been okay in any case. He greeted me with the same matter-of-fact directness that characterized most of our interactions, tucking a plump finger into the pages of his book to welcome me back, then accepting the jacket Shirley proffered without demur. They were gone before I'd even removed my blue coat.

I was tired, and like a child I hoped that Shirley and Stanley would make all right for me, that I could wait at home while they fixed all of it, wove Fred's remorse into a golden purse of academic glory. I don't apologize for being young. Although I wonder at the girl I was.

The front door creaked as I pushed it shut, and all was tranquil inside. To be sure, the house greeted me with a sigh of its foundation, even the walls trembling slightly in welcome as I climbed the stairs, suitcase in hand. I was so tired, and so very relieved to be back there that even the dust-strewn light in the long upper hallway seemed to caress my skin. I went past Barry's room, Sally's, Jannie's,

and down the length of the hall to the back, past all the school draw-
ings and bookcases stuffed with paperbacks to the room that Laurie
had once been king of, the room that now belonged to me. Suitcase
unpacked, toothbrush back in the bathroom. I flushed the toilet and
listened for the water running through the pipes. The bathroom
windows glinted along the distorted planes of the ancient glass, and
the sun divided into separate streams that glowed along the wooden
floor. I almost felt the fingers of the sunlight curling like more cats
against my toes, as if even the sunlight that filtered onto Hymaneal
floors welcomed my return. Hardly a night gone by, but the house
had missed me. If Sally had been home, she'd have felt what I felt,
that I belonged there. Of course, she wasn't. No one was, and so I
went back to my room and waited, princess in the tower, listening
for the car in the driveway, or any other sound of life.

I sat on my bed, against the pillows, and I began to wonder
what the house knew, what it had watched, whether it believed in
me more than Fred or liked us both the same? How did I measure
up to Sally, or she to Shirley or Shirley to Stanley? I floated somewhere between relaxation and sleep, and I felt the pulsing of the
house's life begin to throb inside me as if we shared a single heart.
Not that the walls spoke, nothing so insane, but I could feel the
history of footsteps treading its floors. The slamming of doors, the
rumpled bed linens, the broken glasses and books left abandoned
by bedsides, the arguments and the laughter, the spilled drinks
and worn socks and burnt stews and crumpled pages. I smelled
flowers and semen, vomit and sweat, the sour scent of cigarette
smoke, the achy sweetness of bourbon in the bottom of a glass
come morning. History, the history of lives here lived, our history.

The thought was comforting, like the monotonous churn of the waterwheel down in the village reservoir, over and over and over so that crashing water lost its violence, became its own continuing momentum—

thoughts into words into pictures and i closed my eyes. my brain calmed, slowed, foot soldier words aligned themselves in sentences nonsense thoughts i'd never thought such things and as i woozed and floated embryonic in the clockticking electricity humming heat rising silence i began to know, to know—

i know who i love, i dreamed it, dreamed the words, was i waking or sleeping, i know i know

stanley—i said to him—stanley, stanela

but i was dead, how was it so, that i was dead and i was her and so i told him, stanley listen

when i was alive, i told him, and we were happy (decades of this, and weren't we very?), we made a vow that whichever of us went first would be cremated, and sit in a jar on the dresser in our bedroom, keeping an eye on things.

was i waking or sleeping, i dreamed. i dreamed i was shirley, i dreamed i was shirley. i knew i was shirley i was. shirley

"you, you'll remarry," i told you. "men do. you won't like to be alone." there was no dig in this (i fucked dylan thomas on our porch, did i ever tell you? there was a party, and all our friends drunk as lords inside and it was winter. too much gin and he felt wobbly and i took him to the porch, where he grabbed icicles off the roof and tickled my neck with the cold end, then licked my frozen skin. and me, he lifted my woolen dress and drew down my tights, and yes, he fucked me, stanley, on our very own porch with you inside and some eager undergraduate stroking your shoulders as you held forth. but dylan thomas, stanley, dylan thomas— now that was a man worth holding against naked skin chilled and rubbery, dylan thomas—). i only wanted you to know i would not mind.

"don't love her more than me," i said, and you studied me, noting the brittleness in my tone, unsure whether i was about to lose my temper.

"impossible."

twenty-seven years and if ever any man could kill me, it would have been you, it would have been you, stanley. did i ever tell you—how often did i tell you?—how much i hated you? you loved my prose, you loved our children, i do believe you even loved me, as much as it was possible. you are not you without me.

i asked you to kill me. i said, "don't let me be humiliated." i did not want to see the inside of an institution, the white walls of a hospital, to have my arms strapped tight, to take their pills instead of my own. "save me from—" but i did not know the word. it was *you*. save me from you, is what i meant to say.

"i love you too much," you said, and then, because you

were late for class, you went to work. i followed, stumbling after you on the ice-slicked path through the gates and through the woods to campus, and when i stood outside your office pounding on the door, pounding on the thick wooden door, the snow melting off my boots to puddle on the wooden floor, you kept the door locked, you kept whichever girl it was covered with the flesh of your warm belly, you did not stop what you were doing. not for me. you heard me: "stanley! stanley! stanley!"

but did you stop? stanley, you killed me years before i died. you would not let me go.

you could have let me in.

my mother told me not to trust you. i've always thought she boiled the sheets after we stayed with them, took the silver out and had it polished to a sheen, removed all traces of our lips from her glasses and our hair from her bathtub. not our kind, dear, but then i married you. fornicated with you. bore your children.

how i must have sickened her.

when i was alive, your women haunted me, although i never (rarely?) let you know. now that i am dead, now that i am watching you—your faithfulness is what destroys me. that foolish woman, what gift does she have, what wisdom, what more than tailoring and chopping onions and painting the lips red does she understand? she tinkles the piano keys and thinks herself my equal. and she is the woman who carries on for you, who raises our children, who keeps my own legacy aloft? and you bed her, and her alone?

no one can be wounded the way the dead can. i am the pebble in your italian loafers (also the reason you can own them). i am the shadow that curves over the swollen cracked plaster in barry's ceiling, waking him in fear when the moon is bright. i am the acrid taste that flows from the kitchen taps after heavy rains. i am after you, i am part of you, i am everywhere, i love you.

my mother made so much of caste and class and i rejected it. remember, at that party in rochester, how she insisted we pretend you were not jewish? "they wouldn't understand," she said. and you agreed. you found it funny. She dressed my lumpen form in spinster gray though i was only twenty. she and my father danced instead of us; we sat in hardback chairs, watching. in her defense, i think she had no idea of what to do.

stanley. do not listen to that woman. you made a promise to me, and i am your wife. so many years, stanley, and what we gave each other. and you promised me. don't you remember? *whichever of us dies first will be cremated, and sit in a jar on the dresser in the bedroom, keeping an eye on things.*

we were students; you read my story in *the threshold.* you said to your roommate, "this woman has something. i'm going to meet her," you told him. "and if she's anything like her writing, i'm going to marry her."

wasn't i? wasn't i?

i'm here, stanley, as we agreed. in state, on the dresser, in the jar you selected so carefully and placed with such reverence. the girls laid out the lace scarf from my drawer, and you put the brass jar on it, and opened it, and all of you—even barry—gazed at me for a long, silent moment. i felt it then, all the love, how much i mattered, how very important i had been to you—the air itself pulsed with your loss—until Jannie mentioned that her boyfriend was downstairs and you suggested he come up and meet me. Jannie had a boyfriend, so quickly? me not even weeks dead, and someone new?

"daddy," she groaned. "he'll think i'm crazy."

"you are," barry said.

"too soon to let him know." that was sally. and all four of you laughed, and turned, and it was barry who remembered to put the lid on the jar. without it, a stumble or a shove and i'd have been gone, scattered across the floor like crumbs from a bread knife.

laurence's wife came by to see me—was it the next day? does it matter? time flows so smoothly; i should have seen this before—and she sat down on the bed, her baby weight a flaccid layer atop the springy surface of her skin. it would have stopped my breath, had i any. perhaps i, too, was beautiful once.

stanley licking the new wife, how he slobbers in his eagerness; he can't taste enough of her. she must be delicious. he sleeps, his arms circling her. i'm here, stanley, where you put me. here remembering how you slept turned away, your knees bent into your chest—"i sweat too much, shirl; i can't touch anyone while i sleep."

you seem to sweat a lot with her.

i know what a story is; i spent my life telling them. but you have stolen from me the structure of the only tale i lived. i believed you, stanley; i believed in your endless infidelity, the honesty of knowing you would always lie. the boundlessness of your anger, your lust, your need for novelty: that happiness was beyond your reach. that no woman was ultimate to you.

"so beautiful, the way you smell, your skin, the softness of your hair," and you sigh and hold her tighter. god, stanley, i'm sitting here on the dresser; don't you see me? don't you notice me? do you not even remember me as you take her, night after night, tell her how beautiful she is, how you had never dreamed of holding a woman who felt like her. looked like her. damn you, stanley, was i that ugly?

there is no solace for me here.

clymene, who lost her son because his foolish father let him ride a chariot far too near the sun, she knew. she wandered the earth looking for poor phaethon's bones, and when, at last, she found them, knelt sobbing. her daughters (his sisters) at her side, mourning for their dear lost brother until fully four months had passed. and then, as if they hadn't lost enough, before clymene's eyes the girls complained of stiffness, their silky skin turned to bark, leaves sprouted from the follicles where auburn locks once curled.

"no, mother, please. please stop! those shards of bark are me, don't pull at me, it hurts!"

and thus clymene lost all. phoebus the father still had his days to ride through, drawing the sun across the sky, but she, clymene, the patient housewife, was left with naught. what could she do but kiss the rough trunks of her daughters, stroke the leaves that now adorned them, list from one maiden to the other wondering if there were words she might have left unspoken, honest words, that might have allowed them to live?

dead, i have one thing you do not. i never age. i curse you to wrinkles and strands of gray hair swept across the dome of your balding head. i curse you to erections that do not rise. i curse you to greeting each morning with relief, another night survived, a heart still beating. i curse you and i hate you and i will not leave you.

because i love you.

I WOKE WITH A START, my heart pounding, to the sound of their footsteps on the rickety front porch. Cheerful voices, the slam of the door, Natalie's cry, the concomitant tingling in my breasts. I was not rested, not at all. I was out of breath; I could feel the clamminess of my skin. Shirley's voice downstairs, not dead, despite my dreams. When had I slipped, and into what world, where had my dreams taken me?

I'd dreamt she was dead. No. I'd written her dead. The devil's work was what she said writing was, and now I knew it to be true.

The house had come to me like a person while I slept, *whispered whispered* that everything was about to change. I knew enough about Freud to feel as guilty as if I'd killed her myself. I wiped a hand across dry, swollen lips. Downstairs, the baby's sobs grew louder. Fred's voice trying to calm her . . . afraid to bring her up to me . . . afraid of what I would do. Stanley's voice was loud, almost in song. He was too cheerful.

I swung my feet to the floor, felt for my shoes with my toes.

They were still in the front hall in their coats, all very convivial, as if they'd stopped somewhere for drinks. Shirley took my entrance as her cue to head into the kitchen. The men eyed me warily. I took Natalie from Fred's arms. "D'you need me?" he asked. "Should I come up with you?"

I told him I was fine. He looked away first, answering a question of Stanley's, something ballad-related, in his usual calm voice.

The baby was cranky. I brought her up to the bedroom and tried to nurse, but she wouldn't latch on, no matter how much I petted and coddled her. The truth was my milk was virtually gone. I carried her down the back stairs, to the kitchen, where luckily the milkman had delivered that morning. Shirley was in there, smiling to herself, humming as she rinsed frozen corn to defrost it; I flushed, remembering my dream, and she tilted her head quizzically.

"I fell asleep."

"What else?"

"Nothing."

"You saw a ghost," she said. "It's in your eyes."

I opened the icebox door and took out the milk. Shirley handed me one of the clean baby bottles, filled a saucepan with water, lit the burner. "Give me that," she said, and placed the bottle in the water while I dandled fretful Natalie. She shook the bottle, spreading the warmed milk throughout. Natalie settled into it with gusto, then proceeded to fall asleep before even a minute had passed, the nipple still clenched between her gums.

"What did you dream?"

I couldn't meet her eyes.

"Tell me, Rose. Whatever it is."

I did not plan the words. "My coat," I blurted. "My good blue coat. I stole it, from my sister Helen's employer."

Shirley's eyes went shiny and expectant. I sat down at the table, the baby in my arms, and I said, "It was about money, you see. I'd never had any."

She waited, the way you do when a cat is coming closer.

"I had to walk to school each morning, and then to work each afternoon, and home again in the dark. It was right before I met Fred. Not the coldest winter in history by any means, but I did need a coat. And Mrs. Cartwright had so many. Cashmere, wool, fur; black and gray, jaunty plaid, fox fur stoles, mink wafting around her ankles; car coats, evening coats of stiff satin, a velvet opera cloak, my god, she had so many. Her things filled closet after closet, she had so much and I had nothing."

Shirley's back against the counter, she was peeling carrots while she listened, dropping the peels into the hand that held the carrot so she could face me as she worked.

"She offered it to me. That blue wool coat. And then I put it on and she liked the way it looked. She took it back. Mrs. Cartwright took back her promise." I stopped, took a breath.

Shirley

"Don't you see? When people do bad things, don't you see? They make everyone else around them bad. She broke her promise and made me a thief. I don't want to rub off on someone else the way that woman rubbed off on me."

"You stole a coat."

"She went to answer the telephone, and I put it in the bag of things she didn't want. My sister Helen let me."

"That was kind of her." Oh, and there was one other thing Shirley said. "You and your devilish blue coat. And you look so sweet." She laughed to herself, gave the baby a pat, turned back to the pile of carrots on the counter. It was true. She always put the devil in shiny blue. Called him James or Jimmy or Jim, and always Harris. The demon lover had a name, and a look—tall and slim—and he was a writer, wasn't he? Shirley's devil was a blue-clad, slim aspiring writer. She had known about me before she ever met me, known I was coming. Just as she had known the truth of what happened with Stanley. Before it ever happened. Her only mistake was in getting angry a week too early.

Twenty-one

AFTER NATALIE FELL ASLEEP, and before I went downstairs to face Fred and have him face me, I went to look for Sally. It seemed imperative to make peace with her. To explain myself. If we were to be family—I was staying, wasn't I?—I would have to find a way. To be both one of them, the daughters, and also Shirley's friend. I saw that now. She wasn't in her room, although the toss of clothes on her unmade bed and the tumbled sweater and mud-damp boots nestling her open overnight case told me she hadn't yet returned to school. I stood in the hallway for a moment. No life up here, save mine and the baby's. No pulsing blood, no lungs expanded in quiet breath, nor air seeping in nostrils—just me, really, and those voices downstairs in the living room, tones humming and pausing, feeding the air. She wasn't home.

Back in the room, back on the bed, the baby's snuffling snores, the walls hovering around her crib like fairy godmothers—but the baby bestows the gift, that as she sleeps we imagine peace.

I took the back stairs again, letting myself quietly out the kitchen door. I borrowed the buffalo plaid jacket from the hook by the door—still muddy from when Shirley'd fallen (or said she had) while wearing it weeks before—stuck my hands in the pockets, curled my fingers over the book of matches I found there. There were matchbooks everywhere in the house; we bought two boxes at a time. God forbid a reader or a writer had to break a train of thought in order to find a light! But these matches, advertising Charles Atlas's weightlifting course like all the others, had been crushed, even though half the book was still unused. As if someone, in a hurry or in excitement, had made a fist without realizing what they were. I palmed them thoughtfully.

I passed under the parlor windows. Marvelous that Stanley and Fred's endless ratiocinations continued even on an afternoon like this, not even a moment of respectful silence to mark the dramas of the weekend. If anything, Stanley's voice seemed to drum at the clouded window glass with a more enthusiastic tremolo than ever. *Damn Iago,* I muttered to myself, stamping through the back gates of the college, chilled despite the huge jacket, which came down far below my knees and probably made me look like a hobo.

And *Damn Iago,* I muttered again, a few minutes later, passing a group of girls huddled in the shelter of the barn entrance, trying to light their cigarettes. They were bare-legged despite the weather, in shorts and kneesocks topped by winter peacoats, and each girl seemed more assiduously to avoid my nod than the one next to her. Campus gossip was like city gossip, apparently—less than two days and even perfect strangers could identify the pathetic spurned faculty wife at a glance. Iago with his drive toward troublemaking for entertainment had met his equal in Stanley, I thought, a fellow who tempted a good man to destroy his own love and then went after the foolish wife. Why not bed her, reap a practical benefit from the season's entertainment? *Damn Iago.* But how could I be mad at Stanley, who had never deceived a soul? Shirley knew him for who he was, as did his kids and his students and everyone else who met him. Scratch Stanley and there was only Stanley beneath the surface. Brilliant, childish, generous, selfish Stanley.

Scratch Shirley at your peril. Hadn't Stanley's lover Caroline discovered this? Shirley was no pitiable Desdemona. Action did not frighten her. "I am pragmatic," she had said. And I believed her. I wanted to be like her, and so I sought her daughters. Peace was a practical solution. Nonetheless, I liked knowing the matches were in my pocket.

I wasn't sure where Jannie's room might be, nor did I feel comfortable asking any of the girls I saw, so I went down to the dormitories and began walking through the buildings in search of her nameplate. She was on the second floor of the third building; her door was ajar; she was in there with Sally, cuddled together on the bed like puppies, both asleep. I cleared my throat.

Down the hall I heard giggles through another open door. Somewhere a shower ran, and a toilet flushed, and a violin made nearly pleasurable sounds. The hallway rug was worn almost to the wood, patched in places, smelling of old perfume and pencil shavings. My damp loafers felt heavy.

On Jannie's floor was a pile of partially knitted wool, a scarf she had undertaken before Christmas. Back then I'd been jealous watching Shirley teach her a better way to cast on stitches, and I'd been pleased to see how Jannie dropped the project when Shirley stopped paying attention to it. But here was the scarf, at least a foot longer than it was the last time she'd had it at the house.

"You keep secrets, too," I said. But Jannie remained asleep. She was short, like Shirley, with pale brown hair that swirled limply on the pillows without tangling into Sally's blonder curls. They breathed the same way, shallowly and through their nearly touching noses. Sally's hand slept on Jannie's; I imagine their feet were intertwined beneath the patchwork quilt. I cleared my throat. Loudly. I wanted to have it out with them. I think I had the idea that if they forgave my rudeness I'd be able to go back to the house a grown-up, someone that Fred and Stanley and of course Shirley would have to take more seriously as well.

"Wake up," I said. "Wake up." But nothing. I stood for a moment longer, and then turned and walked slowly down the hall. Just before I entered the stairwell, I could swear I heard Sally's giggle, suppressed by a sweatered elbow or length of quilt, but audible all the same. I stopped. I didn't hear her again.

I stayed in the hallway, my heart pounding. Everywhere around me the sounds of life being lived, laughter and running water, someone jumping, another girl's high voice recounting the story of an evening debacle at rapid, excited speed. I held my breath, tiptoed the length of the hall to Jannie's door.

They were cheek to cheek, still, sitting up now, heads against the wooden headboard. As I entered the room, their smiles froze.

"I didn't think you were asleep."

"How dare you come here?" Sally said. She swung her legs to the floor, began digging around for her shoes with stocking feet. Jannie sat up straighter against the headboard, silent.

"I wanted to explain, to tell you why we came back," I said.

Sally shrugged the shoulder of her brown cardigan back up,

checked the buttons, drew the sleeves carefully down to her wrists. "It's not as if we're interested."

"I don't want to have trouble, I didn't want you to be angry."

"Why would you care?" She stood, began rooting in the tangle of sweaters and slippers and books and notebooks on Jannie's floor for her jacket.

"Because you were right, what you said to me. I am the same age as you"—I looked to Jannie—"and I have been trying hard, so hard, to be a good guest at your house, to be part of your family—"

"Part of Shirley's family," she said snidely.

"Yes. And for Fred, to make sure Fred makes a good place for himself here."

"He's certainly done that."

"I know," I said, and again I started crying. Even I was tired of my tears.

They watched me coldly.

"I wanted it all to be different, to be special, don't you see? And now look what's happened. What he did."

"What did he do?" Jannie asked. She honestly did not seem to know.

"Screwed a student. At least one." God, Sally's voice was cruel. Just the tone of it was like being stabbed.

"He did?" Jannie asked with interest.

"Your father taught him exactly what to do."

Jannie blinked several times, took her glasses off, cleaned them, and replaced them on the bridge of her nose. "My father?"

"You know what he is."

Sally said, "Don't listen to her Jannie, don't. She's making it up."

Sally's pale skin was as red as the jacket Paula Welden wore the afternoon she took off from campus and headed for the Long Trail, bright, bright safety red—Had this been her room, I wondered, and why not? It could have been—and Sally took Jannie in her arms and lifted her to standing. "We're going to dinner," Sally told me. "You can tell them we're eating on campus tonight." A sheen of sweat glistened across Jannie's forehead.

"Are you ill?" I asked, but no one answered.

She went down the hall to where the bathrooms were. Sally said, "She doesn't think about our father the way you do, she doesn't like to. So save your histrionics for the house, for people who have no choice about listening to them."

I was stumped. I said, "You know about Stanley, don't you?"

"I'm no fool. I see things."

"But she—"

"What's the difference, Rose? Let her cling to what she clings to; it won't hurt you."

I clutched her arm; I could tell it was too hard; she tried to shake me off. "I dreamed she'd died," I said. "Shirley. I dreamed she died and Stanley married someone else and everything was awful."

Sally's breath came hard. She glanced at the doorway, but Jannie was not yet back. "You're crazy," she said. "You're crazy and evil enough for Shirley to write about you, but I won't give you the pleasure. Get out of here."

"I'm trying to help," I said.

"Then go away."

She left me in Jannie's room, and I heard her down the hall, pushing open the bathroom door. After it closed, I could hear her voice but not her words, and I left, walking slowly, fingering the matchbook in my jacket pocket with one hand, the other holding on to the banister for balance.

Outside, I felt eyes on me everywhere, as if the students were mockingbirds perched high inside each dorm window, staring and laughing, sneering and chattering as I made my way up the drive. Their cars blocked my path, their disdain seemed to float in the air like dandelion weed; all I wanted was to get back to the house. I clutched the matches tightly; with my fingers I could tell that less than half the book was used, but all I wanted was to be in my house. My house, Shirley's house, the place where I was safest. Where even if Fred had wronged me, I was needed.

I did not let myself think about the students. How lucky they were to have been loved enough to be there, to be children without babies, to be young enough to fuck their professors and go on with their studies and their dreams. I had never been young enough to take any risks, I told myself furiously. I had never, ever been lucky enough, or safe enough, to make mistakes. What freedom that would be.

I strode back to the house filled with self-pity and rage. When an image of Paula Welden appeared, a captioned picture in the boldly headlined tabloid in my head, I dismissed it and marched on. Whatever Shirley had done to her, there on the mountain, Paula Welden had been loved. Not even she had endured the misery and betrayal that had been my lot since birth.

Oh, I realize how this sounds, how awfully childish, how awfully selfish I was. I do not defend myself. I only want to tell the truth.

Shirley

. . .

I SAID TO FRED, not half an hour later, "Even with what you did, you need me."

"I do," he said. "And I'm sorrier than I can say."

"You need me," I said again.

He nodded.

"We made a promise, we have a life together, our whole life, and now I'll never forget, I'll never forget what you did!" Somewhere downstairs, someone closed a door, perhaps to give us more privacy. Stanley put on one of his jazz recordings. It made me mad. I wanted them to hear us. I wanted everyone to be with us, all of them, I wanted them all to be a part of what had been done to me, to celebrate my injury, to atone for it, to make it right.

"Shh," Fred said. "The baby." But Natalie slept through all of it, and downstairs life went on as normal, and that was the way of it. I know we talked some more, and there were apologies and promises, but honestly, the fact that we were both there, in the same room, made all discussion moot. The inevitability of going on was understood.

213

Twenty-two

STANLEY, OVERHEARD IN THE KITCHEN. I was making my way downstairs in stocking feet, not because I was sneaking but because I intended to return to bed with my morning coffee. I did not feel the need to breakfast with Shirley. I wanted to be alone, in the bed, staring at the floral wallpaper—challenging the house to tell me its intentions. Was I to be ejected like poor Eleanor in *The Haunting of Hill House*? Ejected and then forced by death to be immured in the house forever?

Was I crazy? Well, of course I was. I see it now. I do. I was crazy and I was right, and it was Stanley's voice I heard as I headed toward the kitchen.

Yes, Stanley, overheard: *So we return to normal.*

The hiss of the water as she soaked the still-warm frying pan. She: *I kept my promise. Brought them both back safe and sound. Now you keep yours. No more phone calls.*

He: *No more adventures. No more spells.*

Obediently: *I'll work on my book and see the good doctor.*

Reassuringly: *And Rose will manage the house. It was right to bring her back.*

Shirley

She: *But no more phone calls, Stan. I mean it.*

Whatever he whispered in response made her giggle. When I entered the kitchen, having cleared my throat twice on the last few steps, their faces were arranged to greet me. We made terse morning conversation and I escaped upstairs. I felt the bed sigh pleasantly as I sank against the pillows.

And so began the first morning of that last week.

Twenty-three

THAT LAST WEEK, I spent less time in the kitchen and more in Shirley's library, reading the witchcraft books, of which she had so many. Spells were my focus, so small and so powerful. As the Lancashire witch Mother Cuthbert defined them, *a spell is a piece of paper written with magical characters, fixed in a critical season of the moon, and conjunction of the planets; or sometimes by repeating mystical words. Of these there are many sorts.* If someone had asked me, I wouldn't have said what I was looking for. A charm to keep a husband faithful? To find a missing mother? There had to be a spell to save a doomed friend from death.

I sneaked into their bedroom and took some hairs from her hairbrush. I put them in my dresser drawer, tucked inside my stocking bag. I would have taken a shirt or scarf of hers as well, but I was afraid she'd notice and misunderstand. I'd hate her to believe me a thief.

I went down to the library, and Mrs. Morse seemed to feel it was dangerous to speak to me, as if I'd been infected by whatever curse controlled the household. She nodded formally, and turned to speak to one of the other local matrons, barely meeting my eyes as she checked out my books. But then, just as I was about to turn away, she said, "I suppose you'll be pleased to know his friend is back, the professor's friend. Turned up safe and sound, no matter what that crazy family tried to do to her."

"Oh," I said, relief pulsing through me as if it had replaced my blood. "That's good to hear."

"Won't tell a soul where she went, or why."

"Perhaps it was a family matter."

"She's just too fine a woman to blame others," Mrs. Morse averred darkly.

"I'm sure there's an explanation," I said. Even though I was fairly certain that Mrs. Morse was right. Whether it had been a spell or one of Shirley's more "pragmatic" gestures made no difference. We were Shirley's, each of us her fictional possessions, whether we knew it or not. And then Mrs. Morse surprised me:

"That Mrs. Hyman can't turn us into another one of her evil stories. No, she cannot." And with that, the librarian picked up the books I'd returned and began to pluck out the circulation cards, each flick of her fingers resentfully swiping clean my temporary stewardship of those volumes.

THE MALAMUDS WERE LATE, and Stanley was already pretty drunk. Ann had called to say they'd had a long lunch with the Bellows, who were visiting for the day on their way to Cambridge. Bern had taken a nap afterward. He was making up lost writing time, and she expected they would be at the Hymans' house by eight-thirty, "or nine at the latest." Shirley, who had managed the call with such considered politeness that I knew she was irritated, did not return to taking dried apricots out of the warm cider she'd used to plump them; instead, she left her fingers draped over the telephone receiver as if she were committing the phone conversation to memory. I took a handful of bay leaves from the bag in the back of the spice drawer; when I turned around to add them to the bowl with the apricots, Shirley was gone. The typewriter's click-clack began immediately.

No matter. I could reconstruct the recipe for Shirley's glazed ham with apricots from memory, I was almost positive. Off went the radio, so that I could better dredge the procedure from the cellar of my thoughts, while at the same time heeding the type-writer's rhythms from the library. Melted butter, chopped onion, and then the cider reduced by half. While the cider simmered, I scored the ham, used a skewer to make holes at each diamond edge for the cloves, and patted brown sugar on the entire roast. Already the kitchen smelled marvelously festive, as if tonight might be a bacchanalian celebration.

Malamud was coming! His world was mine. Reading *The Assistant* had been like reading about myself—streets I could picture, stores I'd been in, characters so familiar the book read like gossip from one of my childhood neighborhoods. His people were as endearingly imperfect as Shirley's, but he took them more seriously. His affections were sympathetic in a different way; he seemed kinder, somehow, his intent less ironic. I never thought he was laughing at Morris Bober, or at any of the characters in his short story collection, the one that won him the National Book Award.

Two such important writers in one small village; now that I thought about it, it was surprising I'd not met him before this.

It seemed that life had returned to normal that final week, although in the way of things when one is pretending routine as usual, routines held an element of thwarted fury. Oddly, I had returned to trusting Fred. I had no doubts, now, that when he set out for work he cached his loyalty to me next to his class notes in the soft leather briefcase Stanley had given him at Christmas. Call it another volume toted in from home for use in student instruction. That week, the days were mild and beautiful; after the troubled sleep of the night, I was awakened not by Natalie's cries but by the cheerful morning calls of innumerable friendly birds. Spring on the wing, skies smeared with pale and poignant blue—there was a gentle quality in the air, and in the house, where we were all studiedly kind to one another.

We were past intimacy. No more confiding, although our actions were tinged with the understanding of our mutual affection. Had I forgiven too early, too completely? Remember where I came from—betrayal was what I knew, and I had never seen a man with such remorse—as a tattered extended family, we were past the inevitable and had survived it.

As I read in silence in the living room each day that week, Natalie cooed in her basket at my feet. I knew it was silly, I really did, and yet I made myself believe in Shirley's spells. Her books described the way to make a witch's sacred circle, and most mornings I took time to rig one around Shirley's desk using kitchen string. I'd sit there while she was in the shower or upstairs napping, repeating the silly rhymes I'd written asking protection for the mother of this house, for life and peace and prose that would transcend whatever misfortunes I sensed in the offing. I lit my candles, tucking the matches into the pocket of my skirt as I wished my circle into being, said my foolish phrases. I believed with categorical fervor. I so wanted to believe, I made it so. Sometimes as I heard the loud squeal of the shower faucets being turned off upstairs, I would feel the squawk reverberate down my spine, my essence urgently called home. I'd cease my exhortations with deliberate speed, drawing the kitchen twine back into a little knot that I could store inside Shirley's pencil jar, putting the candles back on the shelf. Even the smell of matches would have dissipated before her footsteps sounded on the stairs, and yet that half-amused smile told me she approved of what I'd done.

Today, however, I'd not had the chance. There were still coffee grounds on the counter by the stove and breakfast dishes in the sink; the ham to prepare, along with mashed sweet potatoes and the frozen peas I would doctor with canned mushrooms and cream. I'd wanted to read Malamud again if there was time, to dip into his short stories or the novels so I might not shame myself in his presence.

Earlier that morning, Shirley had found this laughable. "A few of the short stories are fine, I suppose. He's quite predictable. How he won a National Book Award is a mystery Miss Marple could not solve."

"He's not good enough?"

She did not want to answer, merely tilted her head and walked down the hall to her desk for the first time that day, where I could hear the creak of the typewriter platen as she wound a fresh piece of foolscap around it, followed by the hesitant rhythms of the morning's first typing.

I couldn't help myself, followed her into the study. I selected the Hymans' copy of *The Assistant* from the bookshelves. Without looking up from her work, she said, "He's not as good as me."

He'd won the awards, not her. I couldn't help wondering if I would like him. "I don't know a man like Morris Bober," I said. "But I always believed, I always wanted to believe, that there were people like that. When I was young."

"Bern Malamud did not invent the Jews." The sharp morning light glinted off her glasses so that I could not see if her eyes had narrowed at the thought of him. I put the book down, sensing it was wiser to do so. At lunchtime, when I went in to see how she was doing, she'd closed the volume and replaced it on the shelves.

THE MALAMUDS ARRIVED QUIETLY, knocking on the door and waiting until I went to answer it, standing patiently outside in the still-wintry night air while I struggled with that sticky, obstinate knob. While Shirley paced the dining room on the lookout for badly folded napkins and spotty wineglasses, matters that usually failed to interest her, Stanley read to her from a book review he was writing. He'd stumbled over his own text repeatedly but without comment, as if his inebriation were not worthy of notice. Fred sat on the couch in the parlor, correcting papers.

I introduced myself. Malamud was small and wiry, perhaps my height but no more, while Ann seemed taller and older, a matronly woman with dark owl eyes that tracked through the front hallway deliberately, assessing the quality of the umbrellas in the stand, the gilt on the mirror, the threadbare loveseat where coats would be thrown. I saw the way she examined the sweep of the stairs and the paintings on the wall—Shirley's and the kids' intermingled with gifts from friends, a jumble of collected works and school photographs, all willy-nilly, that I found the essence of what familial life should be. "Shall I place my coat here?" Ann asked, shrugging off her navy cashmere. I took it, not thinking about whether she thought it was my job, but simply wanting to run my hands over cloth as lush and enveloping as this.

I brought her into the living room and introduced her to Fred, who was already handing Bern a glass of white wine. Ann was concerned that Bern not have too much salt, she said; with a heart like his, he had to be careful.

Enter Shirley, with a bowl of peanuts.

Ann refused them, as did Bern, and we arrayed ourselves on the various couches and chairs. Shirley raised the topic of the recent visiting writer whose car tires had been slashed while parked overnight in the village. Did Bern worry that someone was targeting writers?

No, he did not. In fact, he wished there were readers who cared enough to come and slash an author's tires; he feared that in a world transfixed by Da Nang, the Beatles, and Frank Herbert's *Dune*, it was unlikely that anybody would ever be sufficiently interested in him to stoop to violence. Intelligence glittered through the thick lenses of his wire-rimmed glasses.

"Malamud! Here to save the Jews!" Stanley half tripped on the edge of the Persian rug. Vodka splattered from the full martini glasses to the tray, but he managed to keep a hold on his burden. Shirley glanced at me expressionlessly.

"Have some peanuts, Bern."

He made as if to take a few, politely. Ann touched his arm. They did not glance at each other; nonetheless, he changed his mind. "Watching my salt," he said.

Ann began to talk about their lovely afternoon with Saul Bellow and his wife. "Bellow calls himself, Philip Roth, and my Bern the Hart, Schaffner, and Marx of literature," she said, and chuckled, shaking her head from side to side the way an elephant does, as if the work of carrying the trunk is a kind of dignity. Shirley took a handful of peanuts and stuffed them sloppily into her mouth, chewing vigorously.

"Meeting of the National Book Award Winners Mutual Appreciation Society. If only Roethke were still extant, you could have included him." Stanley offered Malamud a martini, was rejected, and drank the entire glass with antic dash. Malamud sipped his white wine, smiling thinly at the wall across the room, where part of Shirley's collection of African masks was arranged.

A silence fell. Bern drew a small reporter's notebook out of the inside pocket of his blazer and held it loosely in his right hand while he drew a pen from his shirt pocket with the other. Shirley watched him with fascination, her mouth twisted in a sad little grimace.

Fred motioned for me to come and sit next to him on the couch, sliding toward the arm so that I'd be sandwiched between his lean frame and Ann's matronly girth. I shook my head. "The ham is calling," I said, and escaped into the kitchen, where the cornbread

I'd made at the last minute was browned and ready to emerge from the oven. I felt tremendously excited by all the tension.

WHEN I CALLED THEM TO DINNER, Stanley did not appear. "He fell asleep, I think," Fred whispered.

"I'll get him." But Shirley said no, to serve the ham and she would wrangle him. Fred and I sat down with Bern and Ann Malamud, and I handed the large platter around. Bern asked Fred about his teaching load, and Fred described the way he was co-teaching with Stanley. Bern asked about Fred's dissertation. Fred glanced at me anxiously, as if he had suddenly forgotten the entire sum of the past two years, had lost track of his own professional interests.

"Are you interested in Jewish folklore, in our cultural myths?" Bern asked.

Fred nodded. "Lately, I've been thinking about the Old Testament as science fiction. Adam and Eve the first colonists after nuclear disaster—"

Bern laughed out loud. "You're a novelist!"

"Oh no, I only meant—" Fred blushed, picked up his fork.

Ann said, "Ham." The one word, flatly.

"I'm so sorry," I said. "I never thought. You don't eat pork?"

"Of course we eat pork. But when she asked us, I told her Bern was trying to avoid salt. His doctor says he should. And here you give us ham."

He reached across the table and put a hand on her arm, a mirror of what she'd earlier done with him. "We'll make do," he said. "It's fine."

I liked the way her fury sputtered at his touch. They seemed married in a way I aspired to, their fortunes managed mutually. Fred offered Bern a helping of sweet potatoes. I passed the mashed cauliflower and explained what it was, that we made it for Stanley. "You're a good girl," Bern said. He patted my hand.

I heard the typewriter start its arrhythmic beat. Had she gone back to work? I swallowed a bite of partly chewed ham and coughed, then told Bern how much I'd liked *The Assistant*, how much I admired his work. "You've caught the world we come from so completely, how there isn't time to protest the war or hear the Beatles, how a neighborhood feels like the universe broken out block by block. I know your characters, all of them."

He offered to read a little bit after dinner. "You'd do that?" I couldn't believe my luck.

Ann spoke loudly, as if she wanted to be heard over the sound of Shirley's typing down the hall. "He'd do that."

I felt a pool of sweat begin to form on the chair seat, under my legs. They were bored and we were not enough to entertain them; she did not like me. "I wonder where Barry's gotten to?" I said, but of course he was at the Malamud house, she explained, eating spaghetti with their daughter and some other friends. I passed the wine bottle and she took another glass, although he refrained.

"Those myths," Fred said. "You use them in your stories, don't you? I'm thinking of *The Magic Barrel*."

"My mother's stories," Malamud said, his face brightening as he began to talk to us about his family, about his parents' journey to this country, about the way he combined superstition and folklore with the culture he'd been raised in—the marriage broker, the princess, the poor schmuck with the good heart who needs guidance to become a wise man in the end. Ann chewed her food daintily, politely. I wondered how tired she was of hearing him repeat his epics at dinner table after dinner table; did that happen to all couples? I was confused; I admired the Malamuds and was ashamed for our hosts, and yet I could see that though she loved him, Malamud was imperfect in his wife's assessment. To my not-yet-twenty-year-old eyes, their stretch of life together was daunting in all ways: prosaic, faintly embarrassing, and astonishing.

I was overfull by the time Bern had finished picking at his plate. I cleared, and Ann helped me, and as I set the coffeepot to heating I suggested we return to the front parlor. She had Shirley's witchy ability to find her way around the kitchen, pulling out the silverware drawer on the first try and piling all the coffee cups and the sugar bowl on the precise tin tray Shirley preferred.

"Stanley, Stanela, wake up there, why don't you?" Bern said. "Company's here." But Stanley snored blearily, stretched out full-length on the less comfortable of the two sofas, as if he'd graciously ceded the better one to those who remained awake. Shirley typed away in the library, her rhythm so steady she might easily have been practicing secretarial exercises: quick brown foxes jumping over lazy dogs. I sat in the chair next to where Bern was perched, on the end of the good couch. Fred took the chair opposite me. Ann, a cup of coffee in either hand, came over and perched on Bern's knee, smiling at me as if our moment of shared labor in the kitchen had made us friends.

"Get off," he said. "You're too heavy." And he pushed her crudely, so that hot coffee splashed like an O'Keeffe flower across the bottom half of her pale green dress.

"For God's sake, Bern!"

Stanley sat up with interest, rubbing his eyes, as I ran into the kitchen to grab a wet dishcloth. By the time I returned, everyone was standing. No typewriter sounds from the other room, either.

Malamud's jaw was set in a mulish manner. "I'll apologize for the coffee, but honestly, Ann. You sat on me without asking."

"Let's go home. I want to go home."

Shirley appeared in the doorway. "But you can't. You've barely gotten here; it's far too early. We'll call some people, have a party. I'll invite Alan and his wife, and the Burkes. And Jules might be free. You can't go now."

"I want to go," Ann said tightly.

There was a long pause. We all watched Malamud as he considered the question of staying or leaving. Stanley's eyes were half open, his posture wobbly and his cheek indented by the seam of the throw pillow on which he'd been sleeping. Shirley leaned against the doorjamb, head tilted: no notebook needed to retain the details of this evening. Fred stood with his palms open; who was he beseeching?

I opened my mouth. "You were going to read to us," I said.

"Oh yes, you must read to us. A veritable Pickwick Society meeting here tonight." It was impossible to miss the harshness of

Shirley's tone. Stanley sat back down on the couch with a *thwap*, lifted his legs, and stretched them out along the cushions.

"I want to read," Bern said to Ann, but it was not as if he had decided, more as if he wished her to accede. Her face was suddenly lovely, so vulnerable and tender. She would agree to anything, if he would look at her that way. Shirley shifted, next to me, and a glance showed her sympathy writ large. Both of them strong, strong women still subservient to their men; I looked for Fred, and he'd gone over to the couch. One hand already reaching for the student papers he needed to correct. Could I ever be so focused on the job at hand that I would stop watching for others' reactions or listening for a baby's cry?

Ann buttoned her cardigan over her green jersey dress, a smile inlaid on top and bottom lips. I was upset for Ann, and for Shirley and for myself. All around us, out in the world, there were Negroes insisting on their civil rights and children insisting they would not go to war and women giving voice to their right to be counted as equals, at work and at home. Women who said, *I want this* or *I will be that*. "I want you to read," I said evenly, to Bernard Malamud. "I think you should read to us now."

"You should read, too," he said to Shirley, politely. His balding pate glistened under the orange light thrown off by the wall sconces.

"Not now," she said. "I'm in the middle of a story. I'll finish it tonight."

The look that passed between them should have been funny.

"I like that story you wrote," Bern said, "the one about the girl who went missing from the college."

Stanley took his glasses off and rubbed his forehead. Shirley said, "Paula Welden? That was before our time."

I jumped up. I said, "I'll get *The Assistant*. You can read from that."

"No," he said. "You have *The Magic Barrel*, don't you?"

"Of course we do," Shirley said. She stayed by the doorjamb, and he remained right there, four feet from her. Ann hugged herself over her newly buttoned sweater. Fred held his students' papers as if there were nothing he'd rather do than correct homework, and Stanley lolled clownishly on the couch.

I found the book filed correctly under *M*, right next to Malamud's other books. The dust jacket was chilly to the touch. I returned to the front parlor, handed the book to Bern, and sat on the sofa, my skirt brushing against the soles of Stanley's shoes. Stanley did not sit up, merely tapped my skirt cheerfully with a clad toe.

Bern opened the book; all of us heard the *cree-ack* of the spine being broken for the first time. "I see you have a fresh copy." Exuding calm, he took the pen from his pocket and turned to the title page, as if about to autograph it.

"It's fresh," Shirley agreed, and then she burst out laughing. The giddiness of it frightening to the ear. It did not stop, the sound caught on itself and amplified, turbulent to hear and awful to watch. She leaned against the wall, the light reflected off the plaster spilling its glow over the paleness of her skin, and she laughed as if the mirth were painful, gale after gale of whooping howls that brought tears to her eyes and bent her over in the middle. "Oh, oh, oh!" she cried, and kept on laughing, shriek upon shriek, so that

Stanley stood and went to her, his drunken pleasure utterly dissipated, and Malamud stood, and Ann with him, and only Fred and
I remained sitting.

"We should go," Ann said, her fingers automatically unbutton-
ing and rebuttoning that sweater, while Shirley went on laughing,
laughing, laughing, and Stanley had his arms around her, saying,
"Shh, shhh, shhh, Cynara, shh, my Shoiley, shhh, shhh."

It was so sudden, the way electricity goes out in a storm. You've
felt the pressure dropping and seen the clouds but now the swoop
of the wind and the pelting rain arrives, and you are shocked by
how abruptly the world becomes dangerous and incomprehensible.

He led her up the stairs; she was sobbing now, guttural belch-
ings between the wails. The Malamuds had found their coats, and
as I showed them to the door, I struggled once again with that god-
forsaken doorknob and had to square my body and shove the knob
against my hip. I could not let them out. I wanted to tell them that
it wasn't anything they had done, that the events of the evening had
nothing to do with them, or their marriage, or his writing—that
the house itself was sometimes inclined to sour even the sweetest of
connections. They were happy to use the kitchen door when I suggested it. Her footsteps crackled on the paving stones. They walked
in unison under the library windows and I did not see a word pass
between them. From the front hall, I listened to the water running
for the tub upstairs, and even through Shirley's thick bedroom
door, I heard the sounds of grief, the grotesquery of despair trapped
joylessly in mirth.

I stood awhile in the hallway, letting the nausea settle in my
stomach, listening for the moment when her sobs would peter into

calm and, I hoped, to sleep. I felt stronger than her, than other women. I thought of my missing mother, of Paula Welden, of those teachers lost in time at Versailles. *And I am of the now, and I am staying in it,* I told myself. *Life will not defeat me.*

I would have gone to do the dishes, but instead I went back to Fred and found him seated on the couch where I'd left him, the clutch of papers still in his lap. His ashen face, I won't forget his face, and I asked if he was all right, and, shaking his head no, he said, "What happened? What was all that?"

I thought of the string I'd left coiled in the jar on Shirley's desk, of the half-used matchbook in the pocket of my skirt. I put Fred's hand between my own and closed my eyes, picturing the walls of the house pulsing like a heartbeat to keep us safe. *Save her,* I implored them. *Save us. Save me.*

I woke an hour later, nearly sliding off the couch in shock when Barry slammed the back door on his return and thudded up the stairs. Only Fred's sleepy clutch kept me from the floor. The lights were still on. "Let's go up."

"The dishes," Fred said, ever the polite houseguest.

"They'll wait," I told him. "They'll wait, and if they don't, I'm sure there'll be more tomorrow. Let's go to bed."

We left the lights blazing. I drew him up the stairs with both hands. Not for sex, not even for forgiveness. Just to prove to both of us that I could.

Twenty-four

THE NEXT NIGHT, Barry's friend Mealtime dropped by with his usual acuity, just as Shirley called the household to dinner. That's when we realized Barry wasn't home. He'd left a note on Shirley's desk saying he was joining his sisters on campus. "They did that last Sunday as well. What is it? I was in the kitchen; why didn't he come in to tell me?" she asked. Mealtime's face was a study in panic. Would he have to answer? The Hyman family was the cinema of his life, but he would die if he found himself a featured player. Not Hamlet, nor meant to be.

For a moment, I thought Stanley might add the proverbial fuel to the fire, invite Mealtime to the table to boost the numbers: the poor kid's skinny chin trembled, anticipating Stanley's imperial command, but it was Shirley who shooed the boy out of the house, telling him to return the next evening.

In all these months, we'd never been seated at that enormous table as a foursome before. We sat at Stanley's end, Shirley on his right and Fred on the left, with me next to Fred. Shirley had made creamed corn and beef stew, served over the recurring mashed cauliflower. Fred, who still ate like a teenager, heaped his plate with food and began nervously to cut the cubes of beef into the smaller pieces his mother had always insisted were correct. I put some corn on my plate, and a heap of cauliflower. I had no taste for meat that night.

I watched Stanley's mouth as he chewed, his lips glistening with the tomato-flecked stew broth, the way he brushed his beard with the side of his right forefinger each time he placed his fork, tines down, at the edge of his plate. Fascinating to watch that mouth, the lips dark with pumped blood, the teeth imperfect in form and yet white as a dairy farmer's, the way his fat tongue emerged to swipe an errant drop of gravy: I could not look away, not even when I felt Shirley's scowl. She had piled stew on her plate but left the corn and cauliflower; it didn't matter, as she was drinking red wine and smoking a cigarette instead of eating at all.

On any other night, there would have been talk of the day's events, discussion of the death of Princess Mary, or of Martin Luther King and his march on Montgomery days before. Stanley was finally reading Bellow's latest and Shirley had been sent a copy of William Humphrey's *The Ordways*, and I suspected she was enjoying it, as she'd had it open in the kitchen while cooking. But none of that came up. The men plowed through the food on their plates without grace or hesitation, and Shirley smoked and drank, and I picked at my meal, all in silence. We were finished in less than fifteen minutes, and Stanley brought out the Scotch and poured a glass for each of us. The candles on the table flickered, and I watched the harmless flames. I thought about getting up to put on a record, one of the plaintive, scratched folk recordings we all loved, perhaps Sam Charters's *The Country Blues*. But with yesterday's events had come a sense of resistance, new for me and quite unlike the survival-focused resistance of my childhood. Thus I would not stand up and help clear the table, nor would I contribute to conversation or put on music. I hunched over my plate and sipped my Scotch and hoped that Natalie would remain asleep until I'd forced the universe to conform to my will.

"Well, the baby seems no worse for wear," Stanley said suddenly, his tone so blithe I had to wonder at it. This was practically the first time he'd ever mentioned Natalie, making the comment even odder. Then he asked about Shirley's work and she said she'd had a productive week.

"The new novel? I'm ready to take a look whenever you like," he said.

She wasn't quite ready, thank you very much. Stanley poured a little more Scotch and sipped it, nodding to me. "She's seen it."

Shirley shook her head no.

I bent my head over the mound of stew. I'd looked at some of it, here and there, when I was straightening up, I admit.

"You've read it?" she said. Her voice was tight. I tried to say no.

There was the sound of something moving in the kitchen, and Shirley went to shoo whichever cat it was down from the counter. Stanley remained undaunted. He took another sip of his Scotch. I turned my glass, letting the brown liquor puddle viscously atop my ice cubes before tilting and jiggling the cubes again. Fred's eyes were very bright; he blinked as if he were holding back tears, and this fascinated me. I'd not yet seen him cry.

Stanley said, "We must walk down to the Rainbarrel and improve the quality of this evening."

Fred wiped his eyes with his napkin.

"The quality of mercy is not strained," Stanley began, as Shirley returned from the kitchen, carrying a jar. It was a brass jar, very simple, with a wide lip and a smoothly knobbed lid. I'd seen it before, I thought, and then I gasped.

"Yes," Shirley said flatly, putting the jar down on the tablecloth in front of me. Her hand was on the lid; she was about to open it.

I swallowed a huge sip of my Scotch and began to cough.

"It's empty," she said.

"One such fascinating revelation will, perforce, beget another." Stanley detested disagreements unless he was part of them. "Grab your coat, Fred. Let's go."

"I can't," Fred said tensely.

Shirley proffered the lid at me, showed me the shiny inside of the jar. "Nothing to see in here."

I was suddenly as frightened as I'd been the night she barred me from the premises. I had to force the words out: "How could you possibly know?"

Stanley took his glasses off and laid them on the table, pouring himself another finger of Scotch. "Has our witch been at work again? Casting spells to soothe the hearts of troubled lovers?"

"Shut up," I said fiercely, surprising even myself.

He chuckled.

"I mean it, shut up."

"Tell me the dream," she said evenly. "Just say the words out loud."

I can remember being too young to read but already understanding what it meant when my father clenched his fists or my mother crossed her arms over her ample bosom. I knew to look straight in my questioner's eyes when I was covering up a sin imagined or real; I knew to lean forward to show that I was interested. Quiet people see a great deal; they aren't listening for the pause in conversation that will allow them to cut in; and someone like me is always looking for a safer place to stand, a spot where the rising water won't wet the only pair of shoes that fit. What I didn't know how to do was deal with someone like her, someone who seemed to see inside me in such a way that dissembling was impossible. "This is insane," I said. "I didn't dream anything."

Fred put a hand on my back, pressing the cotton of my blouse against the damp of my skin so that it chilled me, but still I was grateful. I would be good to him, too, and together we would be better than our beginning. I leaned against his hand, felt the slight pressure of his fingers.

"You might as well say it."

I shook my head no.

Shirley pulled out the chair on my other side, sank heavily into it. "Sally told me," she said. "She's in the kitchen eating leftovers. You dreamed I died, she told me you dreamed it."

I clutched the edge of the table.

"How did I die? What did I die of?"

Stanley said, "You'll come to haunt me, won't you? Or we'll go together. Do we drive up to Glastenbury Mountain and get eaten by mountain lions? Or are we executed like the Rosenbergs? What fate has pretty Mrs. Nemser willed for us?"

"I haven't, I haven't!" I stood, pushing out my chair. "With all that's happened, this isn't funny. It's not right. You're unkind."

"I'm not the one, I haven't dreamed a coffin for anyone," Shirley said, pushing her glasses back up on her nose.

"Nor have I."

She studied me grimly, as if I had disappointed her terribly. "Fine, then, I'll wait for fate to come for me."

The phone rang, and I could hear the satisfaction in Sally's voice, even through the closed kitchen door, as she answered. "That's what mortals do," Stanley said, and then he called through the swinging door: "Who is it, Sal? I hope to god it's entertainment, or this will be the longest night since Normandy." Whoever it was, he intended to invite them over. And he made another call after he hung up, and soon the house was warm with laughter, and Shirley was passing olives and peanuts and Fred was talking about Vietnam with an earnest-looking fellow only a few years older than he, a speechwriter named Alan that the English department was thinking about hiring. I went up to find Natalie pink-cheeked and deep in slumber, and when I returned, I sat on the sofa and was shortly joined by a frail-looking sprite of a girl with a wispy voice and an equally spare blond braid that tickled her shoulder as she nodded. Her name was Maud, she said, "named after Maud Gonne, though I've found no Yeats-like poet to love me, despite it."

I laughed, took the glass of wine she offered, and leaned back against the cushions, tucking my bare feet up beneath me. "You're a student, of course," I said.

She shook her head no. "I'm from the village. Grew up here. A friend of Laurie and his wife"—the eldest son, the one who lived in Manhattan—"and I knew there was likely to be something going on here. Stopped by for some excitement." She sighed, rolling her eyes as if to signify that nothing in Bennington could ever be exciting. "And you're the child bride."

"The child bride?"

"The little housewife who rattles no fences and folds the laundry and fills in the missing pieces."

"The house tells me things," I said, my voice so thin and high it seemed to squeak like bats seeking direction inside the rafters of my skull. "I fall asleep and I dream things. The house owns us, owns all of us." Maud studied me, amused. I could imagine she was friends with Sally. "Not like Hill House," I said. "It isn't evil. But it keeps an eye out. It knows everything that happens."

And then Shirley leaned over, as if she'd been standing behind me all along, and she said, "Our Rose has an imagination to rival any novelist, doesn't she? Hello, Maud." They exchanged hugs, Maud rising slightly and Shirley leaning down to perform the ritual as expeditiously as possible. I stood, offering her my place, and as she sat, Shirley said quietly, "Stay away from what's mine, Rose. Do it now before you ruin everything."

"Novelists are liars," I said evenly. "What I'm saying is true."

"I honored her. Time and time again, I honored the girl. I kept her memory alive," Shirley said. "Only me."

What could I answer? I think I was a little drunk. Maud's eyes were bright, flickering from Shirley to me with interest. I said, "You think we're all characters, don't you? Characters you can move and place, who only act according to your will."

"What I actually think is that it's time for you to go to bed. You look tired. You're not yourself tonight."

I was, suddenly, exhausted, my brain so thick with sleep that my mouth opened without my stopping it. I said, "You didn't write those stories to remember her. You wrote all those stories so there'd be more of them, more stories for people to wonder about, more gossip to cover your tracks."

Maud sipped her wine. Shirley's glasses glinted opaquely. The orange light spun from the fireplace cast shadows on all of us. "You look tired," she said again, and then she leaned closer and confided to me alone. "It won't be fire," she said. "Not for you."

My wineglass trembled in my hand, and I thought it best to leave it on the table. I don't think I said good-bye to Maud, but stood with all the dignity I could muster. In my wake, I heard women giggling. It was gloomy in the hall, and I wasn't sure where Jannie or Barry had gone, but I moved carefully, fancying they might have set a trap for me. I stumbled as I entered the library, where Stanley and Fred and the man named Alan were companionably engaged in denigrating Bellow. It was smoky and the lights were low, and there were cats draped sleepily on the back of each chair. Fred stood immediately, so that the tabby who'd been guarding him jumped to the floor with a baleful glare.

"Have you met Rose?" Stanley asked, reaching automatically for a fresh glass to offer me a drink. Alan stood, extending a hand, and as I took it I heard Fred breathing behind me, and I don't know what came over me. Alan was a handsome man, and I smiled at him, noting the smooth, tanned planes of his cheeks. I felt Fred's lanky presence. The music on the phonograph was jazz, someone I didn't know, and the urge to act came from outside me. I walked past the new man, and over to the table where Stanley had his hand on the glass ready to lift it toward me, but I got to him first. I put my mouth to his, I took his hands and placed them on me, on my breasts, and Fred said, "Rose!"

"Rosie!" Fred pulled at my arm, but I held Stanley tight. He held on to my breasts even after Fred had dragged me from his mouth, and then he laughed out loud, he said, "Mrs. Nemser, I think we've crossed an unexpected Rubicon."

I was breathing hard, of course. I said, "You wanted me to, you said you did. You asked me first and now it's yes, I say yes to you. I'll sleep with you, I'll fuck you, I'll do it."

Fred held my arms as if I would throw myself on Stanley, sink down on him on the floor right there, and I might have, I was angry enough, I might have done it.

"Go upstairs," Stanley said evenly. "Go now, before she tears you to pieces right in front of Alan and whoever else we're entertaining. Go upstairs, Rose." And he turned, and picked up his glass, and said to Alan, "Have you actually tried *Herzog*? If Bellow gets any more self-referential, he'll start writing with his asshole."

Fred walked behind me, all the way up the back stairs, as if he thought I might throw myself down them. In the room I collapsed onto the bed. Now I was crying with my whole body—sobbing, really—and I woke the baby and she began to wail. Fred waited with me until the crying was over, and the baby slept, and he left a hand on my back and sat. So quiet that despite what had happened, I almost fell asleep.

Eventually, he spoke. "We'll go," Fred said. "We'll go anywhere you like."

"Let's go, then." Those long-fingered beautiful hands, the lanky limbs, the bright inquisitive eyes, they waited for me. And I said,

"Why me, Fred? Of all the girls you could have had, why me?" He reddened. "Why me?"

He cleared his throat. "I love you," he said carefully. "And I love the way you look and how you think and who you are. And I don't care who you become, I'll love that, too." I rolled my eyes. "And you're alone, you see? You're mine. And I'm yours. We don't have to share."

And so I stood and wrapped the baby in her blankets. On the dresser, I left no note, only the half-used pack of matches I'd found in the buffalo plaid coat when I borrowed it to walk up to the Bennington campus. I wouldn't need them, after all. And for the second time in as many weeks, we borrowed Shirley Jackson's car without asking and took off for Williamstown. On the way out, we used the front door. It opened for me, easily, and I knew what that meant. There was cigarette smoke everywhere, and a fire in the fireplace, and the sound of high-pitched laughter and Stanley had put Coltrane on the stereo. At the door, I turned around, shrugging Natalie higher against my shoulder. I could swear the house was laughing, as if we'd performed all winter for its entertainment, and nothing more.

Twenty-five

FRED WAS NOT OUT OF WORK for long. Stanley, more gracious than I could ever dream of being, placed some phone calls on Fred's behalf, and we found ourselves in Syracuse early in the summer. We rented an apartment near the campus, a dingy one-bedroom in the basement of a small house. I was tired; it was hot; Fred's mood from day to day impossible to predict.

He had taken a step backward, working as a teaching assistant for an elderly professor named Lord. He made additional money supervising an undergraduate literary magazine. Mostly, Fred focused on finishing the last section of his dissertation, determined to be back on tenure track before the year was out.

I was polite to him, and he to me, and I took it as both job and duty to be assiduous in my wifely attentions. There were good days, such as the hot August afternoon when we borrowed another married grad student's car and drove to the lake in Skaneateles, and I dipped Natalie in the shallow water and then lowered myself into the lake and felt myself weightless and cool, paddling about while Fred and Natalie watched me from the flat sandy shore. We stopped for ice cream at a little roadside shack, and while we sat on a picnic bench, under the trees, Fred fashioned a doll for Natalie out of an oak leaf and two toothpicks and a paper napkin. She glared at it with intensity, as if willing it to come to life. Fred's eyes met mine.

"Another witch," he said lightly. "I can see her mind casting spells, even if she doesn't have the words yet."

"Spells and haunted houses. I've had enough of all that to last a lifetime." I gave her a little taste of chocolate ice cream, but Natalie only licked the cold sweet politely, her attention focused on Fred's oak leaf doll.

"It seems like none of it ever happened. None of it was real," he said.

His tone was wistful. I missed them, too. Already the winter had taken on a rosy tone; even the worst parts had acquired the sweet deckle edges of memory. There were long, long stretches when it was as if someone else's husband had cheated, someone I knew well and liked, who wasn't me. For his part, Fred never seemed to wonder at what I'd done, with Stanley, or why I'd done it. If asked, I swear I would have blamed that monstrous house. It had poisoned me, I thought, as much as slow-dosed arsenic would—I'd not grown immune, but slowly sicker. Now we were alone—for the first time, really—healthier, recovering.

We grinned at one another. It was all good, dragonflies darting near the spilled puddles of congealing ice cream, cars snaking past us on the dusty road—other families out seeking novelty and relief in the summer heat—and I said, "I never asked you, did I? How many times you slept with that girl. And how many others." I kept my voice light and conversational, not wanting to upset the baby.

He put the doll down on the silvery cedar. "You haven't asked, not once."

"I'm asking now."

"We're fine now, it's behind us."

"That's why I want to know."

How mature we sounded, how calm. Without the doll to study, Natalie's eyes closed. Breath slow, she slipped into her afternoon nap against my belly. Not for the first time, I imagined we were breathing in unison.

Fred crumpled his napkin, put a hand on either thigh, and shook his head. "I'd rather not, not here, Rosie. I'd rather talk about this another time, at home."

Near us, a young couple leaned against one another on one side of their picnic table, his tawny curls intermingling with hers as they shared a single cone. They were probably no younger than I was, but I felt ancient in comparison, watching their hands, petting and exploring, the way her hips shifted when he ran his fingers along her neck. Sensing my interest, he turned, his mouth brushing the top of her head. He winked. Affectionate, that wink, as if its maker knew the universe loved him. He lowered his cheek back against the girl's, forgot me.

"I'd like to finish it," I said. "Have it done. Not think about any of it, ever again."

Fred silent, a forefinger tracing little circles into the grimy table. "I figured, I guess I thought that you were over . . . I don't know."

"When did it start? How many of them, Fred? And was it the whole time we were there, one student after another, or only her?"

I did not mean to get louder; Natalie made a mewling sound in her sleep, tucked her chin against my breast.

"Just her. And only twice. I don't apologize, I don't. But there were other, well, opportunities, so many of them. As if I was the fool. They didn't make me do it, it was my fault. I'm not excusing myself, not at all. But the way people talked, what they understood, the way the rules were. I was different. I was the one who was strange."

"What was her name?"

"Don't do this, Rose. It doesn't help."

"You want me to just put it away? Forget about it? Move on?" I was tempted to fling myself away from him, storm off toward the car, but keeping the baby asleep seemed as important. A sparrow pecked at the packed dirt by the table, alert to the possibility that Fred's mostly finished ice cream cone might fall there at any moment.

"Where was she from?" I asked quietly.

"Connecticut, somewhere."

The couple got in their car, a Chevy. Instead of driving away, they sat talking animatedly, as if engaged in making up a story. A story about us.

"I keep wanting to forgive you, I do. I keep trying to figure out the way to do it, to put this behind us, to move on. For Natalie."

"For us," he said. "I don't want to give up on us."

I said, "I'm not the one who did it."

Fred slammed a hand down on the picnic table. The girl in the car giggled loudly. "God, Rose, what am I supposed to do? How can I prove to you how sorry I am? I can't take it away, what happened. I was terrible. I admit it. I was wrong. I'm sorry. I'm sorry. I'm sorry. Now what? How can I fix it? Tell me what to do."

What right did he have to be angry?

"It's not my problem," I said coldly. "I am not the one who . . . I'm not the one who fucked another woman. Fucked her. You did. You have to fix it. You have to make it right."

"But how? I don't know what to do."

"How could I know? I'm no expert. This isn't my area," I said. The boy started the Chevy and backed out, onto the highway, raising a cloud of dust that shimmered in the humid afternoon light. He straightened the car, heading west, back toward Skaneateles. The girl stared at us through her open window, shocked, as if, without meaning to, she'd stumbled onto our horrible secret. Ten years have passed, but still I could blush, thinking of her face.

"Rosie, don't be this way. I'll do anything. I'll do anything you want me to. I'll spend the rest of our lives proving to you what a good husband I can be, how important you are. It's always about you, Rosie, it always is. No matter how badly I screwed things up."

He started to sneeze, an alarming series of explosions that went on and on and on, his eyes growing wider in apology, damp with tears. He could not catch his breath. I had the baby on my lap, could not move without awakening her, and Fred and I watched one another—him sneezing, me guarding our daughter—for perhaps a full minute, until his outburst stopped, as suddenly as it began, and we both started to laugh.

Sometimes that's as good as crying, or yelling, for breaking an impasse. I couldn't help myself. "Okay, Fred," I said to him, the smiles still on both our faces. "We're done with it. That's all."

"I love you, Rosie," he said. He came around the table, and helped me up, balancing for me as I hauled myself to standing, Natalie against my hip. She stayed asleep. We got into the car, and Fred turned on the motor, put the car in gear. I didn't say the words back to him, not then, but I remembered how.

You think you know what you can handle, and what you can't. But the truth is, almost anything is endurable. Because we're made that way, to make the best of what we have. I never told myself, well, this is Tuesday and it's now been a year, or even two, and soon I will forget. I never organized and made a plan to put it behind us, and nor did he. But we went on, and in truth, we got better. And in time, I came to see that I trusted in him more than I had before we went to Bennington: I knew the worst of which he was capable, I knew what it would do to him, and I knew we could survive it.

I'm not saying this was the perfect solution. Only that I don't regret it.

Twenty-six

THE HOUSE, and you don't have to believe this, had told the truth. Shirley Jackson did die that summer, just as I had dreamed she would. So very Shirley-like that this would be the case.

We must have made that trip to Skaneateles Lake on August 7, a Saturday, because Shirley Jackson died in her sleep on the afternoon of Sunday, August 8. She'd gone upstairs to take a nap, apparently in a cheerful mood. Shirley never awakened. She was forty-eight years old.

I found out on Monday, August 9. Fred called from the campus office he shared with five other grad students. Stanley and Shirley had met at Syracuse, in the late 1930s, and news of her death was buzzing down the brick-trimmed paths and through the academic offices, shock passing through the faculty like a virus.

"Shirley's died," Fred said awkwardly, and at first I didn't understand what he meant. And then once I did grasp the words, I could not grasp the reality. Experienced as I was in poverty and abandonment, I knew nothing of death.

He said, "It's too late now. You should have written to her."

I tasted bitterness in the back of my throat. "She could have written to *me*."

"I'm sure there'll be a service."

"Go if you like."

"We could both go."

I unplugged the iron, emptied the heated water into the sink. When he realized I wasn't going to answer, he said, "Never mind. There's no need. With that crowd, nobody will know who shows up and who doesn't."

"I did nothing wrong, Fred. I did nothing wrong."

His voice was stiff. "Do I have to say it again?"

I remember that after we hung up, I sat on the couch, watching saliva bubble at Natalie's mouth, her closed eyelids flutter, some dream overtaking the peace of her sleep. I sat. I did not cry, or sort the dirty laundry into darks and lights, or think about dinner. I did not think. I simply sat, and watched and waited. One road had closed, one path to resolution. I would never make it up with her, never get to apologize or tell her what she'd meant to me. I would not be her friend again. I had not conceived this possibility.

Forgiveness. I hoped she had forgiven me.

Twenty-seven

STANLEY DIED FIVE SUMMERS after Shirley did, five years ago, in 1970. A heart attack at the end of a convivial dinner at the restaurant down the hill from the house. Irony of ironies, he'd married a Bennington student only months after Shirley died. The house had told me that, as well. Who knows if they were happy? I've heard the new wife was pretty, one of his folklore students, well trained in musicology. If memory serves, she was pregnant at the time of Stanley's death.

Stanley's Iago book had just come out. It was not a huge tome like most of the other Hyman books, but Fred nevertheless deemed it Stanley's culminating masterpiece. In examining Iago's motivation using a multiplicity of critical techniques, Stanley demonstrated how much prejudice comes built in to a particular methodology. Reading the book, I could hear Stanley's voice, could hear him arguing with Fred—that note of amusement that always tangled through even his most pompous assertions, as if to make clear that he was smarter than even his own language would demonstrate.

Stanley, by the end, was no longer interested in producing a critical technique that met Aristotelian standards, in developing an overarching scientific standard for analyzing literature. He'd come to believe that every method of analysis was flawed, that the wise critic had to draw on a multiplicity of disciplines at once, keeping a keen eye out for his own prejudices and biases. I found his Iago book accessible and fascinating, and often thought about it afterward, imagining how Stanley might have read a new Roth novel, or Joyce Carol Oates or John Barth, or Iris Murdoch.

Fred cried when I handed him the folded-over section of *The New York Times* with Stanley's obit. We were still in Syracuse then, the dog days of the August of 1970, swimming in dank upstate humidity as we raked through our gloomy basement apartment, packing five years of our lives into cardboard cartons, this in preparation for the move to Stanton. A temporary downgrade to the English department at a prep school would be a little side note, dinner-party fodder, a rest stop on Fred's professional journey. Just because Syracuse had denied Fred tenure didn't mean he wouldn't find another tenure track position elsewhere the following year. Still, we were silent as we crated books and sorted winter clothing, each of us isolated in separate sulks, bitter thoughts.

Well, yes, I admit that I was disappointed. Fred was the star to whom I'd hitched myself, and while, on the one hand, I knew how special he was, how brilliant and hardworking, how deserving, there was that other hand, the one that resented him for not vaulting past his earlier errors. His dissertation, the one that had garnered so much attention while still in progress, had been defended, accepted, and published with little notice and even less acclaim. So much for the Child ballads and their repressive, pasteurized variations in American folksong. Fred had broken with Stanley over subtleties in the lineage of intellectual reasoning that led from Frazer and ancient ritual, through Freud and Malinowski, to Kenneth Burke and the question of the way the individual's understanding of his or her culture is transformed by the very words the culture uses to describe the symbols and ideas it values. Perhaps Fred resented Stanley's adoration of Burke on a personal level, and let it cloud his professional judgment. Ironic, isn't it, that a set of symbols deriding Burke transformed Fred's position in their common culture precisely as Burke might have predicted?

Thus, although Fred had been diligent with his students and dutiful in attending faculty meetings, volunteering for committees and shouldering scut work, he'd not made the tenure grade. Financial security first. Fred wasn't even thirty yet; there was ample time to regroup.

We were pragmatic when we had to be. Fred had been given fair warning by his department head; no surprises there. We spoke of our situation the way one speaks of an illness, as if it were outside us, at a distance. Situation, I said, do you see? We never spoke of it as failure. And I think it's true of both of us that we loved our little family more than any title or place to live, any power to be earned. We were delighted to shepherd our pretty girl around the central campus; we protected our group as if it were an indivisible unit, the prime number of our collective well-being. And so we soldiered on, past this unattractive reality, without going through sessions of blame and recrimination.

But the news about Stanley seemed to tap a well of sorrow in Fred. He finished reading the obituary, placed it on the table, and began to dig through cartons of packed books until he pulled out

Stanley's *The Armed Vision*. The pages were that tissuey paper pub-
lishers use for huge academic books and volumes of collected Shakespeare, and Fred gently ran his fingers over the pages as if they
were love letters he'd stumbled on, sitting on his heels in front of
the box. Rocking from toe to heel, back and forth, silently crying as
he stroked the pages of Stanley's book.

Natalie had been napping and now called loudly from the bedroom, signaling delight at having found herself awake. Fred did not
look up. Instead, he closed the book, sat down hard on the wooden
floor, and leaned back against the wall, squeezing his eyes shut
tight.

"Someone should write about him," Fred said. "He'll disappear,
he won't matter, and it's wrong."

Twenty-eight

FRED WAS RIGHT, OF COURSE. For all his bombastic relevance in the forties and fifties, and even the early sixties, Stanley's energies, his status as a public figure began to fade almost immediately after Shirley's death. If there is any proof of how vital they were to each other, it is that he did not know how to be Stanley without Shirley there to make him so.

Shortly after Fred's father died in 1975, we decided together that our small inheritance should permit Fred to take a break from teaching. He wanted to write about Stanley, and I agreed; I thought it might right his course. I trusted Shirley that much, still. Ten years dead, and yet I still believed she had our answers.

We went together to visit the Library of Congress archives in Washington, on the way dropping Natalie in Philadelphia to stay with Lou, his wife Sandy, and their six-year-old son. I had a sense of pilgrimage, as if somewhere in this visit I might discover for myself a way to think about the wrong turn we'd made all those years ago, to finally settle what might have happened if my turn had been the left one, not the right.

The security guard, a lanky white-haired man in a black policeman's uniform, nodded to me with a friendly air that seemed like recognition. The manuscript reading room was a grand one, with high ceilings and a terrazzo floor. I imagined that, come afternoon, when the light hit the row of windows along the western wall, it would grow warm in there. I filled out an application card, told the wide-eyed sprite of a librarian that I was helping my husband to do research on Stanley Edgar Hyman, that I was assisting him in writing a book. I gave our address and telephone number, affirmed my honesty, and went back to the guard, who gave me a locker key so I could hang my coat. Then I found Fred at the edge of the room, where connected desks were arrayed in austere rows.

This reading room was a repository of lifetimes of essay drafts and novel drafts and letters and birthday cards and diaries all bundled into cartons by bereft children and mournful helpmeets. Stationed at the reading room tables were researchers eager to wrest history from all those frankly uncollatable life moments. Fred already had four cartons of Stanley's papers on a book cart at our desks. I pulled out the heavy red leather chair next to his and sat.

"What should I do?" I whispered. "Read some of these? Take notes?"

"These are Stanley's class notes, from the early years, when he was working out the details of the folklore course."

Line after line of seemingly disconnected thoughts. Page numbers, proper names, names of books and ballads and poems. "I wouldn't have been able to teach the alphabet using these," I said.

"But I know exactly what he's saying." Such wistful lingering of his fingers on the thin typescript. "I could teach it right now, using this."

I looked up, saw that one of the librarians—a man in his thirties, casually dressed, with the requisite wire-rimmed eyeglasses—was staring at us down the long length of the room with a curiosity bordering on disapproval. We were about to get shushed. "How can I help?" I lowered my voice below a whisper, barely mouthing the words.

"I don't know," he said absently. "Why not look through her stuff, Shirley's?"

"Shirley's? She has papers here, too?" I couldn't imagine what it would be like, to look through her things. After all these years, to paw through the remains of her writing life, like a Peeping Tom in a lingerie drawer. My heart began to pound excitedly.

Fred handed me the cloth-covered notebook listing the contents of Shirley's files at the Library of Congress. Oh my. There were her high school journals, old photos and papers—letters, novel drafts, Christmas lists! Cartons upon cartons of Shirley. "Can I?" I asked him breathlessly. "What would I look for?"

He shrugged. "Anything. Look for what interests you."

I almost couldn't believe it. Even as I filled out my first request form, I was certain something would go wrong. It wasn't possible, was it, that I could actually be with her again? But the librarian took my request without questioning my right to Shirley Jackson. Her files were on-site and available. It would be a few minutes; he would bring the cartons to me at my desk.

Cartons of Shirley. I imagine it was much the way one feels about a loved one's ashes, seeing all that accumulation of personhood reduced to several dry, crumbly cups of undistinguished afterlife—and yet feeling certain the essence is in there, quietly seething with watchful expectation. Empty and full at the same time. For me, she was about to be alive again. The most important woman I had ever known. *My Shirley,* I told myself. I would see her once more, after all: her mind at work, her thoughts active, no expectation of death. Perhaps I would find forgiveness here, or understanding.

I sat as quietly as I could, but even the blood coursing through my body pulsed a little faster in anticipation. It was the moment just before, that most delicious cresting that jolts one aloft, time paused, time delicious—if the heart could salivate, it would.

The cart grumbled toward me, paused next to my seat. The librarian showed me how to manage the files. "This piece of cardboard is to save your place, so you remember exactly where the file was and can replace it in the same order. No copying without permission."

"Why?" It seemed so silly to have to go up there over and over, request page after page, such a tedious, childish overlordishness.

"Bring whatever you want to copy up to the desk, still in the folder, and we'll look at it, and let you know. Anything that might be hurt by the machine, or damaged by the pressure of the lid, you won't be able to do." He nodded at the small Kodak Fred had left on the table, and said, "You can take pictures with that, too. We don't want the originals folded or bent by the copiers."

Most of what these files contained seemed to be Xeroxes already. Hardly damageable, but why point this out? Besides, I only wanted a little bit of time with Shirley. Why make copies? An hour of this would do the trick, probably leave me surfeited for the remainder of the years ahead.

I pulled out the first folder, placed the cardboard in its place, and let the librarian signal his approval. Fred, over by the issue desk, preparing to make copies, waved at me agreeably. I opened the folder without examining its title. Whatever surprise was in store was fine with me. The first page was typewritten, single-spaced, with little punctuation and no capital letters. I ran my fingers over the surface, felt for the indents of the typewriter keys on the paper.

My eyes? They would not focus, would not unblur, as if the mechanism that usually handled this activity had stopped performing. Blink, and blink again, but nothing doing. I could not see. It wasn't until my ears heard the nearly silent water droplets hit the table that I realized what it was. My own tears, warm to the touch and slightly oily.

At a table, in a public library, on a winter Saturday, and yet I felt as if I'd arrived home. That house in North Bennington, another winter ten years earlier, and I as young as a girl could be and yet as old as any other Mother Earth, and I had learned what it was to love. How to be loved and how to provide love, and how to be of service as a gesture to the gods. Had I known how fast it would all go, how little it would amount to, would I have lived each day more consciously? Ah, me. I don't have the faintest idea.

FROM SHIRLEY'S JOURNAL, dated December 3, and the year was 1964, and I am certain I was in the house. I was upstairs in the house, and this is what she was writing.

all day yesterday and this morning i have been thinking of
these pages as a refuge, a pleasant hiding place from problems

and troubles; that i suppose is because i told the doc yesterday that the writing was happy, which of course it is. writing itself is a happy act, and when i can remember the future and plan for it i am very happy indeed. i am oddly self-conscious this morning because stanley is at home and there is literally no telling him what i am doing. i think he would regard me as a criminal waster of time, and self-indulgent besides. but the endless explanations involved in merely telling stanley anything he does not immediately understand are beyond me right now; it would take all my writing time only to tell him what i am doing.

writing is the way out writing is the way out writing is the way out. too early to think of plots.

there is a calm that begins to come. and my fingers are more limber.

While Shirley wrote this, I had to have been in the house. Upstairs. Perhaps napping. Or maybe I was reading in the living room, or doing dishes. A slim possibility that I was out, in the village, visiting the library or buying groceries. And if so, as I did those errands, they were done for her, for the life I shared with her family, in that house on the hill in North Bennington. But in the writing, there is only Shirley, Shirley and Stanley. As if the world held no one else. Lower down the page, she wonders if she should invite Barbara for coffee? Who is Barbara? Why don't I remember her?

I opened the next folder and riffled through it quickly. And then the next, and the one following. Where was I? Where was I mentioned? I had been there, every day of that entire winter. Where was my name? Was all of it imagined?

I found it difficult to read further. I closed my eyes. As if imprinted on the inside of my eyelids, I could see the walls of that bedroom upstairs, the one Stanley and Shirley gave to us, the one we slept in all that long winter. I'd believed myself a grown-up, hadn't I? And the room itself served better than the mother I'd been born to, its windows looking out onto those huge, threatening, snow-covered trees, that steep climb up the icy hill to campus, but me held safe inside. I'd never lived another place, before or after, in which a house itself had so protected its inhabitants. The house had loved me, hadn't it?

So Shirley didn't see me, not as I saw her. I hadn't known. Ah, the snufflings of scholars: noses sniffed, throats cleared, pencils tapped, chairs shifted. With my eyes shut, I could hear paper sheets being turned respectfully over, the squeak of one resentful library cart's wheels, and under it all, the constant whining rhythms of the photocopy machines. My stomach growled. How very, very anxious I was, suddenly.

I felt the air shift as Fred sat back down, placed a pile of Xeroxed sheets on our table. "You can staple these," he said. Offering distraction at a most opportune time.

Mostly, Stanley's papers were endless listings of course plans, notes for lectures, ideas for articles—how familiar the sight. They were always scattered around the house, on tables and chair arms, piled on the window seat, or left abandoned on the kitchen counter.

One thing Fred had copied that caught my fancy was a handwritten document from Box 33, Stanley's early writings. It was called "Me—In Outline" and began with the lovely phrase: *My ancestors were normal people . . .*

I showed it to Fred, but he barely glanced at the paper, didn't bother to smile.

And then I picked up the next folder, the one Fred had set aside to look at next. Oh, god. That list of names, that single sheet of paper atop a pile of lecture notes and book reviews. Fred had not read it yet, or he'd have seen her name there. Maybe, without examining the list, he thought he'd look them up, the students from the fall of 1946, look them up one by one and find out how brilliant each of them found Stanley. I couldn't breathe, couldn't lift my eyes, couldn't move my elbow: What if Fred realized what it was? What if that overly responsible librarian chose this moment to glance my way? But Fred was standing now, about to go ask permission to photocopy more pages. And the librarian watched as he advanced, and I did it without thinking: I simply folded up the original page and tucked it in my bag. Two quick movements and it was over.

I told myself she'd have done the same for me.

"Look," Fred said, returning minutes later, "another letter from one of Stanley's childhood friends. I bet you'll find this interesting."

It was dated December 8, 1946. The first two paragraphs were inside jokes to Stanley and Shirley, mentioning their old friend

June and her reaction to the sale of Stanley's first manuscript. "*The Armed Vision?*" I asked. Published eighteen months later, this was a celebration of the brilliant pioneers of literary criticism Stanley had been trained by, a widely lauded, career-making treatise that I knew was now considered to be hopelessly optimistic about the future of the craft. Even Stanley, twenty years later, when we knew him, believed he had been wrong—the brilliant techniques for reading and analysis developed by Blackmur and Burke and Empson had become unusable tools in the hands of lesser scholarly minds. Stanley would, in moments of unbridled (read: inebriated) self-pity, include himself in the latter company.

"Not that," Fred said. "Keep reading."

The next paragraph:

What with all your young lady students disappearing as they are . . . if she turns up mumbling hysterically about Tammuz we will know who to look for and if she turns up mumbling hysterically about Cthulhu we will know who else to look for.

I knew who Tammuz was, the god of the harvest, who was slain by the cruel and selfish goddess of love, that courtesan of all courtesans, Ishtar. But who was Cthulhu? I nudged Fred and pointed to the word.

He whispered, "It's from a science-fiction story, by Lovecraft. Cthulhu is the high priest of a cult, I think he's from outer space. Gargantuan. Hideous. Shirley must have liked the story. Stanley didn't read anything so lowbrow, nothing that wasn't quote-unquote literature."

"And so?"

"Your girl, the one that disappeared, the one you thought about so much—"

"Paula Welden?"

He nodded. "She disappeared in 1946, didn't she? Right after Thanksgiving? I thought they didn't know her."

"What? Don't be silly, Fred. This guy's joking. It's only a joke."

He sighed, turned the page over carefully, and closed Folder 11, placing it back into Box 13. "I thought you'd like to see it."

"They didn't know her," I said loudly, not caring when researchers at other tables turned curiously to see who the rude scholar was. "They didn't know Paula, she told me."

Fred shrugged, put a cautionary, comforting hand on my arm. I did not glance down at my purse, where the class list, from the fall of 1946, the class list with P. Welden's name the last alphabetical entry, was neatly folded. This was one thing I could do for Shirley, one way I could thank her, no matter how little she had thought of me.

For, in fact, I was the same as Paula, wasn't I? Rose Nemser: cipher, dream, fraud. I didn't exist. I'd been through all the later boxes—letter, journals, photos—and found nothing. Not a word about us, not anywhere in this accumulated detritus of a life. She had not thought enough of me, she had not thought to record even a mention of my existence. Not for a moment, not for a meal, not for a conversation about fidelity and marriage, not for an arduous, extraordinary winter. Not for the darning of a sock or the roasting of a chicken. Not even for a crying infant.

Rage tingled the length of my back, between my breasts and

across my scalp, as if my whole life had been a sprinter's burst and I was pushing through those last arduous strides. Before I left the reading room, I checked to make sure my husband was okay. Wasted worry: his nose was buried in a folder from Box 41. He had returned to studying what he'd come there to find, the folders with Stanley's lectures on myth, ritual, and literature—the part of Stanley Hyman's life that Fred Nemser most wished had been his own.

It was cold outside, achingly so, and the streets correspondingly empty of people. I paused in front of the library, tightening the scarf around my neck, checking the buttons on my jacket. Fred appeared next to me; I'd known he would, I suppose. That's why I waited.

We strode briskly down to the Mall, not talking. His breath coming in foggy bursts that puffed from his nostrils, dragon's smoke. I could barely feel my fingers, or my toes, but I liked how cold my brain got, how my thoughts slowed and my cheeks burned.

It was practically deserted—only temperatures this cold could keep the tourists at bay. We began to march down the path, wind cutting at the exposed skin of my neck and face. The anger dissipated, my whole being taken up in resisting the bite of the frigid air.

Our footsteps crunched on the icy gravel. Fred's boots damp at the toes and limned with salty residue, the hems of his trousers speckled with mud. When he spoke, I thought at first I had imagined the words:

"Why'd you do it?"

Walking faster to keep warm, our strides matching despite the difference in our heights, we would be at the Washington Monument in two minutes. It loomed ahead of us and made me think of a sword, the kind a knight would use for battle with an enchanter. "Do what?" I asked.

"All those years ago. When we knew them. Why'd you throw yourself into the breach? You were the only person in the right. And you made yourself more wrong than anybody else."

"Stanley must have hated me," I said. "For what I did to you, for taking you away from him."

"I wanted to leave, I wanted to go with you. And there's time. There's still time for us to matter." He'd never before admitted that he wanted to.

"That house," I said. "I had to get out of there."

"There are better ways to start a marriage." He touched my hair, a tendril escaping from under my scarf. "But why, Rosie, why'd you kiss him? Why'd you say that to him?"

"That's easy," I said. "I made a choice."

I simply meant that I'd decided. To be as wrong as the rest of them. Just as I'd decided on Fred, that afternoon on the Temple University campus years before. And then I'd decided to make it work. Because I needed him and he me. I took his gloved hand between my own, pulled him to a stop. We were both shivering.

"They didn't remember us."

"I suppose."

"I'm as absent from the world as Paula Welden. Or my mother."

"Absent from their world, but the center of ours. We have our world, Rosie. We have each other, we have Natalie. We didn't need theirs, we didn't."

"I trusted her," I said bitterly. "She didn't even notice. No record. Not a word, not in all those days we spent together. Not even a note that I hung her laundry out on the coldest afternoons, that I cracked the icy sheets before I brought them in. That Natalie was born. That we talked. Oh god, Fred, she was my friend. I was certain of it."

He was silent.

"We have our world," he said stubbornly. "She doesn't make our life. We do."

"My name is nowhere! I pawed through every single page of her journal. I read her letters. I don't exist! In her mind, I was never alive!"

"We'll write about them, we can do it, we'll bring ourselves to life." As if that was the answer. Fred stared up at the monument, reverential, determined.

"I envy you your faith," I said. And then I opened my purse and took out Stanley's class list from the fall of 1946, consigning his connection with Paula Welden to the place where it belonged, one of the dark hooded trash bins that sat like chess pieces taken prisoner along the edges of the Mall. I shoved my hands back into my empty coat pockets, stretched my cold fingers into the stitching at the corners.

WHEN WE RETURNED, I felt distinctly better. I went directly to the last box I'd ordered—Shirley's Box 29, the one with her incomplete literary manuscripts. I wanted to find the book she'd been writing at the time of her death.

I pulled out the first folder, opened it, and looked at the densely typewritten sheets. If I closed my eyes, I knew I'd smell her cigarette smoke. Harum-scarum punctuation, yellow paper, handwritten corrections: I could hear the proud flourish of the typewriter roll as she drew forth the finished sheet. There was always a louder one, at day's end, as she pulled that last sheet out and tapped the day's pile into place. That sound marked the end of labor, the beginning of our evening celebration. Oh, I could still hear it now!

I extracted the first of Shirley Jackson's unpublished manuscripts from the stack, and began to read.

i know where i'm going
and i know who's going with me
i know who i love
but my dear knows who i'll marry . . .

It was to be a novel about the yearning to be an artist, the story of a woman who believes she can make an art form out of the life of an artist without ever actually doing the work to become one. Shirley wrote, *This is to be the story of a strangely haunted woman, whose life becomes a cheap tragedy because of her anxiety to be an artist in the sense in which she sees art, as irresponsibility and lack of discipline.*

There was no date anywhere on the file. I had no recollection of her mentioning such a project, of her reminiscing about beginning it or why she abandoned it. I wondered why she did. Was this the project she'd begun when she discovered Stanley was in love?

Was this an early project she later deemed beneath her evolving talents? I tended to doubt that. This plan was good; the story had everything—characters, plot, ominous threat, fantasy, gossip and petty nastiness, farm fields and urban settings. It was rich in the psychological; the characters were whole. I would have loved to have the volume now, to have one more work of Shirley Jackson's I could read. Even the notes had extraordinary lines, as in her description of Oscar as a husband who believes *any woman will make [a] good wife in the country if he is fond enough of her.* The plot was rife with devil imagery and dreams, with ominous self-delusion and the ever-present potential for tragedy and violence.

I would write this book myself, if I could. It seemed to me a universal tale. I pushed back my heavy armchair, made my way to the front desk, and received permission to photocopy all ten pages of Shirley's proposed plan.

I know who I love, she called it. I liked that phrase enormously; it rattled my tongue as if it were pinballing between the different areas for sweet and salty, bitter and sour. Ah, this was the thing she taught me, isn't it?

AND THEN, as if the witch of Bennington had waited in these cartons a full decade for the moment when I'd do this, I selected the last file from the folder.

Her last novel had barely six chapters completed when she died. It was to be the story of an older woman who sells her possessions and leaves home, takes a new name, sets herself up in a new city.

Makes a fresh new life. The novel begins with the cheerful comment: *I always believe in eating when I can.*

I always believe in eating when I can.

I said that.

I said it, and the words must have tricked Shirley into action, thrilled her, driven her to her desk. I remember the kitchen that morning: water steamed over the breakfast dishes, the sponge dropping from Shirley's reddened hand, the pause as she took the words in and moved them through her brain, the way her shoulders stiffened and her smile went vague. I should have known.

Coffee grounds on the counter, a curtain partly twitched by a cat skulking at the window ledge in search of stealable leftovers. The air still charged by her exit. *I always believe in eating when I can.* I remember that I put my toast down and stepped to the sink to finish the washing up.

With my eyes closed, I saw it perfectly. Yes, I remembered precisely how her face changed, and what followed. How even Stanley had to thank me, everyone knew there were moments of relief I'd brought into the fraught landscape of their home.

It was the very first sentence. *I always believe in eating when I can.*

See, world, I was there!

"We're boring," I whispered, and Fred nodded, not really listening. The word felt glorious, an enveloping sea of comfort and understanding. I tapped his hand, said, "Our boring little family— I miss our girl. Let's drive back tonight; let's get Natalie and go home."

"We'll finish here, we're almost done."

And then Fred sighed as he moved the holder card to the next place in the file box, removed the next folder. I put my hand on his and squeezed it gently. His thumb shifted and pressed mine, and then we both returned to work. It was good.

I, too, know who I love.

Acknowledgments

My interest in Shirley Jackson has an arc all its own. I first read *We Have Always Lived in the Castle* and *The Haunting of Hill House* when I was around thirteen, the age when I also discovered Baroness Orczy and Judith Rossner and Daphne du Maurier and Iris Murdoch—like Jackson, women writers whose female characters managed to be both part of and resistant to what can only be called "normal" life. But I had never considered Shirley Jackson from a writerly point of view until I had the good fortune to meet the novelist Rachel Pastan in 2007 at the Bennington Writing Seminars. It was Rachel who encouraged me to examine Jackson's gift for mixing the mundane and the fantastic. For that, and for her patient, intelligent readings of this novel through many iterations, I will always be indebted.

This book has had so many friends. Thank you to readers Dinah Lenney, Renée Shafransky, Maggie Merrell, Lou Ann Walker, Martha Cooley, Ellen Prentiss Campbell, Melanie Fleishman, Joe Stracci, Ian Williams, Ann Fitzsimmons, Julie Sheehan, Jennifer Pike, Jake Merrell, Martha Samuelson, and Herb and Maggie Scarf. Thank you to Bob Reeves and everyone else at Stony Brook Southampton's MFA in Creative Writing & Literature; Jed Turner, Antonio Romani, Ann Brandon; the Library of Congress, particularly Dan DeSimone and Carolyn Sung; Benjamin Dreyer, Cathy Creedon, and Jackson biographer Judy Oppenheimer. At Bennington, particular thanks to Sven Birkerts, Lynne Sharon Schwartz, Alice Mattison, and Joe Tucker at Crossett Library.

Unlimited gratitude goes to the three people whose belief in this book has been a game changer: Henry Dunow, Sarah Hochman, and Jim Merrell.

Last but far from least, I must acknowledge Shirley Jackson and Stanley Edgar Hyman. I have conflated their residential history, and restructured facts and details to serve the purpose of my story, much as Shirley did with the story of Paula Welden or that of the two young schoolteachers who visited Versailles. My hope is that Shirley and Stanley would be amused by this fictional exercise.

About the Author

Susan Scarf Merrell is the author of a previous novel, *A Member of the Family*, and a nonfiction work, *The Accidental Bond: How Sibling Connections Influence Adult Relationships*. She is a professor in the MFA in Creative Writing & Literature program at Stony Brook Southampton, and is fiction editor of *TSR: The Southampton Review*.